HOLLYWOOD DOUBLE DOWN

A SCREAM QUEEN DETECTIVE AGENCY NOVEL

DAVE SINCLAIR

ALSO BY DAVE SINCLAIR

Scream Queen Detective Agency

Hollywood Double Down

L.A. Fade Out

California Screaming

Mason Nash Novels

Past Transgressions

Shadow Hunting

Devil's End

Atticus Wolfe Novels

Out of Time

It Takes a Spy

The Coldest War

Charles Bishop Novels

Kiss My Assassin

Agent Provocateur

Venetian Blonde

Eva Destruction Novels

The Barista's Guide to Espionage

The Rookie's Guide to Espionage (novella)

The Amnesiac's Guide to Espionage

The Dead Spy's Guide to Espionage

Nina has a Spotify Playlist ~

For Kristi.
My cheer squad, my muse, my love.

FADE IN

ACT I

I'd like to thank the Academy.

Wednesday, 4 September 1984

CHAPTER

ONE

No one walks in LA.

Especially not in Bel Air.

Nina Maddox trudged up the lawn on the wide palm tree-lined street toward the police cordon. She left her jet black '68 Dodge Charger baking under the annoyingly bright Californian sun.

Despite their abundance of funding, the Bel Air Police Department hadn't managed a more elegant solution than a strip of yellow and black plastic to keep the gawkers at a distance. At least it was doing its job. A small clump of onlookers stood dutifully mute behind the obstruction, hoping for some excitement. It was a crime scene; Nina wasn't entirely sure what they expected to see. They'd missed the exciting part by at least five hours.

The immense estate was the residence of TV star Hank "The Tank" Trank. The gaudy faux French chateau-style mansion was the epitome of what the super-wealthy confused for taste. Trank was the star of one of TVs hottest shows, *Vengeance Inc.*, which *TV Guide* had labelled a "must watch of Fall '84." Who was Nina to argue with *TV Guide*?

Actually, he was the *former* star, Nina corrected herself. The coroner's van in the driveway reinforced that fact.

Celebrity murders always shock the general public. Usually, the victim too.

Tugging at her very un-LA leather jacket, Nina lifted the crime scene tape and ducked under it. She made it all of two steps.

"Uh-uhh."

She glanced up to see a cop with pursed lips and a meaty hand on his sidearm. He was young, bald, and overweight. It was like someone had put a baby hippopotamus in a blue uniform and hoped no one would notice.

Casting the young cop a cheesy *you got me* grin, Nina held up her hands.

Fingers still hovering over his pistol, the Hippo-Cop growled. "Behind the line, citizen."

Shrugging indifferently, she said, "The name's Nina Maddox. I'm a private investigator and I'm looking to get in there."

"Well, I'm looking for two weeks in Baja. Get behind the line." His fingers twitched. "This is your last warning."

"What's going on here?" A cop in a cheap suit bounded over to them. Straight out of central casting for a world-weary senior cop, the tall, thick-necked homicide sergeant recognized Nina and grunted. "Uhh, it's you, Maddox."

The Hippo-Cop's head snapped around. "Birmingham, you know this... woman?" He relinquished his grip on the gun.

The newcomer's nose was apparently aggrieved by some irritant. "There was a time when every teenage boy in the country knew her." Ignoring the confused expression on Hippo-Cop's face, Birmingham turned to Nina. "How is it being the studio's little bitch, Maddox?"

"Pretty good, Birmingham," Nina replied apathetically. "Beaten any good confessions out of anyone today?"

The two fake laughed at one another. It was either that or a start a shoot-out.

Nina addressed Birmingham. "Mickey Boehler sent me." She tilted her head to the bemused Hippo-Cop. "You know Mickey, right?"

"Lady, everyone in this town knows Mickey."

Mickey Boehler was the tyrannical CEO of Phoenix Studios and a legend in the industry. Not in a good way.

Nina went on. "Well, he invited me here to poke around. Incidentally, he owns this house, and the studio where the deceased worked. I believe he's also the leading contributor to the annual Bel Air Police Department ball." Nina flashed her once-famous smile, much to Birmingham's irritation. "He said I should mention that."

The homicide cop's face twitched involuntarily. Eventually, with a mouth like he was sucking lemons, his shoulders slumped and he motioned for Nina to follow.

"But Sarge!" Hippo-Cop started to protest.

Birmingham silenced him with a weary wave of his hand. He and Nina knew the same thing; if you wanted to last in this town, you didn't make an enemy of Mickey "The Steamroller" Boehler.

The wide, paved driveway was jammed with police cars, marked and unmarked, as well as the coroner's van. A clump of uniformed cops stood before the closed double garage, apparently having nothing better to do than smoke and laugh boisterously in reverence to the dead.

The two walked in silence for a moment. Nina spoke first.

"What can you tell me?"

Birmingham mulled this over. He must have already

worked out that refusing Nina could be a career-limiting move, and getting in Boehler's good books might be a fast track to a promotion. "I suppose it's nothing we're not going to make public anyway."

It was a lie, but Nina let him delude himself. No point in pressing her luck.

"A studio minion arrived at the scene a little before 6 am to drop off a new script revision for Trank. He had a key so he could leave it on the hall table—I guess you don't leave a script to a hit show in the letterbox. When he saw a bloody footprint in the front entrance, he got the heebie jeebies and followed it to its source upstairs."

The story gelled with the brief she'd been given.

"A straight-up murder, then." Nina's words were more for herself.

Birmingham grunted. "If it's not, then it's the most violent suicide I've ever seen. No forced entry; whoever did this was known to the victim. There's blood all over the crime scene. Trank didn't go quietly, that's for damn sure." He raised an amused eyebrow. "This'll probably go down as one of the most Hollywood deaths ever."

"Why's that?"

"You'll find out."

Nina let it slide. Her job was normally getting stars out of trouble of their own making. A drug bust here, a dead hooker there; she'd made most of them go away. She was doing her best to build a reputation as the go-to woman for when Hollywood was in trouble—and it was always in trouble. She'd performed miracles in the past, but this case was beyond her significant capabilities and more George A Romero territory.

The entrance to Trank's mansion was as gaudy as the exterior would suggest. A grand staircase split into two, then rejoined itself on the first landing. Along each stair-case, the walls were adorned with framed posters of Hank Trank, and only Hank Trank. The first had him decked in his 49ers uniform in a heroic football-carrying pose. There were *Buster Higgins* movie posters, commemorating his unlikely transition to successful movie star after a knee injury put paid to his sporting career. Further up were successive posters from each season of *Vengeance Inc.,* in which the poor and helpless needed a violent avenging vigilante to assist them every week. The entire entranceway was the story of Hank Trank. And one hell of an ego trip.

On the golden hall table sat a script, no doubt the one dropped off by the studio runner. There was also a framed photograph of a teen Trank standing with his Ivy League parents in front of an equally Ivy League school.

Nina and Birmingham trudged up the marble staircase in silence. On the first landing they made a left and entered the main bedroom. Unlike the rest of the mansion, this was a hive of activity. The space was massive. Gaudy red wall-paper on all sides, gold light fittings. At its center there was a huge bed, and above that, an equally huge mirror.

It was unfortunate that the mirror on the ceiling offered a technicolor view of the victim in all its gory detail. The crème silk sheets were stained a deep crimson. At the end of the bed, the bloody and battered corpse of Trank lay on an open body bag.

Nina moved closer to get a better view of the victim. The late Hank Trank was in a bad way—well beyond the part where he was dead. Clad only in leopard-print under-wear, the famous actor was unrecognizable. When alive, the ex-footballer had a stocky and imposing physique, which meant whoever killed him must have been pretty powerful themselves. His upper torso was a gory, bruised mess. There were no entrance or exit wounds that Nina could see. His head and lower arms showed extensive blunt force trauma, probably defensive wounds sustained during the attack. His face, if it could still be called that, was a bloody, fragmented mess.

Nina was the only woman in the room, an all-too-common occurrence. As one of the few female private investigators in the city, Nina was used to being the only woman present. She was just as used to the multitude of men's gazes cast in her direction. The looks were either judgmental, dismissive, contemptuous, or lustful. Sometimes all at once. Ignoring the glares, Nina did her job and observed.

The coroner and medical examiner stood in the corner fussing with an object of some description, placing it in an evidence bag. Whatever it was appeared to be caked in blood. They were performing the act with such reverence it caught Nina's attention.

"What do they have there?" Nina asked Birmingham.

"The murder weapon." Birmingham's mouth twisted into the closest the man ever came to a smile. "Trank's Academy Award. Best Supporting, if memory serves."

"He was beaten to death with an Oscar?"

"Have you ever heard anything more Hollywood?"

Nina let out a low whistle. She had no doubt the image of a bloodied Oscar would grace the cover of at least one true crime book before the year was out.

Two scruffy men entered the bedroom, chewing gum. The logo on their off-white lab coats advised that they worked for the coroner's office. The mortuary cot they wheeled in advised what their role was. Their job was to drive the van and remove the deceased once the preliminary examination was complete. The only time a deceased person was placed in the back of an ambulance was in the movies.

The two half-heartedly pushed the cot over by the bed and set about zipping up the body bag, readying Trank for one last descent down his grand staircase. A man emerged from what Nina assumed was an en suite. He was tall, dark haired, and with a chiseled jaw that would give Kirk Douglas a run for his money. Two cameras were strapped around his neck, and he carried a silver photographer's case.

"All done here," the newcomer said to the medical examiner.

He turned and saw Nina. The two exchanged fleeting glances, then immediately looked in opposite directions. The forensics photographer packed up his gear and headed toward the door, but not before casting Nina a brief glimpse.

Noting the silent exchange, Birmingham asked, "You know Lang?"

"We've bumped into each other from time to time." She hurriedly changed the subject. "Anything taken?"

Given the highly violent nature of the murder, Nina didn't suspect this was a burglary gone wrong, but her job was to investigate all angles.

A young kid approached and handed Birmingham a Styrofoam cup of coffee. He did so with such cowering subservience, Nina assumed he worked for homicide in some capacity. His eyes darted to her, then back at Birmingham, who gave a slight shake of his head. His meaning was clear: *she doesn't get one.*

"Thanks Kevin." Birmingham turned to Nina. "Nothing taken as far as we know. Looks like someone rummaged through his private cinema downstairs. One of the boys thinks it could be a superfan searching for unaired episodes of *Vengeance Inc.* or a kinky sex tape. Nothing else was disturbed that we know of. There was a few hundred bucks in cash in a key bowl in the study, so if they were burglars, they weren't very good ones."

Nina nodded. There wasn't much else for her to do. "I'll let Mickey know what a helpful little soul you've been."

Birmingham simply grunted in reply, then peeled off and left her alone in the corner of the enormous bedroom.

From what she could see of the crime scene, there was nothing untoward—other than the savage murder, that is. There was no evidence of a sex game gone wrong. No one was strapped to anything incriminating. No vials of pills, piles of white powder. No paraphernalia unbefitting someone who had thrice graced the cover of *People* magazine. She could confirm for her employer that everything *else* appeared above board and scandal free, which was no doubt why she'd been hired.

Though she was sure her employers would argue otherwise, Nina wasn't there to save Hank Trank's reputation. She was there to save the studio from scandal. The only time a studio relished a scandal was when it involved another studio.

Birmingham stood by the doorway, satisfied he'd done the bare minimum required of him. The removal technicians untied the straps and pulled the sealed body bag unceremoniously onto the mortuary cot.

The taller of the two elbowed the other, motioning in Nina's direction, and in a low voice asked, "Isn't that Nina Maddox?"

Nina ignored him and examined the room with her hands planted behind her back. Recognition came with the territory. Her past followed her relentlessly like a slasher from one of her films, and was just as welcome.

"Yeah, I used to have a poster of *Scream Queen 2* on my wall."

Blatantly ogling the woman standing right next to him, the taller technician sleazily replied, "I wouldn't mind having her up against the—"

The end of his sentence was cut short when Nina kicked the latch release of the cot, causing it to collapse on his hand. As he screamed, Nina leaped over him, gesturing as if she was helping the writhing man, all the while pushing on the rail, causing him to scream all the more.

A group of helpful onlookers extricated the whimpering man. Nina plastered on her most innocent expression before hastily exiting the bedroom. Birmingham, who was propped against the wall in the hallway, shook his head and tutted.

"You realize you just assaulted a member of the coroner's office with a dead cadaver, right?"

Nina gave him a blank gaze. "Well, attacking him with a live one would be apocryphal."

After a deep growl, he said, "I think it's time you left."

Watching the technician cradle his hand, Nina replied, "Yeah, maybe you're right."

Birmingham gestured downstairs, in case there was any possible ambiguity about the fact that she'd outstayed her welcome.

Outside on the street, Nina mingled with the gawkers, purely because she had nothing better to do. Mickey had paid her for the day, so she felt obliged to hang around. She was surprised there were no TV crews yet, and suspected that was Mickey's doing. Or maybe he was delaying it for prime time? Imagine the ratings.

Even if the media were kept away in the short term, Trank's house was destined to be a morbid stop on the crime tours, entertaining ghoulish, starry-eyed tourists for years to come.

She wandered around the periphery of the assembled masses. There were countless whispers of, "What's going on?" and "Whose house is it?" It was all of two minutes before Nina was thankful she'd hung around.

A well-tanned but bewildered-looking man stood across the road. Obscured by a tree and beyond the onlookers' line of sight, he held a grease-stained In-N-Out bag.

Nina scratched the back of her head and wondered for a fleeting instant if she'd seen a ghost. Then she remembered she didn't believe in ghosts.

Besides, this man wasn't a ghost. It was the man the world knew as Hank Trank.

TWO

Glancing around to see if anyone else had spotted the supposed dead man, Nina briskly crossed the street, doing her best to move calmly. The man was likely spooked enough already.

It didn't work. Catching sight of Nina making a beeline toward him, Trank dropped the takeout bag and sprinted away. She raced after him as he rounded a corner, Nina quickly gaining ground. He was a big man whose football days were far behind him.

Drawing parallel with him, Nina called out, "I'm here to look after you, Hank." When his pace didn't slow, she added, "Mickey sent me."

The big man slowed, then completely stopped before doubling over with a wheeze. Nina let him inhale deeply for a time. When he'd recovered, she patted him on the back.

"You're breathing pretty well for a dead man."

"Thanks." He straightened up, startled. "Wait, what do you mean dead?"

Nina flicked her finger toward the corner they'd just

rounded. "The crime scene tape and all the cops didn't give it away? You're apparently dead, Hank."

The alarm on Hank "The Tank" Trank's face was palpable. It wasn't every day someone told you you're dead, Nina supposed.

His mouth flapped open and shut several times. "But... I'm not."

"I can see that." Nina tried hard not to smile.

"Mickey sent you?"

She nodded and flicked her head, gesturing for him to follow her back toward the house. As they walked, Trank gave Nina a once-over. He didn't appear to like what he saw. "Are you the police?" His tone seemed to suggest that someone who looked like Nina could never be a cop.

"Thankfully, no. I do a lot of work for Mickey, he sent me over. You're more alive than I was led to believe." She took a card from her back pocket and handed it to him. "The name's Nina Maddox."

"Scream Queen Detective Agency? Cute."

"A marketing guy came up with it. Said I'd be drowning in cash after twelve months."

"Were you?"

"It's been eighteen months and I'd be lucky to get my feet wet." They rounded the corner just in time to see the mortuary cot being wheeled toward the coroner's van. "Any idea who that it is? From what I saw, it was a male roughly your age, same build and complexion. Was anyone staying at your house, Hank?"

Nina used his first name in an attempt to appear more friendly in an unfriendly time.

In a daze, Trank stared at his mansion, stunned. "Seth. Seth Wagner. He's my, uh, he's my stunt double."

Up close, Nina could see that there were bags around

Trank's bloodshot eyes and his hair was unkempt. This was not the face for a magazine cover.

Checking his hands, Nina found them perfectly manicured and blemish free. Not hands that had recently brandished a weapon to inflict the damage she'd seen. He'd need an iron-clad alibi, but Trank didn't strike her as a killer; he seemed more like someone who'd come home to a surprise murder scene.

Nina checked for prying eyes. "My car's just over there —the black one, see it?" She waited for him to nod in response. "We're going to hustle over there and you're going to get in the passenger side, okay? Then we can talk where we're less exposed. Come on."

She practically led him by the arm, guided him into the bucket seat, and closed the door. She moved to the driver's side of the Charger, making a slight detour to pick up the dropped In-N-Out bag laying at the base of a tree. Nina was famished.

Inside the car, she opened the bag and asked, "This for Seth?"

Tearing his eyes away from the unfolding crime scene, Trank turned to Nina, looked down at the greasy bag and back at her. "I dropped that on the ground."

Nina shrugged. "And?" She took out a fistful of fries and stuffed them in her mouth. With her mouth full, she said, "I'll ask again, did you buy this for Seth?"

He gave an affirmative dip of his head. "I... I was out late last night. This was meant to be a surprise."

Despite his disheveled state, he was handsome up close. Even with the Hollywood tan and teeth whiter than the keys on a brand-new Steinway, Trank had a rugged manliness to him.

"There's no In-N-Out in Bel Air, so I'm assuming you drove. Where's your car?"

His finger drifted toward a late model Mercedes, immaculately white and shiny, parked on the opposite side of the road. They watched the proceedings in silence for a moment.

"Seth was in your bed. Was that a frequent occurrence?"

Hank's complexion finally developed some color. "What are you insinuating?"

"Mickey Boehler sent me to protect you, Hank, so that's what I'm trying to do. I don't give a shit if you have twenty pigs with lipstick in your bedroom, I'm not here to judge." Nina sighed, realizing her usual brashness wasn't exactly endearing her to the startled man. "But Hank, in order to protect you, I need to know everything, good, bad, and especially seedy. You get me? Save the pearl clutching for another time. Were you and Seth lovers?"

Blinking several times, Hank pursed his lips and stared mutely forward.

"Fine, keep that one to yourself for now," Nina said evenly. "Just so we're clear, I'm here to save your career, if I can."

"You could use a little more tact."

"So I've been told." Nina unwrapped a burger and took a bite. "I'm going to assume you and Seth were lovers, okay?" Receiving no answer, she added, "You sleeping with your stuntman? Your lookalike? It'd be like fucking a mirror."

Hank frowned. "This is you using tact, is it?"

"I don't get paid to be nice."

"How much would it cost?"

Nina gave the slightest of smirks. "You couldn't afford it."

The brief moment of levity evaporated quickly. Trank's morose gaze returned to his house as he watched Hippo-Cop lift the crime scene tape to let the coroner's van through. He looked on forlornly as it turned onto the road and disappeared around a corner.

Once it was out of sight, he exhaled. "I suppose I better go and talk to the police now to get this cleared up."

Nina took another bite of the burger and shook her head as she chewed. "No."

"No?"

"No. Good talk." She realized Trank needed more. "Chatting to the cops is exactly what you *don't* do."

"Why?"

Casting greasy fingers toward the crime scene, Nina said, "That man, Wagner, was murdered. In your bed. That most likely means someone tried to kill *you* and missed. If that's the case, the murderer is still out there and you're in danger. Best not to poke your head up so someone can have another go. Right now, no one knows you're alive, besides me. I wouldn't recommend wandering around in public before we figure out who wants you dead. That's where I come in."

Nina didn't think it was possible for Hank to grow any whiter, but she always left room to be surprised. Unfortunately for Trank, she wasn't finished yet.

"Alternate take: Wagner was the target and the cops pin the murder on you. After all, it was your house, your bed, your lover." She turned to him to ensure she had his full attention. "Either way, walking over there right now would be a mistake, and Mickey hired me to look after your interests, so that's what I'm doing. Talking to the cops before we know what the hell is going on would be capital D dumb. You might look it, but you're not dumb, are you Hank?"

Trank breathed out through his nose slowly. "You don't have many friends, do you?"

"Let's get this straight: I'm not your friend, I'm your fucking guardian angel."

Trank's gaze drifted to the crime scene once more. "Who would want to murder me?"

Nina turned the key in the ignition and the beast of a V8 roared to life. "Let's go and find out, shall we?"

Driving out of Bel Air always made Nina feel like she'd stolen something. She assumed the guardhouse on the corner of Bellagio and Sunset was there for that exact reason. It may as well have been a giant sign that read, *You Don't Belong Here.* Just the way the mostly white residents wanted it.

She and Trank drove in silence, and it wasn't long before they hit the interstate. It took all of two minutes before they ground to a halt in a traffic jam.

LA's freeways crisscrossed the city like veins feeding red taillights from one side of it to the other, keeping it alive and strangling it at the same time. Locals nicknamed the 405 the "four or five," because that was either how many miles per hour you travelled or how many hours it took to get anywhere.

As they drove at a glacial pace, Nina filled Trank in on the gruesome details of what she'd learned so far. Which wasn't much, but it was still too much for Trank.

She waited for him to respond.

They passed out-of-date billboards advising that Atari and Budweiser were the official sponsors of the Olympics. The posters were peeling at the edges.

After a long silence, Nina finally asked, "How do you feel about that?"

"About which part? That my friend was viciously murdered? That it was in my own home? That this could be a career-ending scandal? The fact that someone could be looking to murder me right now? Or frame me? Which part precisely do you want me to have feelings about?"

"Maybe start with the death of a man you knew intimately?"

"Yes, that's a tragedy."

He delivered the line with all the sincerity of a table read. It was hard for Nina to determine if it was shock, or if something else was going on. Trank's emotions seemed far removed from these events. He drifted off into a sort of stupor, methodically gnawing his once well-manicured fingernails to stumps. Nina let him. She needed time to think.

She'd long ago stopped being awestruck in the presence of celebrities, though Trank was still an imposing physical figure. Handsome in an old-Hollywood kind of way, bulky without being fat, he exuded a commanding presence.

"I recognize you, you know?"

The break in silence was so jarring, it took Nina a moment to realize her companion had spoken. Focused forward, his facial features were as neutral as they had been for the last fifteen minutes.

"You were the Scream Queen, right?"

Everyone she'd ever met for more than five minutes eventually asked the exact same question. "For a time."

Her screen career, if you could call it that, had lasted a grand total of three and a half years.

"You threw me for a bit, not having blond hair." He

thrust a finger at her raven locks. "Those movies were pretty big there for a while."

"Yep. The budgets got bigger and my outfits got smaller."

"How many of those movies did they end up making?"

"Four. Two with me before I... left. I hear another one is in pre-production."

"And now you're a..."

"Private investigator," Nina said quickly before he suggested something less flattering.

"Do you miss it? The acting, I mean?"

"No more than an abuse victim misses their tormentor." Nina shook her head and shifted down a gear, both metaphorically and physically. "When I retired at the ripe old age of twenty-three no one gave a shit if I lived, died, contracted leprosy, or moved to Azerbaijan. I could have moved to New York to tread the boards on Broadway, or to San Fernando Valley to become a porn actress. No one cared. It was pure unadulterated freedom and skull-crushing claustrophobia at the same time."

"But you became a private eye? Why's that?"

She watched the traffic. This line of questioning was heading down a road Nina didn't want to travel. Her reasons for her career choice were far too private and dark to be shared with a client.

Tapping the steering wheel with her nails, her mind ticked. Now that Trank was lucid, she may as well get the investigation back on track.

"Where were you last night, Hank?"

Thrown by the change in subject, he fumbled for words, eventually stammering, "I drove out to Runyon Canyon. Had to do some thinking."

"Good hiking up that way. Did you go for a walk?"

"A run, actually. Like I said, needed to clear the old noggin. I'm still a country boy at heart, and sometimes I need the wide-open spaces. Even back in my football days, when I was under pressure I'd find an open space and run."

"Okay, I'm going to stop you there." Nina clenched her eyes shut, opening them just before she rear-ended the Pinto in front of her. "If you were in a police station right now, I can guarantee you'd be about to be charged."

"What? Why?"

"You just bullshitted me, Hank."

"I most certainly did not."

"There's more bullshit in that story than in the Calgary Stampede. Let's ignore the fact that I was, briefly, an actress and can spot a phony a mile away. Let's stick to the facts, shall we? First, it's been a long, hot summer. Lots of dust up in those canyons. I saw your Mercedes, there's not a speck of dust on that thing. it's been off road as much as a bumper car. Second, new moon last night, you couldn't see shit on those tracks. Third, those loafers you're wearing aren't trainers. You couldn't run ten feet in them, and they're whiter than the front row of the Academy of Country Music Awards. So, are you going to tell me where you really where?"

Trank folded his arms and stared forward at the glacial traffic. "No."

"Fine. Just don't bullshit me. I'm trying to save your life here."

Nina gripped the wheel tightly. She hated being lied to, especially by the people she was trying to help. Wherever he'd been, he was keeping it close to his chest and she had to wonder why. What would be worth keeping secret when it could prove your innocence? It made no sense. The pieces just didn't fit. Perhaps this wasn't going to be as open and shut as she'd first hoped.

This case could really put her agency on the map. So far, she'd only had a handful of studio heads as clients. They paid well, but work could be sporadic. Currently, the agency consisted of her, a dive bar phone number, and her cat. If Scream Queen Detective Agency was to survive, she'd need a few high-profile cases, and they didn't get much higher profile than Hank the Tank. All she needed to do was keep him alive.

An awkward hush that fell between them, and Nina turned on the radio to fill the silence. They were discussing the upcoming Presidential election between Reagan and Mondale. All pundits had it as a landslide for Reagan. They were interviewing the Los Angeles mayor, who was making a senate run. The soft interviewer credited him with the recent success of the Olympics, pointing out it had been the first Games to turn a profit. Nina noticed that the mayor didn't take credit for the months of traffic chaos it had generated. In fact, the traffic jam they were stuck in now could be the same one from the Olympics, months after the fact. In LA, all traffic jams looked the same.

This mayor had been in power since before she'd arrived in this smog-ridden city with stars in her eyes, fire in her belly, and seventy-five dollars in her bra. She was about to change the station when the announcer came on with breaking news. Both Nina and Trank tensed.

"This just in, ex-footballer, TV and movie star Hank Trank was found dead in his Bel Air home early this morning. Details are still coming in, but police sources state that the death is being treated as suspicious. We will share more details as they come to hand, but for now, just repeating the top story of the hour, Hank Trank, star of TVs *Vengeance Inc.*, is dead at forty-four."

Clearly Mickey's lid only stayed on for so long.

Nina switched the radio off. "How does that make you feel?"

"Pissed." Trank folded his arms. "I'm only forty-two."

Nina didn't know if it was a joke or not, so decided not to react. Slinking down in his seat, Trank eyed the slow-moving cars around them, probably scared every occupant was a reporter or a hitman.

"Here," Nina said, reaching into the glove box.

She handed him a pair of old sunglasses. They were tacky and feminine for her, but they were big. Trank snatched them and put them on, slinking further into his seat. Nina felt like Elton John's chauffeur.

She changed lanes to make sure she didn't miss her exit and Trank spoke up.

"Where are we going?"

Nina was surprised it had taken this long for him to ask. "My place."

"Why there?"

"It's as good a place as any until we find out what's going on." Nina honked at a red Chevy trying to merge into her lane. "Do you have many enemies, Hank?"

"As many as anyone else with my success, I guess."

"Not helpful. Let me rephrase. Has anyone threatened to kill you of late?"

Rubbing his stubble, Trank mulled it over. "I had an assistant a few months back. He hated my guts, even filed a suit claiming that I verbally abused him, but the case was dismissed when no witnesses came forward."

"Was it true?"

"That no one came forward?"

"What he alleged. The verbal abuse."

"Oh, yeah, I was an asshole." He poked the big glasses back up the bridge of his nose. "*Vengeance Inc.* looked like it wasn't going to get a fourth season and it was all I had. Do you know how humiliating it is to be dumped on a show that was beneath you to begin with? I thought my career was in the toilet, and I took it out on poor Marvin, the quintessential 98-pound weakling. I tormented him for months, belittled him in front of others, chastised him for the tiniest of mistakes, trivial insignificant stuff, just so I could feel like the big man."

"And no one would corroborate his allegations?"

"In this town? You testify against the powerful and you can kiss your career goodbye. The industry doesn't forget. Ever. The poor bastard couldn't get another PA job because his old boss was an insecure lying sack of shit."

"Do you think he hated you enough to kill? It's quite a leap from not being able to get a job to bludgeoning someone to death with an Oscar."

"I don't know. He hated me, I know that much, and I despised myself for the longest time after what I did to him."

"You achieved some personal growth, yay you." Nina gave the Chevy driver the finger as she passed. "But this isn't about you. It's about him. Would he be capable of killing?"

"I... I just don't know."

"Okay," Nina tried to conceal her irritation at the non-answer, "let me ask this. Did he know?"

"Know what?"

"That you're a homosexual?"

"What? That's an outrageous slander. I'll have you know—"

Nina planted her hand on the horn, shocking everyone around them, especially Trank. "I call this the bullshit horn. It goes off whenever I hear bullshit. As I keep explaining, I'm not here to judge you, Hank. I'm here to protect you."

She gave him a moment to gather his thoughts. Nina had spent enough time in the industry to know that homosexuality was far more widespread than the newspapers would have you believe. "Gay" was becoming the preferred term. The fact that her best friend was gay was irrelevant to the current conversation. The only time gay men were in the media was when the story involved four little letters starting with A. Trank likely had images of Rock Hudson dancing in his brain.

Her voice was the softest she could make it. "Hank, where you and Wagner lovers?"

With an almost imperceptible movement, Trank gave a nod. Maybe he thought the car was bugged. Perhaps he couldn't verbalize it. Either way, at least Nina knew the truth now.

"Okay," she said. "So I'll ask again, did your former assistant know?"

Trank wriggled uncomfortably in his seat. "Yes."

Nina jiggled her shoulders. The California sun was beating down and she was slowly roasting in her leather jacket. The leather upholstery wasn't helping. "Seems to me it would be a hell of a lot easier to make a call to the *National Enquirer* and pocket a few bucks than to break into a house and murder an ex-footballer twice his size, wouldn't you think?"

"So, you're saying..."

"I'm saying Marvin's not your man."

Nina took the exit to Wilshire Boulevard. She could have taken Venice, the most direct route, but she preferred

Wilshire. Plus, cutting through side streets would tell her if they had a tail. This case gave her the jitters. In her profession, being cautious was never ill advised.

"If it's not your old assistant, who else have you got?"

Staying mute for a good minute, Trank finally spoke. "I can't think of a single person. Everyone else I know owes their living to me in some shape or form. Managers, staff, lawyers, accountants, drivers. They all rely on me to keep the gravy train running."

Accepting the statement without further comment, Nina's mind raced. "Tell me about Wagner."

"Not much to tell, really. Met him on set about six months ago when my last stunt double quit to work on *Magnum PI*. He wanted to live on the beach in Hawaii. Wagner and I hit it off. We shared similar interests."

"I bet."

Continuing as if he hadn't heard her, he said, "It was never a serious thing, just occasional."

"Serious enough for him to stay at your place when you were running the canyons," Nina said, emphasizing the last part.

He ignored her sarcasm. "His place was being fumigated so I said he could stay at mine."

"How magnanimous of you."

"I thought so."

Making her way toward the ocean, Nina's mind raced. Where had Trank *really* been last night? Did he have an airtight alibi? If he did, why the hell wasn't he willing to share it? What was he hiding that was more important than avoiding a murder conviction?

If Trank was being truthful—something she'd established was dubious at best—about having few deadly enemies, who would be willing to beat his brains out with an awards statue? What if he had enemies he never knew existed?

Of course, there was another possibility: that Wagner was the true target. But why would someone risk breaking into the mansion of one of the biggest stars on TV to murder him? They must have *really* wanted him dead.

Now that the news was out about Trank's murder, it was her job to make sure it didn't actually take place. Whatever was going on, Nina sensed her work had barely begun.

CHAPTER

THREE

"You live in a *bar*?"

Trank somehow managed to make "bar" rhyme with "dumpster."

"In a bar?" Nina turned off the engine. "No."

She checked Abbot Kinney Boulevard for photographers or news vans, not that she expected any—this wasn't the popular part of Venice. Seeing nothing untoward, she stepped out of the Charger.

Following her lead, Trank exited and took in his surroundings. His expression was that of a man who'd eaten a dozen lemons and been handed a dozen more. Bel Air, this wasn't. He turned his attention to Nina's car.

"This is LA. Ferraris, BMWs, and Mercedes are de rigueur, yet here you are driving around in this relic."

"It's not a relic. It's destined to be a classic."

"Destined, perhaps," Trank lowered his head, "but it's not there yet. It's completely out of place in this city. It has no style, no grace."

"I think it suits me perfectly."

"Oh, I didn't say it didn't suit you."

"But you just..." Nina squinted. "Oh. I see what you did there."

Trank's frosty demeanor was starting to thaw. She made her way to the bar with the actor in tow.

"Why do you live in Venice?" The screwed-up nose remained firmly in place, as if Nina's suburb of choice had an aroma akin to an abattoir.

"If it's good enough for Kerouac and Ginsberg, it's good enough for me. It's full of subversives who say fuck you to the man. Some stiffs tried to gentrify the place a couple of years back and were firebombed out of here." She beamed. "*That* suits me just fine."

Trank smoothed out his suit jacket. "Charming."

Asta's wasn't much to look at from the outside, which was fitting, because it wasn't much to look at from the inside, either. Nina pulled the weathered red door open. Trank didn't step inside.

"What if I'm recognized?" Fear returned to his chiseled face. "A public bar isn't exactly a place I can disappear until you figure this out."

Nina realized Trank was still sporting her ridiculous sunglasses. She took them off him and slid them into her pocket.

"The clientele in here wouldn't give two shits if the Pope turned up riding a unicorn, as long as he paid his tab. They keep to themselves. You do the same and you'll be golden." Nina was getting tired of holding the heavy door. "You either trust me or you don't. Which is it?"

Trank appeared to weigh up his options, or lack thereof. He entered the bar silently.

It took a few moments for Nina's eyes to adjust from the bright Los Angeles sun to the gloom of the bar. Gloom was an apt description. The dark wooden floor was stained with years of traffic, spilt beer, and blood.

The few barflies barely lifted their weary heads to assess the newcomers. They mostly wore dog-eared military green field jackets and sneers. The patrons were a mix of hard-looking black, white, Hispanic, and Asian men nursing beers, surrounded by a miasma of melancholy and discontent. It was the United Nations of drunkards.

Trank gulped and whispered to Nina, "This place is a little rough."

"It's a dive bar, not the Biltmore." Her tone softened. "This ain't rough, darlin. It's the only bar in this city where I haven't had my ass pinched or been hit on by some coked-up executive producer wanting to reveal the big part he has for me. Here, people keep to themselves. Most of these guys are ex-servicemen, and the owner runs a tight ship, doesn't allow any disrespect. This place isn't rough," she slapped his shoulder, "it's home."

The chipped oak bar had been worn smooth by thousands of burdened elbows. Behind it stood a heavy-set black man drying a glass with a dishtowel; another was draped over his shoulder. His severe gray crew cut was nothing compared to his disposition. His casual, yet guarded stance screamed ex-military. He dipped his head in greeting to Nina as she entered.

"Titus. Any messages?"

The big man shook his head, then swiveled his gaze to Trank, then back to Nina. He raised a quizzical eyebrow. Titus Jones was a man of few words.

"He's with me. Might stay a few days." After receiving the slightest movement of his head in acknowledgement, she asked, "Phoebe around?"

Titus shook his head, then poured a beer and handed it

to a grizzled old man propped up at the corner of the bar. The barfly appeared so ingrained he may have been a permanent fixture. Nina thanked Titus with a wave, then strode to the far side of the bar and opened a door labelled "Private." She ushered Trank through.

Behind the door, a rickety set of wooden stairs snaked upward. Nina led the way, her charge close behind.

"The barman seemed most loquacious," he observed with a distinct accent of disdain.

"Titus? I've known the man for years and I've never seen him smile, not once. Not when I tell him my best jokes, not when I do my Groucho Marx impression, not even the time I fell off the end of the bar and chipped a tooth. Never. He's a diamond in the rough, though. Absolutely someone you want in your corner if shit goes down." She paused at the top the stairs while she extracted her keys. "And he's not just the barman, he owns this building." Nina relished the surprise on Trank's face. "Underestimate people and you'll always be surprised."

Nina opened the door to her apartment and Trank audibly gasped. In contrast to the dank claustrophobic confines of the bar below, her home was bright, open, and welcoming. The entire left side of the loft space boasted high glass windows opposite an exposed brick wall. Shelves were filled with plants, books, and records. Mismatched furniture was covered in random colored cushions, and in the corner sat a large mid-century bar that wouldn't have been out of place in Dean Martin's house. It was eclectic and random, yet inviting at the same time.

"Speaking of underestimating people," Nina dropped her keys in a colorful Moroccan bowl, "you were expecting a hovel, weren't you?"

Fleeting amusement crossed Trank's lips, but he moved on quickly. "You live alone?"

The mirth was slapped from Nina's features. "I do now."

Not picking up on the sudden mood shift, Trank asked, "Isn't that dangerous, a woman living alone?" Noticing Nina's disdain at the question, he quickly added, "In your line of work."

"My work is Byzantine and often dangerous, but if I was ever in trouble the *rough* lot downstairs would come running in an instant, and believe me, no one, and I mean *no one* ever wants to get on the wrong side of Titus Jones."

Satisfied with her answer, Trank asked, "No TV?"

Of course the TV star asked that. Before Nina could offer a smart-ass reply, he'd moved to a bookshelf and picked up the only photo frame in her apartment. Trank studied the picture of a smiling Nina, younger and blonde, with her arm around an equally young beaming redhead, laughing on set.

"A friend?"

Nina snatched the picture from his hands and realized the forcefulness of the action. She did her best to soften her stance and her voice. "She was." Regarding the picture for the first time in a long time, she added, "Not anymore."

Taken aback by her abruptness, he said, "No wonder you live alone."

Nina regarded the photo, realizing she actively ignored it most days. She couldn't recall the last time she'd paid it any attention. It's amazing how one picture can mean so much all at once. Juliet had been her best friend when the two were busting their asses trying to get their big break in this unforgiving city. They bussed from one lousy audition to the next, living off whatever can of beans was cheapest that week, doing their best to avoid the casting couch no matter what promise was dangled in front of them. Juliet was the first person Nina told when she got the *Scream Queen* role. Not her family, Juliet. They'd splurged and bought a can of beans that were *not* on sale—the extravagance!

The picture also reminded Nina of the day she lost her best friend. The day Hollywood stopped being a rollicking adventure. The day Nina lost Juliet. The day she quit acting and became an investigator. Nina placed the picture reverently on the shelf, face down.

An orange and white cat stepped from the open kitchen, causing Trank to jump. Ignoring his alarm, the cat rubbed against Trank's leg. Nina was thankful for the distraction. Trank leaned down to give the purring creature a scratch behind the ear.

"That's Sputnik. He doesn't usually like people, but he seems to like you."

It was a lie. Sputnik was a friendly cat who approached most visitors, but Nina found people got a kick out of thinking they were somehow imbued with Doctor Doolittle abilities. And she certainly needed Trank onside.

Nina hung her jacket on a hook. "Bathroom's on the right, my bedroom's on the left. You can sleep on the couch." Seeing the look of fear on his face, she asked, "You need a drink?"

"It's a bit early, isn't it?" Shaking his head as if remembering the day he'd had, he added, "Cognac, if you have it. Can I use your bathroom?"

When Trank returned, he dropped heavily onto the green velvet sofa. Nina handed him a bright blue bone china cup and saucer. Creases of confusion crossed his forehead as he accepted the cup. He took a sip and almost did a spit take.

"This *is* cognac."

"That's what you asked for." Nina slumped into the leather armchair opposite.

"I didn't expect it to be served in a fancy china teacup."

"Why, what do you normally drink cognac out of?"

"I can't work out if you're completely nuts or not."

"It's going to be fun finding out, huh?" Nina drank her vodka from a coffee mug with the words *Inch High Private Eye* emblazoned on it. "Is there someone you want to call, to let them know you're okay? Someone close?"

Trank's gaze drifted and he scratched the back of his neck. "My agent?"

"I said close. Your folks? I saw a picture of them on your hall stand."

"I guess. It's been a while."

"How long?"

"Years."

"Years?"

"I've been busy." Trank swirled the contents of his teacup.

Nina thought that was the saddest thing she'd come across in a while, and she'd seen a murder victim that morning. She reached over to the side table and opened a leather notebook.

She tapped the pad with her pencil. "How often did you and Wagner... see each other?"

"Occasionally. Maybe a few times a month, I guess." He ran his hand over his trousers. "I usually called... except last night. Last night, he called me."

"Why's that?"

"Like I said, his place was being fumigated and he needed a place to stay."

"Pretty forward for a casual arrangement."

He sipped his cognac contemplatively. "I didn't think anything of it at the time, but even when I told him I was busy, he pushed, which was... unusual."

"When he arrived, did he act differently? Say anything out of the ordinary?"

"Normal, I guess. Perhaps in retrospect he was a bit more jittery than usual. He was bragging about getting out of the stunt business. His knees were shot, you see. He'd been saying for some time that he was sick of being taken advantage of, that sort of thing. So it wasn't totally out of character for him to say he wanted out." He leaned forward. "Last year he was off work for a couple of months. He was working on some movie I can't remember the name of, and a harness he'd been issued with wasn't up to code. It was a familiar story—the production was ten days behind schedule because of a rookie director, safety meetings were cancelled, corners were cut. He was injured."

It seemed to Nina that Trank knew quite a lot about Wagner for such a casual relationship. She let him talk. He was filling in the blanks, and if she was going to crack this thing, she needed all the information she could get.

Nina lifted her pencil. "A couple of months off is a lot of time to think."

"I guess. Wagner wasn't much of a big thinker, though." Trank winced, instantly regretting the jibe. One shouldn't talk ill of the dead.

"What else can you tell me about him?" Nina asked innocently, her tone belying her intent.

"He is... was... a Louisiana boy through and through. Tried to hide the accent around new people, but once you knew him, he sounded like he'd walked right out of the bayou. Don't know much about his family. Ah..." he scratched the back of his head, seeming embarrassed he couldn't say more about the man who'd died in his bed.

Nina stepped into the silence. "I need you to walk me through last night. Tell me everything, no matter how unimportant it may seem. Minutiae is consequential."

"Now there's a five-dollar phrase. You could be a screenwriter with lines like that, and a damn sight better than the ones writing my show, that's for sure."

Deliberately not answering, Nina let the silence speak for itself. Trank shifted uncomfortably in his chair and went on.

"He arrived at about six, I think."

"How? Did he drive, get dropped off?"

"I, uh, don't know. I assume he took a cab. I didn't see his car."

"What sort of car does he drive?" Nina asked, pencil poised.

"One of those land whale things. A Buick Riviera, deep chestnut. It's the only thing he loves."

Cabs have logs, Nina thought, and a private car may still be in the neighborhood. So far, she wasn't getting anything remotely murder related. Nina motioned for him to go on, and Sputnik leaped onto the armchair and curled up in Nina's lap.

"We had a whiskey. And..." He gazed sideways at Nina. "In the cabana by the pool. I poured. He had a second, which I also poured. With ice, two cubes, I think."

"Maybe not that much minutiae. What did you guys talk about?"

"He was telling me he'd be rich soon, saying he'd be able to buy a place like mine. I know what stunt workers earn, even the big stunt coordinators, and he wasn't one of those. Believe me, he couldn't afford my letterbox."

"Okay." Nina made notes. "Then what?"

Trank became very interested in swirling the contents of his teacup. Nina leaned forward, annoying Sputnik, who stretched and wandered off.

"Hank?"

"Hmmm?"

"What happened next?" When she received no further answer, she huffed in frustration. "You were doing well for a while there, but now you're tighter lipped than a Gorilla Glued clam. Did you and Wagner engage in... activities before you left?"

Trank's lips pursed.

"I'm not trying to trick you into anything, Hank. If you did, there will be evidence at the crime scene. If I'm to protect you, I need to know."

His eyes met hers. "Yes."

"Thank you." She tapped her pencil on her notebook. "Okay, so, greeting, welcome drink," her mouth shifted to one side, "activities. What else?"

"That was it, really. I showered and got dressed. He made himself a sandwich and watched TV in the downstairs screening room."

"Made *himself* a sandwich. No staff at all last night?"

"No, only daytime. Gardeners, maids, chefs. They all finish at five."

"Tell me about him, Wagner. Did he have close friends? Ones he mentioned to you?"

"A few. He often mentioned a close friend. Ah..." Trank cast his gaze toward the ceiling. "Lewis something... last name is like Dale or Deal... Dean?" Trank swirled the cognac again. "Although..."

Nina leaned forward; something in Trank's manner suggested this was important. "Now we're talking about it, he mentioned the Lewis fellow last night. In relation to getting out of the business. He mentioned that the three of them—I don't know who the third person was—had found a way out."

"That's the wording he used? This is important."

Trank rubbed his stubbled chin. "No. He said..." His eyes gravitated to the ceiling again, as if willing the words to manifest. "He said something had fallen into their laps, meaning they could get out of the stinking business, or to that effect. He definitely used the phrase 'fallen into their laps,' because I remember I made a lap-dancing crack he didn't appreciate."

Transcribing the note, Nina underlined it. Twice. She also made a note, *Possible third person???*

"When did you leave?"

"About ten."

"Anything else you can recall? Any detail could matter."

He scratched the back of his neck. "No, nothing. Just that he was jittery. Outside noises made him jump. When I left, he asked me three times if I was going to lock the door."

Studiously making notes, Nina made another column. Birmingham stated there were no signs of forced entry. Wagner was home alone. She hardly thought he had beaten himself to death. So, who let the murderer in? With no ready answer, the finger of blame had once again swung back to Trank.

No time like the present. Nina picked up her cordless phone and dialed the number she knew by heart.

"Who are you calling?" Trank asked.

"An associate member of my detective agency."

Someone picked up. "Yep?"

"Hey Phoebs hon, it's me. Got a job for you."

"Anything for you, darlin', except murder, incest, and square dancing. Shoot."

"I need you to find the current location of a Lewis. Last name could be Dale, Deal, or something similar. He could be a stuntman, might not; currently working in LA in the film industry in some capacity. Known associate of one Seth Wagner. This one's important, okay? Anything you can give me in the shortest amount of time would be appreciated. Got all that?"

"Yep. I'll get back to you within the hour." Her friend paused. "You alright, Nina? You sound a bit...?"

"I'm fine. Let me know how you go."

She rung off. Noticing the time on her antique wall clock, Nina turned to Trank and asked, "You hungry?"

"Famished. Someone ate all my burgers."

Ignoring the jibe, Nina said, "I'm going to have a shower—I rushed out the door so fast this morning I didn't get the chance. I smell like Wayne Gretzky's jockstrap." She stood and walked to the kitchen, opening the fridge, then a cupboard. "There's bread and whatnot, make yourself some toast."

Trank's reaction was part stunned, part contemptuous, part bemused. It was as if she'd asked him to perform open heart surgery while landing a plane. He obviously hadn't touched a toaster in years, probably couldn't use one even if he wanted to. Toast making was a task for the help, not someone of his caliber. He was a capital S Star.

Nina was not a Star, or even a star. And even for those twelve seconds she had been, she'd still made her own fucking toast.

"Or starve." She turned away. "Up to you."

Nina showered, staying in there for as long as the hot water held out. She wanted to wash the stink of the case from her, but realized it wouldn't be that easy. She took her time to blow-dry her hair and emerged an hour later feeling marginally more human.

Tank hadn't moved an inch, still nursing his drink in the dainty teacup. Sputnik had curled up beside their guest —whether to protect her or guard him, Nina wasn't sure. She strode over to her extensive record collection, selected *Ellington at Newport* and entered her happy place as the first chords chimed.

Cooking helped Nina focus. Right now, she needed to process what she knew. A mindful activity turned down other thoughts and freed her mind to explore ideas. Her best friend Phoebe used the inelegant metaphor that it was it was like a mental enema. Crude, but straight to the point, a Phoebe specialty.

Searching the available ingredients, Nina went to work making herself and the pampered star some lunch. It had been hours since she'd eaten the pilfered burger and she was starving.

First, she warmed milk in a saucepan, as she'd been taught. In another she carefully melted the butter then added the flour, being careful not to let it burn. After a few minutes, she added the warm milk, stirring continuously before adding nutmeg, pepper, and salt. Once satisfied, she crafted the sandwiches, spreading the fresh bechamel on thick slices of bread, then adding butter, Dijon mustard, sliced gruyere and Swiss cheese, and smoked ham. She fried it in a pan, then finished with grated parmesan on top.

All the while, her mind processed the information she'd accumulated, rearranging it and pulling it apart. The puzzle pieces didn't fit. The trouble was, she didn't know the size or importance of the missing parts. She needed to collect as many of them as she could to form a picture. Wagner's friends were the likeliest of places to start.

Nina put the two sandwiches on mismatching plates, handing one to a baffled Trank.

"What's this?" he asked, part awed, part curious.

"Croque monsieur."

He screwed up his nose right until the moment the sandwich hit his tastebuds. With eyes wide, he held up the food with reverence. "My god, Nina, you're a gourmet chef!"

"It's only a sandwich."

She took a bite and realized she'd outdone herself. She stood corrected.

"This is fucking great," Nina announced, receiving no argument.

After a few more bites, Trank gently put his sandwich back on the plate and shook his head. "You were a pin-up actress, now you dress like Joan Jett but live like a bohemian. You're a gourmet chef and a private investigator. You're an enigma wrapped in a paradox encased in a leather jacket."

Nina wiped her mouth with a napkin. "Who says human beings need to fit some predetermined form? We're an amalgam of experience, trauma, triumph, and happenstance. We're all complex and fucked up, and none of us make the damnedest bit of sense." She flashed her teeth. "Some more than others."

"Do you enjoy being a private eye?" Trank asked before savoring another bite.

"It's been a hard slog. Thankfully Mickey and a few other studio types have given me sporadic work, but I won't claim it hasn't been tough. Made harder by the fact I'm not the usual type who does this kind of work."

A quizzical expression washed over Trank's face.

Nina pointed downward. "Vagina. I probably wouldn't have gotten this far if Mickey hadn't believed in me. He's pretty much the only one who has. I guess I owe the big lug."

Sputnik leaped onto the bench, apparently experiencing a sudden rush of affection for his owner. Nothing to do with food, Nina was sure. She gave him a scratch behind the ear and a piece of cheese she'd sliced off in anticipation of this completely random appearance.

The knock at the door made them both jump. Sputnik didn't care, he was too busy enjoying his cheese. Nina stepped cautiously toward the reinforced door and wrapped her hand around a baseball bat in the hat stand.

"Who is it?"

"Marie Antoinette, y'all got any cake?"

Laughing, Nina unlocked the door and yanked it open, revealing a casually dressed woman with a well-crafted afro and a wide, toothy grin. The two hugged, chuckling at Phoebe's lame joke.

The new arrival made herself at home, throwing her jacket in the general vicinity of the hall stand and her keys in the Moroccan bowl. She took all of two steps inside before she pulled up in surprise.

Grasping her friend's forearm, Phoebe whispered, "Ah, darlin', you've got *Vengeance Inc.* in your kitchen."

"I know, I've tried absolutely everything to get rid of it."

Phoebe turned to Trank. "I don't mean to be rude..."

"That'd be a first," Nina cut in.

"... but aren't you meant to be dead?"

Trank leaned in conspiratorially. "If I've learned

anything in this industry, it's that you shouldn't believe everything you read in the daily rags."

Nina motioned between them. "Phoebe Jones, meet the not-late Hank Trank."

Trank extended his hand. "Any friend of Nina's…"

Phoebe's mouth slanted to one side. "You're not going to finish that sentence, are you?"

"Not in polite company, no."

"You're funny." She turned to Nina. "He's funny."

Not ready to agree, Nina had nothing to say, so did exactly that.

"You're an associate member of the detective agency?" Trank asked Phoebe. "What does that mean exactly?"

"It means I don't get paid."

"But you will," Nina added quickly. "As soon as I start making some money."

Phoebe helped herself to half of Nina's sandwich. She didn't protest; such was the nature of their friendship. They shared food as freely as they shared clothes.

Taking a folded newspaper from under her arm, Phoebe handed it to Trank. "Now I get why Dad said I should take this upstairs."

"Your father?" Trank asked.

"The mean bar owner downstairs," Phoebe said between bites.

"Titus certainly was… intimidating."

"You should try being a teenager and getting caught creeping through your bedroom window at 5 am."

"I'd rather not."

"Smart man."

Trank unfolded the afternoon edition of the *Los Angeles Herald Examiner* and instantly huffed. The front page was mostly dedicated to a missing teen star, a pretty blond girl with big teeth who looked far older than the fifteen years she apparently was. Rising star Alicia Morrison had been missing for three days. The newspaper also mentioned Trank's murder.

Holding the paper at arm's length, Trank made a noise that could have been a shriek or an exclamation of agony.

"What?" Nina asked.

"I was murdered and I don't even merit a front page!"

Nina peered over Trank's shoulder. "Yes, you do. There." She pointed. "Hank Trank, star of the *Buster Higgins* movies and *Vengeance Inc.* found dead this morning. Even has a flattering photo."

More details could be found on page six, the newspaper proclaimed. She waved a palm as if to say, *what more do you want?*

"Below the fold!"

Nina gave him a half-hearted pat on the back. Her job wasn't to appease his fragile ego. Her job was to find who the real murderer was and keep Trank out of jail.

She led Phoebe away from the sulking Trank and his progressively higher pitched grunts.

"How did you go?"

Phoebe pulled out a crumpled piece of paper. "Lewis, last name Diehl. Age forty-seven. Works for Star Turns out of Fairfax. He's working today in West Hollywood on a movie called, uh, *Lethal Heat.* Sounds awful. Got the address and the name of the First AD if you need."

"Phoebe Jones, you're a marvel."

"I am, aren't I?" She chuckled. "Going to tell me how you came to be having lunch with a dead guy?"

Nina turned to Trank, then back to her friend. "When I can."

Phoebe gave her a knowing look, then proceeded to screw her nose up. "What is this shit you're listening to?"

"Duke Ellington." Nina raised her voice as Phoebe strode toward the turntable. "Don't you dare turn this off during 'Jeep's Blues.' Don't you dare."

"It's old!"

"It's better than what you listen to. Toto, Hall & Oates, Steely Dan. Christ, Captain & Tennille! Yacht rock is awful."

"I like it."

"But you're black!"

"Are you saying black people can't own yachts?" Phoebe planted her fists on her hips theatrically. "Racist!"

Nina broke into peals of laughter, Phoebe joining her. They hugged, regaining their composure eventually.

"You two have a very strange relationship." Evidently, Trank had recovered from his newspaper shock.

Nina folded the piece of paper Phoebe had supplied and put it in her pocket. She turned to her friend. "You good to hang here for a few hours?"

Phoebe gave a thumbs up.

Trank sneered. "I don't need a babysitter."

"Says the man who can't make his own toast."

"Needing a minder is humiliating." Trank folded his arms. "And I know humiliation, I had a guest role on *Manimal*."

"You'll be fine, Hank," Phoebe said. "If you're a good boy maybe I'll take you out for ice cream." Somehow, her sarcasm didn't sate Trank's decaying dignity.

"Plus," Nina eyed her friend, knowing what was to come, "Phoebe knows how to feed Sputnik."

Phoebe let out an exaggerated grunt. "Fine." She bent down to the cat and rubbed his fur the wrong way, literally. "I'll feed the feral little flea trap!"

Sputnik hissed and Phoebe gave him the bird. Theirs was a hate/hate relationship.

"Thanks, Phoebs." Nina picked up her jacket and keys. "I'll be back soon enough." She yanked the door open. "I have a case to crack."

FOUR

A thin bead of sweat coated on the man's upper lip. The day was warm, but not enough for the volume of sweat this man was exuding. Lewis Diehl stood on the roof of the Emser Tile Building, his feet perilously close to the ledge. His hands were in the air—not all that surprising given the sheer volume of guns pointed in his direction.

Gulping, Diehl's gaze darted to those responsible for his fate before he finally closed his eyes, resigning himself to his plight. An odd calm descended over the scene. It lasted mere moments. Shouting erupted from multiple areas and Diehl's chest exploded into a mass of red. He teetered backward, his feet tripping ever closer to the edge, until he toppled over the ledge into the abyss above Santa Monica Boulevard.

There was a brief silence before the roof erupted into applause. The director shouted, "Cut!", prompting a flurry of activity as crew threw themselves into their assigned tasks. The First AD barked into a walkie-talkie and gave Nina the thumbs up, her cue to move around freely.

She peered over the ledge to see Diehl roll off a massive blue airbag and raise his fists triumphantly. Technicians removed his so-called "dead-character costume" containing the exploded squibs that simulated the bloody bullet wounds. Another assistant handed him a can of Budweiser, which Diehl snatched without thanks and gulped, followed by a "Yeah!" that Nina could hear seven floors up. No one else seemed particularly eager to join Diehl in his revelry.

Minutes later, Nina was on the street waiting for Diehl to finish talking to his stunt coordinator. Stripped of his costume, he wore a white singlet and jorts. He took a Camel from a soft packet and lit it, taking a long drag. The man was built like a fire hydrant and appeared about as smart. His complexion was like the inside of a tin of spam.

He leaned against a beat-up Camaro that had seen better days. The passenger door was black while the rest of the car was a faded red. When he was finally alone, Nina stepped over.

"Excuse me, Mister Diehl, I wonder if I could have a minute of your time?"

Diehl took his time sizing Nina up from top to bottom, taking particular interest in the former.

"For you, darlin', I'll give you two." Draining his Budweiser, he crushed it and threw it on the ground. Lowering his gaze, he sized her up like a buffet at a strip club. "Maybe we could do this in my trailer."

"Out here is fine." Nina had no intention of being alone with this man.

"You sure about that? The old stunts get the blood flowing. Man needs to do something about it, if you get me?"

"I got you before you even opened your mouth."

Diehl's expression morphed into semi-confusion, like

a dog who knows he's been told off but doesn't understand why. Nina was surprised he didn't try and hump her leg.

"My name is Maddox, I'm a private investigator."

"A *woman* PI?" He made it sound like it was the equivalent of an axolotl piloting the Space Shuttle. "And you have a PI license?"

"I do."

She unfolded her wallet to show him. It was always men who were surprised. She was so tired of having to explain herself and her profession. Male private investigators didn't have to explain their choice of vocation; it was just accepted. But Nina was constantly being asked to explain, purely because she had the audacity to walk around without a penis. The nerve.

It was no coincidence there was a distinct lack of women on set, other than the ones who were fetching coffee. She'd seen a couple of make-up artists and a script supervisor, but otherwise, the set was Wang Central.

She reminded herself to stay on subject. Nina pointed toward the airbag. "Impressive stunt."

Diehl brandished his cigarette. "You should see what I can do with a horse."

"There are so many ways I could take that statement." Receiving only confusion in response, Nina pressed on. "I believe you know a gentleman by the name of Seth Wagner?"

The faux-affability and underlying sleaze disappeared in an instant. Nina could have sworn he turned four shades whiter. He took too long to respond.

"I know him."

"That's a guarded response."

"I'm a guarded kind of guy."

Quelling the urge to groan, Nina projected her most professional voice. "You and Seth were friends?"

"You could say that."

"I did. When was the last time you saw him?"

"Been a while."

He let the sentence dangle there, offering no more. Taking a long drag of his Camel, he gazed around the set, as if searching for any kind of distraction. None were forthcoming.

Normally, Nina thought, when a private investigator turned up asking questions about your friend, the first instinct would be to ask what it was about. Diehl had asked no such question; instead, he'd automatically gone on the defensive. That suggested he already knew why she was there, or at least thought he did.

"If you don't mind me asking, where were you last night, Mr Diehl?"

"Lewis, please."

"Where were you last night, Lewis?"

"None of your fucking business, bitch." He abruptly pushed himself up from the Camaro. "We're done here."

Diehl went to leave, but Nina stood in his way. "I still have questions."

"And I don't give a fuck."

He pushed her shoulder with far more force than was warranted. Nina reacted without thinking; her hand grasped his right wrist in a fierce pincer grip while simultaneously taking hold of his elbow with her left hand. Finding the natural bend in the elbow, she dropped into what her karate teacher called the "horse stance," rotating his elbow 180 degrees. Pushing up, she used his forward lean to compromise his balance and bent him over the hood of the Camaro where he landed ingloriously, face down. The whole process unfolded in three seconds.

Leaning down, Nina whispered in his ear, "Do you give a fuck now, *Lewis*?"

"Let me go, whore."

"Now, is that any way to speak to a lady?" She paused a beat. "Or me?" She pushed his elbow further up his back, causing him to inhale sharply. "Are you going to play nice or do we stay like this until the entire crew get to see the big tough man laid out by a girl?"

"Fine," he spat. "Fine."

Releasing him, Nina stepped back in case he was stupid enough to throw a punch. He didn't, but she wasn't ruling out the possibility.

"When was the last time you saw Seth Wagner?"

"Day before yesterday."

It was hard for Nina to gauge the truthfulness of such a short sentence. She decided to take it at face value, at least for now.

"I have reason to believe you and Wagner are working on getting out of the business. Is that correct?"

She chose her wording carefully. She had no idea how much Diehl knew, or if he was in fact the one who'd facilitated Wagner's transition to the past tense.

His eyes narrowed. "Along those lines, yeah."

At least that was something. Now was the time to offer an olive branch.

"I can help. I have a friend who wants to look after Seth. He can help you too. All you need to do is let me."

There was a visible slump in the man's shoulders. His countenance was still tinged with dread, and it was nothing to do with Nina pinning him to the hood of his car.

"Can we talk about this privately? In a trailer?"

The offer was of a different nature than it had been minutes before. The first was born of sleaze, this was born of fear. He was sweating, and it wasn't the heat.

"In a minute. Seth said you'd found a way out." She watched his face closely. "What did he mean by that?"

He gulped. "We... found something big. Huge. Well, Seth stumbled onto it, I kind of helped." He leaned forward. "*Helped*, okay? This wasn't my idea."

"Helped with what, exactly?"

He shook his head. *Not yet.* "Do you know where he is?"

"I do." But she wasn't about to give him the address of the morgue; instead, she gave her own shake of the head. *Not yet.*

He dipped his head in response. *Touché.*

Asking about Wagner's whereabouts suggested he thought his friend was missing, not dead.

Lighting another cigarette, Diehl leaned against the hood. "If you're a PI, who exactly are you working for?"

"Mickey Boehler."

Diehl leaped up as if jolted by electricity, his head bouncing around like a pinball. "You're working for *The Steamroller*?" He shook his head, reeling back in fear. "Lady, you just got me killed."

"I don't know what—"

Nina stopped as the First AD approached, concern etched on his face at Diehl's obvious distress.

"Uh, Lewis, Martin wants another take." His gaze bounced between the pair of them. "Everything alright?"

"Fine." When the First AD took a few steps back, giving them space, Diehl lowered his voice. "You have to tell Mickey I had nothing to do with it. *Please.*"

"I haven't told Mickey anything, okay? I'm just investigating a case."

"Lewis," the First AD called, motioning for Diehl to follow, "we have to get you prepped and ready in twenty. Let's go."

Diehl touched Nina's arm. "Look, I'm sorry about the shit I said earlier. I'm not a fucking asshole, alright? Please, you gotta believe me, the three of us only wanted to make some nice cash. That's all. We weren't going to use it, alright? Jesus, tell Mickey he can have it." Turning away from the glare of the First AD, he added. "Just stay here, okay? We can talk some more. Do that for me, please?"

The three of us. That confirmed what Trank had told her.

Nina gave the slightest of tilt of her head. *Fine.* Relief washed over his face. For a fraction of a second she thought he was going to hug her—not a pleasant thought. Instead, he bowed in gratitude several times.

"Who was the third—"

"Now, Lewis." The First AD waved apologetically to Nina. "We have to get this shot in before we lose the light."

Diehl bobbed his head apologetically to Nina and followed the agitated First AD. First ADs were always agitated. That was their function in life. The role of the First AD was managerial, not creative. They were pushy, nagging, managing those who frequently outranked them, often the loudest and most frequently heard on set. As a result, they were usually the most hated person on any production.

As Nina watched them go, her mind raced. What did all this mean? Wagner had discovered something that had gotten him killed. It apparently required at least two accomplices. And now one of those accomplices was plainly scared out of his mind. *Scared of your client,* Nina reminded herself.

None of this made a lick of sense. At least not yet.

There were shouts of, "Quiet on set" from the First AD and a flurry of activity from the department heads. Nina watched the same movie death scene unfold again, but this time from the ground. The view was more spectacular as she saw Diehl writhe and twist in the air before landing. This close to the ground, there was far more of a thud than she'd expected; no *whoomph* of the airbag.

For several moments, nothing happened. Then the shouting started, each cry growing ever more distressed. A woman screamed from the rooftop. Crew sprinted in all directions.

Something had gone wrong. Very wrong.

The stunt coordinator was the first to set foot on the scarcely filled airbag. Within seconds he cried out, "Someone get an ambulance!"

In the mayhem that followed, Nina was able get close to the deflated airbag. She leaned in to see where the air hose inlet was connected to the two air blowers, or rather, where they *should* have been connected. On the bag itself, two inlets were labelled "In"—to inflate it quicker, she assumed, or for safety reasons. One was completely detached, while the other was almost entirely unfastened. The result was enough to keep the airbag slightly inflated, but not enough to support a man falling seven floors.

This wasn't an oversight.

It wasn't an accident.

This was a deliberate act.

Through the mass of rushing bodies, Nina saw Diehl's motionless body, his lifeless eyes wide in surprise. She pulled her leather jacket around her and walked away. She would get no more from the scene. Lewis Diehl was dead.

She crossed Santa Monica Boulevard and walked toward her car, parked on Croft Avenue. She was doing her best to wrap her head around the stuntman's death when she saw her Charger slanted on an odd angle. When was close enough, she saw why.

"Motherfucker."

Someone had slashed her tires.

Nina walked around the car to assess the damage. There was a piece of paper folded under her windshield wiper. Unfolding it, she saw it was a newspaper ad promoting the first Scream Queen movie at a local revival house. The poster image had been defaced with thick red ink. A red x adorned each of her eyes and a crude knife had been drawn plunging into her chest. Messy scrawled letters across the top declared, "Nosy bitches are dead bitches."

It was clear Diehl had been killed for talking to Nina. Another thing was equally clear: whoever slashed her tires wasn't going to stop there, unless Nina ceased her investigation.

Shit just got real.

CHAPTER
FIVE

Nina knew she should have been more concerned. After all, she'd seen a man fall to his death in front of her, and then there had been a threat on her own life. But right now she was just pissed at having to replace four practically brand-new tires.

"They weren't cheap either," she said to no one, feeding a quarter into the pay phone. Hardly any phones accepted dimes anymore, which only added to her sense of irascibility. "Fuckers."

She called a local mechanic and explained that no, she didn't have four spares in her trunk and would they be so kind as to send replacements. They sold her four new tires, as well as four second-hand wheels. She'd have to make an appointment to swap the tires again if she wanted to keep the rims. She could have sworn they were laughing as she hung up.

"Also, fuckers."

Nina paced for a good fifteen minutes. She wished she was at home in her kitchen to work this one through.

Stomping around West Hollywood in the heat would have to do.

Diehl's death didn't negate the possibility he'd killed Wagner, though it did make proving it a lot harder. Who the hell was going around killing stunt guys?

As soon as she'd mentioned Mickey's name, Diehl had freaked out. He was terrified. Minutes later he was dead. Had Mickey called in a hit? Sure, he was a powerful studio executive who hadn't gained his position through privilege or nepotism, and certainly not by playing nice. Mickey Boehler had started as a runner at Paramount in the fifties, and through pure tenacity and guile had worked his way up until he was the most feared studio head in the industry. *But was he a killer?*

He'd worked with the Teamsters during his ascent. Then there were the mob rumors. You didn't get the sort of power Mickey Boehler had attained without backing. It was a known secret he'd used hired thugs to break the WGA strike in 1973. Then there were the rumors of money laundering productions. How else do you explain *King Kong* '76?

Stories of The Steamroller's long-term vengeance were legend. One said he'd made a deal with the then head of Warners to trade contracted directors for specific projects. He'd held up his end of the bargain, but the Warners chief hadn't. Boehler waited years, but managed to kill their grossly expensive Oscar bait production two-thirds into the shooting schedule. He didn't stop there. He personally saw to the construction of an ugly five story apartment block in front of the executive's prized holiday mansion, blocking their view of the ocean. The rumor that Mickey had also fucked the man's wife was apparently just that, but Nina knew for a fact he'd never denied it.

The lesson was clear, and the whole town understood it: you crossed the head of Phoenix Studios at your peril.

Did all this mean he was capable of having a man murdered? Two men? Nina didn't know. He was certainly a fear-inducing individual, but a killer?

There was one way to find out.

Nina dropped another quarter into the pay phone. Not many people had Mickey's direct number. He answered after four rings.

"Speak."

Mickey wasn't one for airs and graces. *No time for that shit,* he'd said at their first meeting.

"Hey Mickey, it's Nina."

"Anything to report?"

His question could mean everything and nothing.

Up until she'd met with Diehl, she'd been debating whether to tell Mickey she'd found Trank loitering out the front of his own murder scene. At the time, she'd thought she was protecting her charge until she knew more. Now that she *did* know more, she had to wonder if her initial trepidation had been something else entirely. Given current circumstances, Nina decided keeping Mickey in the dark was the wisest course of action, though she was all too aware what her fate would be should he ever find out.

"Not really. Trank's house didn't contain anything incriminating, other than the guy who'd been beaten to death with an award, that is. Just another glorious day in the City of Angels."

"Good, good."

What was he eating? Whatever it was, it was crunchy. Could be anything from a Caesar salad to a charred pig carcass. Given the size of the guy, she suspected the latter.

"What else you working on?"

For someone as busy as he always claimed to be, the question stood out like a turd in a fruit bowl. Boehler rarely took an interest in anything not directly related to himself. The question made the hairs on the back of her neck stand on end.

While Nina was on the phone, the tow truck arrived with her wheels. She waved them toward her car. Two beefy mechanics in filthy unfastened overalls grunted in her general direction. They labored away, displaying far more butt crack than she was comfortable with.

"You know me, Mickey, I've always got my finger in many pies."

"I've heard that rumor." *Crunch.* "Whatever floats your boat, toots."

The banter was classic Mickey, crass with a heavy dollop of misogyny. But the delivery was flat, like he was going through the motions. None of this did anything to ease her all-encompassing feeling of disquiet.

"Anything else you need from me on the Trank thing?"

"No, you're done, Nina. Been a pleasure."

She was only too keen to ring off. Nina folded her arms and exhaled slowly, trying to rid herself of the unease swirling inside her. It didn't work.

Doing her best to shake it off, Nina's thoughts moved to planning her next steps. She wasn't about to wait until someone threw her off a building. Whoever was coming for her would surely underestimate Nina Maddox. It would be a mistake they'd only make once.

As Nina stepped inside the warm embrace of Asta's, Titus waved her over. He waited until a member of the United

Nations of Drunkards had collected his Miller and slunk off into a dark corner, then spoke.

"Man called. Said it was urgent." Titus's voice was molasses laced with shards of glass. He handed her a napkin with the message written on it, but didn't let go. "You know they have message services and pagers these days."

When Titus finally released the napkin, Nina read the message. The name Andrew Ross didn't ring any bells, but it was a Beverly Hills number. In her line of business, it was generally a good idea to return calls from Beverly Hills.

"I could, but I'd miss our little tête-à-têtes Titus, and that I simply can't abide."

The big man grunted. Most people couldn't see past his gruff exterior—Mount Rushmore if one of the Presidents was really mad—but Nina could sense the amusement in the old soldier. Not that he'd ever admit it, of course. She blew the crotchety old softie a kiss and headed upstairs.

Nina expected to find Phoebe and Trank arguing. Or Phoebe and Sputnik. But upon entering the apartment, she discovered there was no Phoebe. There was no Trank. But there was Sputnik with one leg in the air, licking his butt. He issued her a curious expression then, once he'd determined it wasn't dinner time, resumed the task with renewed vigor.

Maybe they had *gone out for ice cream?*

Dialing the number Titus had provided, a prim English-accented voice answered. "Kellerman, Ross and Associates, how may I direct your call?"

"Yeah, I was given this number to call Andrew Ross. The name's Nina Maddox."

"He's awaiting your call, Ms Maddox, putting you through now."

The call was picked up seconds later. "Nina Maddox, Andrew Ross. This is a supreme pleasure." Nina could hear the porcelain teeth through the phone. He had the faux-familiarity that was stock-in-trade for agents the world over, but none had the intensity of those in Hollywood.

"You called me?"

"Yes, yes, I did. I represent a most select group of clients, and I urgently need your assistance with one in particular."

Nina waited. She assumed he was waiting for her to ask who. She didn't. Nina didn't have time for games. This imitation human was wearing her already threadbare patience to the bone.

"Uh," he started, rattled, "you would have seen the news stories about the missing young actress, Alicia Morrison?"

Nina recalled the story above Trank's on the front page of the newspaper. The missing fifteen-year-old with the big teeth and blond hair.

"I have."

"Well, she's my star client and I'd like to hire you to find her. She hasn't been seen for three days."

"I'm kind of busy."

"You are? Sergeant Birmingham, who gave me your details, said you were cleaning up after the Trank murder. Terrible news, terrible. I tried to nab him as a client a couple of years back, but no luck I'm afraid. Fortunate in retrospect, I suppose." He paused. "Anyway, if you'll excuse my candor, what assistance can you offer him now? He's dead, it's not like he's going to get any deader."

And Nina thought she was renowned for her bluntness. She shook her head. Agents. Vultures, the lot of them.

"You have a point." Nina's thoughts turned to her

charge. *Where is Trank?* "I guess. Give me all you have on her last movements."

Nina wedged the receiver against her shoulder and took notes in a leather notebook as he spoke.

"She was last seen the evening before last, leaving the Phoenix Studios lot around 6 pm, on foot."

"On foot?"

That was odd. No one walked in this town.

"Yes, that's what the guard on duty reported, Reg Pillar."

Nina knew Reg well. Nice guy.

"Where did she go from there?"

"No one knows."

"Helpful."

She asked a few more questions, took some contact details and rang off. Did she have capacity to find a missing starlet? It all depended on what she could uncover in the next twenty-four hours. It was getting dark outside. She couldn't start on the Morrison case until the morning. Tonight, she planned to find more details about who killed Wagner. It could be possible to work both cases.

Nina's thoughts were stopped by the sound of a flushing toilet in her bathroom. When the door opened, she expected to see Trank.

It wasn't Trank.

The figure who emerged jolted in fright when he saw Nina. He was like a particularly startled deer.

He recovered, and a familiar suave, self-assured grin spread across his lightly stubbled, chiseled face. "After I saw you this morning, I decided to come by and surprise you."

Planting her fists on her hips, Nina asked, "And you decided you'd go ahead and let yourself in?"

"You told me to last time, remember?" Armin Lang said innocently. The forensics photographer appeared genuinely concerned. "You showed me where you hide the spare key."

"I did?"

"You were a little drunk, I'm not surprised you don't remember."

"I remember everything after we got in."

"You remember the good parts, then."

He smiled. *Damn, that smile.* Nina and Lang had a casual arrangement. It wasn't love that kept them reconnecting, but it had the same number of letters.

Her head swiveled around the apartment. "There, uh, was no one else here when you came in?"

"Uh, no." His brow furrowed. "Competition?"

"Not at all," she answered honestly.

All alone, then.

Nina let her jacket slide off her shoulders. It landed with a *plop* on the floor. She turned to her newly arrived guest. Removing her black T-shirt to reveal a black lace bra beneath, she threw it into her bedroom.

"Well come on, then."

THE NIGHT WAS HOT.

Nina's bedroom window was open, but the curtains refused to move. It felt like there hadn't been a breath of air since the Carter administration. The sweaty body beside her rolled over her equally sweaty form to swipe two of her cigarettes from the nightstand. He lit both, then placed one gently between her lips.

In the movies, a couple generally have a convenient L-shaped sheet, exposing the man's torso while covering the woman's chest and other unmentionables. There was no L-shaped sheet in Nina's world. In fact, there was no sheet. It had been tossed aside as soon as they tumbled into bed. Modesty had no place within these four walls.

Lang said, "Penny for your thoughts."

Nina simpered. She wasn't about to tell him what she'd been thinking. She'd been devising next steps in finding out who'd killed Wagner, and likely Diehl. She wanted to search Wagner's place for any clues as to why he'd been targeted. *If he had,* Nina countered. She still wasn't completely convinced Trank hadn't been the target all along, though any bookie in Vegas would put money on Wagner, given the evidence so far.

"A penny per thought?" she replied, giving him a playful elbow. "If so, you'd better have a big ol' bag of pennies."

He chuckled. "One will do."

"Cheap ass." Nina took a deep drag of her cigarette, buying time to come up with an acceptable reply. "I was wondering if you would have turned up at my place if we hadn't crossed paths this morning."

He gave her that smile again. "You have been on my mind of late."

Her hand snaked down his chest, exploring further. "And what thoughts would they be, I wonder?"

"If you'd like to go for dinner some time?" There was a note of trepidation in his voice.

Nina's hand stopped moving. "I thought we discussed this?"

She removed her hand and pushed herself upright.

"We didn't discuss it." He picked up on her shift in demeanor. "You said you wouldn't talk about it. That's not the same thing. You always do that, push me away." His finger gently traced the outline of her cheek. "Is that what you do whenever anyone gets too close?"

Nina didn't reply as her thoughts returned to the face-down photograph on her bookshelf. She took another drag of her cigarette, hoping he would drop the subject. She knew he wouldn't.

"Oh, I'm sorry," she glanced at the non-existent watch on her wrist, "our therapy session has come to an end. Please make a follow-up appointment with my secretary on your way out."

"I don't have to be a shrink to know your past is preventing you from—"

"Don't." Her voice was soft. "Please."

"Alright."

Early on, she'd given him an outline of what had happened years before, to Juliet, and the horrible truths later revealed. She told him why she couldn't commit, couldn't let herself get closer than the occasional sweaty roll in the sheets and a post-coital cigarette. He wasn't the first she'd told, but he was the first to come back afterward. She respected him for that. It hadn't changed her mind, though. She doubted anything could. Her bed would forever be a transit stop at best; she'd spend most of her nights alone, with her ghosts.

"What's the scoop on Trank?" she asked the ceiling.

Matching her position, Lang propped himself up on one elbow and smirked. He knew it was a blatant ploy to change the subject. He let her get away with it. "Are you asking out of curiosity or in a professional capacity?"

"Mickey said I was done with Trank."

Technically, she didn't lie to him. *Technically.*

"The boys downtown say he was tortured before his death."

"Who would torture a stuntman?"

Fuck. Nina tensed. *Did he notice?* Damn personal talk had put her off her game.

Lang's forehead crinkled. "Trank wasn't a stuntman..."

He noticed.

"He was built like a stuntman, is what I meant to say."

Smooth.

"Uh, I guess." His tone turned businesslike. "The bruising to the wrists and upper torso indicated blunt force trauma prior to the fatal head wounds. The chief medical examiner is under pressure from the DA to issue the death certificate, but he hasn't been able to verify the deceased's identity yet. Dental is out, given the extensive teeth damage. No tattoos, pacemakers, identifying moles, or birthmarks. They have the vic's prints, of course, but so far there's no match. They've been sent to the national register, but if Trank was never arrested, I doubt they'll turn up much there either. The DA chewed out the boss in front of everyone, but the old bastard held firm. No confirmation, no cert. He'll probably lose his job come next review. It was all a bit tense."

Nina understood why they were having such a hard time confirming the body was Trank. Unfortunately, she wasn't in a position to help Lang's boss. At least not yet. She still didn't know if Wagner or Trank was the real target. She felt a pang of guilt for remaining mute on the subject, but keeping Trank safe was her priority.

"Is there any word on—"

Nina stopped herself when a *clunk* emanated from her closet. Lang heard it too; his eyes darted around the room. She moved on, fearing what it could mean.

"What I meant was, is there any word on time of death?"

Still distracted by the unexplained noise, Lang answered absentmindedly, "Uh, around midnight. Did you hear—"

Lang was cut short when the slatted closet door flung open and Hank Trank stumbled out. His hand grabbed at his right calf and rubbed vigorously.

"Sorry, killer cramp."

Nina sat up. "Have you been there the whole fucking time?"

Trank laughed awkwardly. "That's an apt way of describing it."

Lang leaped out of bed and pointed to the newcomer. "That's Hank Trank!"

"I heard him fumbling with the lock," Trank pointed apologetically to Lang, "so I hid in your room. Then you two decided to, you know... It was either there," he pointed to the closet, "or under the bed. Given the last hour or so, I'm glad I chose the closet."

"He's alive!" Lang shook his head, his hand still pointing. "How is he alive?"

Nina picked the sheet off the floor and wrapped herself up. "I'm not sure how I feel about that, Hank."

Lang's mouth dropped open. "Can someone please explain to me how the man I saw dead on a bed this morning is coming out of a closet?"

That caused Trank and Nina to laugh. Seeing the distinct lack of humor on Lang's face, Nina's expression turned somber.

"Sorry, private joke."

Trank pointed to the naked forensics photographer. "Good to see you don't take bit parts, Nina."

"Nina..." Lang said seriously, "I think you better start at the beginning."

CHAPTER
SIX

Lang didn't leave until just before midnight. It had taken several hours and even more coffees to convince him to keep Trank's non-cadaver status to himself. Without giving away details about Wagner, Nina had advised there was far more at play than she was able to explain right now. She promised he'd be the first to know when she was free to reveal more.

Nina explained she was trying to find the killer before she took Trank to the cops, otherwise he'd be prime suspect number one. She'd been hired to keep him safe and that's exactly what she was trying to do.

In the end, she wasn't sure what convinced Lang to leave—that he was satisfied with the explanation, or he knew Nina wasn't going to give away anything further. Probably both.

The ominous part for Nina was when Lang was departing. He waited at the door, kissed her, then checked to make sure Trank was out of earshot. He'd whispered in her ear, "Are you sure he didn't do it?"

The comment gave her pause, but she completely dismissed it as soon as she closed the door. Well, almost completely. Somewhat completely. Semi-completely. A bit completely.

At least now she had a bit more information. Wagner had been tortured. That meant someone wanted information before they killed him. It also strongly suggested the torturers knew it wasn't Hank Trank, unless they were complete morons. It didn't mean Trank was in the clear, but so far, she hadn't turned anything up to suggest anyone was out to get him. Given the twisted serpentine nature of this case, she wasn't ruling it out either. Or, as Lang had suggested, perhaps Trank was the perpetrator.

As Nina sat on the sofa in her bathrobe and rubbed her temples, Sputnik curled up on her lap. Trank sat opposite her, sipping cognac from a teacup.

"He seems nice." The comment didn't seem loaded.

"He has feelings about you too." Nina didn't elaborate on what those feelings where.

"In all the commotion, I didn't ask, did you see Diehl?" he asked.

"Yes. He's dead."

Head reeling in shock, Trank's voice rose an octave. "What?" He lowered his gaze. "Did you kill him?"

Nina rolled her eyes. "Yes, all the best private investigators interview people and then throw them off a building. It's how you crack cases, don't you know?"

"Thrown off a building?"

Nina saw Trank's fear and realized she'd gone too far. She exhaled slowly. "Sorry about that, I'm still a bit rattled by the closet thing." And, if she were honest, Lang's question about Trank being the murderer, which she chose not to verbalize. "Plus, I don't normally see people die in front of me." She paused. "I don't crack cases by killing people. But he did die after falling from a building, that bit was true."

She told him what she'd witnessed, more tactfully this time. She left out the slashed tires, fearing it would only frighten the rattled star even more.

He took it all in and stared into the middle distance, likely trying to make sense of events. She wished him luck, because it was something she'd thoroughly failed to do herself. They sat in silence for a few minutes.

Trank stifled a yawn. "I suppose I should make up the couch. After what you two did in there I'm not keen to share a bed with you."

"Lucky it was never on offer, then." Nina stretched her arms above her head. "But we're not going to bed yet, my friend."

The friend part was a stretch, but Trank let it slide.

"We aren't?"

Nina shook her head. "No. We're going to pay your friend Wagner's place a visit."

"*We* are, are we?"

"Yup. You know where it is, and you knew the man far more intimately than I do. You might find a clue I'd miss."

"Do I have a choice in the matter?"

"Absolutely not."

"Marvelous."

THEY STEPPED out of Asta's onto Abbot Kinney Boulevard. Except for the requisite staggering misplaced drunk and a wild, bearded homeless woman pushing a shopping cart full of her earthly possessions, Venice was thankfully uninhabited at witching hour.

"What the hell happened to your car?" Trank waved at Nina's Charger as he approached. "It looks like some kid's been swapping parts off his Hot Wheels."

He was right. Her beautiful beloved Chevy was now a patchwork of other, less cool, vehicles, no longer a cool black steed and now more suited to a demolition derby. The vibration from the mismatching tires made her teeth rattle.

"It's a long story."

It wasn't, but she didn't want to get into it right now.

They drove though the warm night. The streets were mostly empty, save for the occasional prowl car or delivery van. There were no doubt parties in the hills, where opportunistic players deflowered the innocent, pouring promises of stardom in their ears while plying them with all sorts of illegal substances. If New York was the city that never slept, LA was the city where you slept it off.

Another reason for the late-night investigation was that Nina wanted time to search for Alicia Morrison in the morning. The teen star's agent sounded worried for his charge, or meal ticket, a more cynical person might suggest. Nina wanted to start investigating the young woman's disappearance first thing in the morning. She checked her watch; two fifteen. Sleep was for the weak, apparently.

Beside her, Trank yawned. He was tired too. Nina had to fight to keep her eyelids open and hold the vibrating car on the straight and narrow. She should have had an extra coffee before they'd left.

She'd say Trank was dead on his feet if it wasn't too close to home. It wasn't every day you faced your death and not only lived to tell the tale, but to investigate it.

Stretching, Trank asked, "Care to explain what you

expect to discover in an apartment in the middle of the night?"

"The same thing we'd find in the middle of the day, but with fewer witnesses."

"Smart-ass."

"That's me all over." Against her better judgment, she was beginning to like Hank Trank. Or at least get used to him. Once you got past the hoity airs and graces, he could be amusing and unpretentious. Becoming familiar with a client was always perilous. Lang's warning about him potentially being the murderer still rung in her ears. "It shouldn't take too long. When we finish, we'll go back to mine and I'll cook up a nice brekkie."

Trank sat up. "A what?"

"Brekkie," Nina said with a laugh. "Australian slang for breakfast. My homeland sneaks out every now and then."

"You're Australian? I didn't know that." The revelation seemed to energize him. "I assumed you'd hopped on a Greyhound bus from the Midwest somewhere with stars in your eyes and walked straight into Phoenix Studios for day one of principal photography."

Trank was revived and amused, the slump in his shoulders all but gone.

"My story's almost like that. Just swap the bus for a plane, and the walking through the front gate for two years of waitressing and endless auditions, and you pretty much have it."

"You really wouldn't know. There's no accent."

"It only comes out when I'm tired. Or drunk." Amusement danced on her lips. "You can talk, weren't you actually born in Canada?"

"My mother is American." Trank didn't seem to find the conversation as amusing when the topic turned to him.

Nina chuckled. "The straight-shooting all-American Hank 'The Tank' Trank is none of those things. Especially the straight bit."

Trank crossed his arms. "You really don't give a, excuse the parlance, fuck, do you Nina?"

"I give plenty. The time just has to be right, and the people, too."

Trank's words were harsh, but there was a friendliness that had been lacking before now. Perhaps he was warming to Nina like she was warming to him. She questioned herself about the conflict of interest. Objectivity should be paramount, especially as there was still a question mark around his part in all this. Hell, she didn't even know his alibi. That still riled her professional sensibilities, but his proximity was a necessity for now.

"Nina?"

"Hmmm?"

"Who's paying you right now?"

"Andrew Ross, Alicia Morrison's agent is paying for—"

"No, I mean, what we're doing now. Tonight. My investigation. I assume Mickey only paid you to show up at my house and look around, nothing more?"

"That is true..."

He sat up straight and ran his palms down his thighs. "I would like to hire you to uncover the truth about my—"

"Murder?"

"I was going to say predicament. But yes."

"Okay, you're my client, Hank. A thousand bucks retainer and four hundred a day, plus expenses."

"Do you take credit?" Trank exaggeratedly patted himself down. "It could be difficult to walk into Wells Fargo to cash a cheque at the moment, but I'm good for it."

Nina nodded. "Deal."

It was a topic she'd been meaning to bring up, so she was glad Trank had done it for her. Her grocery bill would thank her.

Trank's tired eyes stared forward. "Do you think we've messed things up with your photographer beau?"

"Did you just refer to a grown man as a beau?"

"You're avoiding the question."

"You're avoiding the fact that you speak like you're living in the '40s."

Trank offered no reply, waiting for Nina to say something. She frowned to herself. *That's my thing.*

"Fine," she eventually said. "He'll be okay. We're not getting married or anything. It's a... relaxed kind of arrangement."

"It didn't sound very relaxed on the other side of the closet door, I assure you."

"You know what I mean. No commitments. I'll wait a few days, bake him a cake, pour him some wine, hang from the chandelier naked, he'll get over it."

"You like him."

Nina turned to him before her gaze returned to the road. "I wouldn't let him in my house if I didn't."

"No, I mean you *like* him."

"He's a good human. He's been tutoring me on forensics. Blood splatter patterns, rates of decay, that kind of thing."

"And this is what passes for pillow talk in your world, is it?"

"Kinda, yeah."

Trank shook his head. "Do you have any breath mints? Gum?"

"You going on a date?"

"No." He opened the glove compartment. "It's two o'clock in the morning, my mouth feels like the floor of a New York cab." He pulled out a folded piece of newspaper. "What's this?"

She'd hoped to avoid telling Trank, but now the cat was out of the glove box. "Just a little message someone left me when they slashed my tires today."

Trank turned to her in alarm. "Why are you still investigating? They're threatening you, Nina!" He shook his head. "I'll give myself up, you can prove me innocent once I'm in custody."

"Thanks for the offer, but no." Nina issued a bored sigh. "Intimidation doesn't work on me."

"It's working on me!"

"I refuse to be intimidated by bad grammar. There's not even a full stop."

"Can I be intimidated enough for the two of us?"

"Knock yourself out."

"If only that were an option."

He put the piece of paper back into the glove compartment and they drifted into silence for a time. Nina drove down an eerily empty West Pico Boulevard in Central LA. The Pico Union neighborhood downtown had some nice historic parts, but there were sections real estate agents would refer to as "up-and-coming" with "local color," meaning you're more likely to be mugged on your way to the grocery store than not.

Trank pointed out a rundown three-story terrace. "That's the one, on the left."

Nina pulled up, killed the engine, and checked the street. No cars pulled over, and none that were parked had occupants.

She dipped her head to see the whole apartment complex through the windshield. "This place isn't being fumigated."

"Then why did he need to stay at my house?" Trank asked.

Nina gave him a quizzical shake of her head, opened the door and got out. Trank followed suit.

Trank nervously scrutinized the surrounds, jumping at the slightest movement. The TV star clearly wasn't used to lurking around in the middle of the night breaking laws. "How are we going to get in?" he asked breathlessly.

"It's okay, I have a search warrant."

Opening the trunk, Nina pulled out a battered military duffle bag. She unzipped it and showed Trank its contents: bolt cutters, a crowbar, screwdrivers, a small sledgehammer, an angle grinder, cordless drill, slim jim, and multiple lock-picking kits.

Nina zipped it up and gave him a wink, pointing to the words written in faded black ink. "Search warrant."

She tapped her jacket, feeling for the Beretta beneath. Girl had to take care in a city like this.

Trank followed her up the path, search warrant slung over her shoulder. "You're a woman of surprises," Trank said in a heavy whisper.

"You have no idea."

They walked around the perimeter of the apartment block, then out the back where a small parking lot was mostly filled with cars. There were separate entrances to each of the apartments off a central open-air corridor. Nina checked the bank of buzzers. A faded hand-printed label advised that Seth Wagner was in apartment 1A, the closest to the street on the ground level. Nina took note of the other names on the list.

Making her way to Wagner's door, she placed the heavy bag on the ground and cracked her knuckles.

"That you, Sethie?"

The two turned, startled to see a frail, weathered little old lady in her night dress, squinting beneath the bright bare lightbulb. She would have been well into her seventies at least. Seeing past the wrinkles and wear from a hard life, Nina could imagine the woman had been quite the looker back in the day. She stood outside the door to 1B.

Her face dropped. "Oh, I's sorry, thought y'all was..." The lady's accent was thick, Cajun inflected.

"Well hey, y'all wouldn't happen to be Mrs Bennet, by any chance? Seth told us you was his neighbor. This here's Levi and I'm Ellie. We're Seth's cousins from Lafayette, paying him a surprise visit."

The old woman's suspicious demeanor morphed to warm and friendly in an instant. Her eyes were brighter than summer fireflies.

Nina recalled the name on the buzzer listing. The split-second decision to pose as Wagner's cousins came when she heard the woman's southern accent. She figured an accent in common might lend Mrs Bennet to make friends with Wagner, who hailed from Louisiana. Nina had almost said sister, but if the woman knew him well enough she might know if he had siblings. No one went into details about all their cousins, especially if they're from the South.

"I am mightily pleased to meet you Ellie, Levi," the old woman said brightly. She pointed to Trank. "I can see the family resemblance, thought you was Sethie there for a minute." Her face turned more serious. "Bit late, ain't it?"

Nina nodded her head sagely. "We got shafted, excuse me ma'am, messed around with flights. Weren't nothing we could do. Don't ever fly Eastern Air's all I'm sayin'."

When she noticed the woman's gaze drift to the duffle bag, she added, "This is the only bag we got. Rest on their way to Alaska, I reckon."

Mrs Bennet straightened her back, accepting the explanation. "'Fraid you're plum out of luck. Sethie ain't been home in a couple of days. Never left no note nor nothin'. I hope y'all got a key?"

Doing her best not to glance at the bag, Nina replied, "Sure do, ma'am, from last time. Sorry if we woke you."

The old woman gave a dismissive wave of her hand. "Damn rheumatism, keeps me up all night. You kids come see me in the mornin', y'hear? I'll cook y'all up some biscuits and calas. Just knock, I'll be up."

"That's mighty kind of you, ma'am, mighty kind. We will." Nina leaned forward. "Mind if I ask how a good ol' girl like you ended up in Los Angeles?"

The old woman smiled and Nina could see it would have been dazzling back in the day.

"Arrived 'ere in '28, just in time for them talkies to ruin evyt'in for someone who sounded like me. Came out to be a movie star, ended up marryin' a brick layer i'stead." She shrugged. *What you gonna do?*

Nina bobbed her head in understanding. "Mind if I ask another question?"

"Don' have much time left on this earth, but I got time for a question." She cackled at her little joke.

"Seth mentioned they was gettin' the place fumigated sometime soon. You know when that'll be?"

The woman puckered her brow. "Don' rightly know where he got that idea. Place ain't been fumigated in years. Dey should though, with the residents inside, do the world a favor." Giving them a slight bow, she added, "Night, young uns."

She gave them a friendly wave and disappeared into her apartment. When they were sure she wouldn't reemerge, Nina extracted her lock picks and made light work of the apartment's cheap lock.

Once inside, Trank whispered, "Where the hell did that accent come from? You sounded like you were New Orleans born and bred."

"Actress, remember?" She pointed to her face. "Some shit you don't forget."

She couldn't help being a little impressed by Trank's compliment. It shouldn't have mattered to the give-no-fucks Nina Maddox, but she had to admit it put a little spring in her step.

Nina turned on the light switch and gasped. The place had been ransacked. All Wagner's earthly possessions were strewn across the lounge. The kitchen, off to the left, had been equally tossed. Someone had conducted an exception-ally thorough search. *For what?*

"This changes nothing," Nina said firmly. "Whoever did this may have missed something. We search everything again. I don't want to come back here, okay? Let's get it done in one fell swoop."

"Righto, ma'am." Trank tucked his hands under his arms and flapped his elbows.

Stifling a laugh, Nina asked, "What the hell are you doing?"

Chuckling at his own silliness, he replied, "I'm a chicken. Like, a fowl. Fowl swoop."

"It's fell. F.E.L.L. Fell swoop."

"No, it's not." Trank ceased flapping and placed his fists on his hips. "That doesn't make any sense. It's a fowl swoop. Fowl. They swoop."

Amused, she shook her head. "How on earth do you

even remember your lines with a brain like that? Actually, it doesn't matter. Let's get this done. You take the kitchen, I'll take the lounge."

The apartment was small, with minimal dated furnishings, it wouldn't take long to search. Wagner had an extensive collection of VHS videotape cases, a lot of gay porn titles. Every single case was empty. *That's odd.*

After ten minutes Trank emerged from the kitchen. "Nothing I can see. Every inch of it has been searched, including the lining at the back of the cupboards. They even threw everything out of the freezer."

"Has it all thawed?"

"Yes, why?"

"If there was still ice that would mean they'd been here recently."

"Smart." Trank exhaled sharply through his nose, impressed. "You're good at this detective stuff, aren't you?"

"Sometimes. We're still no closer to the truth, though."

They searched the bedroom, but besides a pair of handcuffs and some lube there was nothing of interest. What little clothes he had were all on hangers, meaning they held no interest to the intruders. All drawers had been upended and searched thoroughly. Suitcases had been sliced open, every cavity explored. Even the heating vents had been ripped from the walls.

Nina put the clothing in piles and did some mental calculations.

"Planning a rummage sale?"

Nina shook her head, pointed to the clothes in the closet and the now stacked piles. "All these clothes would fill the drawers, and there's only space for these two cases on the shelf in the closet. That means he hadn't packed anything. Whatever compelled him to lie to you about the place being fumigated so he could stay at yours, it was urgent, and he wasn't planning to come back here to pack. That suggests he was on the run, meaning he suspected his place was being watched. The question is, who was after him. And why."

Trank's demeanor indicated he agreed, but he said nothing. Her logic was sound, but it brought them no closer to answers. Among the detritus on the floor she noticed a discarded checkbook. Whoever turned the place upside down clearly didn't think it important enough to take. She flicked though it. The current total indicated he had a little money—not a fortune, but enough to afford a hotel room if he'd wanted. A few hundred bucks would have gotten him a nice place for a few nights, even in this town. The money was about what you'd expect from a stuntman's pay.

She flipped through the stubs. Dry cleaning, equipment, union dues, car repairs. The last one got her thinking.

"Are you sure he didn't drive to your place?"

Trank gave a slight shake of his head. "Didn't we go through this? I assumed cab because I didn't see a car."

Nina recalled the conversation. "But his car wasn't parked out back." She was exhausted, and had to fight the building fatigue. "If he didn't drive the car to your place and it's not in his car space, then where is it?"

Trank frowned. *I don't know.*

Nina tossed the clothes around, ensuring they left the place as they'd found it. On the way out, she wiped the front doorknob before closing it. Walking past 1B, she saw movement through the light under the door. She knocked lightly.

"Hey Mrs Bennet, it's Ellie again. Can I ask a question?"

The door opened and the old lady beamed. "Everythin' a'ight, darlin?"

"Oh, fo' sure. Seth told us we could borrow his Buick, but it ain't out back. I was jus' wonderin' if you know where he parked it?"

She was counting on the old biddy's eagle eye and wasn't disappointed.

Mrs Bennet's face turned sour. "Some rude man took it a coupla' days ago. Said he was Sethie's friend. Was too old for that, if y'all ask me. Had dark hair, but gray at the sides, made him look like a skunk, and he slicked it back like 'e was some sleazy used car salesman. Said he was a frien' from work. Didn't trust him none, never trust those car salesmen. They're all crooks."

"Did this friend have a name?"

"Clem." Mrs Bennet squinted, trying to recall. "Clem something."

"Who's called Clem outside a western?" Nina asked.

"That's what I thought!" She scratched the back of her neck, mind focused, and then exclaimed, "Kaufman. Clem Kaufman, that was 'is name. Told me 'e was a stuntman like sweet ol' Sethie."

Nina made a mental note. Was this the mysterious third member of Wagner's gang who believed they'd found a way out of the business? She'd get Phoebe to work her magic and track down Clem Kaufman.

She thanked the old lady for her time once again and bid her farewell. Nina remained silent on the walk back to the car, mind racing. Why would someone need Wagner's car? She pondered the point right until the moment the engine started in a nearby black Plymouth Barracuda coupe.

The fact that the car started as they reached the road was of mild interest, but when its headlights stayed off as it pulled out, Nina's focus shifted. When it raced toward them she acted on pure instinct. Grabbing the back of Trank's meaty neck, she lifted both feet, using her full weight to shove him to the ground.

"Get down!"

Her beloved Charger's windows exploded in a hail of bullets as the occupant of the Plymouth peppered it with automatic weapons fire. Extracting her Beretta, Nina fired after the car as it raced up West Pico Boulevard. Her shots were rushed and mostly wide, adrenalin and weariness pushing her gun off-target. She lowered her weapon in anger.

That was nothing compared to how she felt when she turned back to her car. The mismatched wheels only amplified how quickly her gleaming pride and joy had fallen from grace.

Trank stood awkwardly, his dilated pupils fleeing from the expanding whites of his eyes. No one came out of the nearby houses. In this part of Central LA you tended to ignore gunshots unless you were in the line of fire.

"Mother fucker." Nina ran her hand over her beloved bullet-riddled vehicle. Every piece of glass had been shattered, bar one, the rear passenger window.

Unsteady on his feet, Trank pointed toward the one remaining piece of glass. "At least you have one—"

Nina punched out the window, shattering it.

"—more reason to solve this case," Trank finished. His gaze drifted to where the Plymouth had turned the corner. "Are..." His jaw moved, trying to lubricate his dry mouth. "Are we going after them?"

Trank's tone was that of a man who very much hoped Nina would answer in the negative. She understood why. It wasn't every day you got shot at. Or that someone was killed in your own bed. With the deaths of Wagner and Diehl, and now nearly himself, Trank no doubt wanted to be as far away from the people dispensing death as possible. Nina was of the opposite opinion right now.

Placing the gun back in its holster, she felt the adrenalin draining from her body. "No need to go after them. I know where they're headed."

"How could you possibly know that?"

"I saw the license plate."

Trank shook his head, not comprehending. "And?"

"It wasn't real."

"The car?"

"No, the plate. It was made up."

"Made up?" Trank lent against the car, a move Nina would have found offensive mere days before but that mattered little now. "I don't understand."

"The plate was 2GAT123." Seeing the confusion on his face, she expanded. "The three letters GAT aren't used by the California Department of Motor Vehicles. Like SAM and FAN." She pointed toward the space where the Plymouth had been. "It's a prop plate. Not real."

"And you know where 2GAT…"

"123."

"That. You know where it resides? There must be hundreds of studio lot cars in this city. Thousands. How could you know?"

"There was only one person who knows I could still be investigating your case, Hank. Only one person with enough power to cause a stunt to go wrong. Only one person who could get a studio car off the lot in the middle of the night."

"Oh…" Realization finally dawned on the big man's face. "You think it's…"

"Yeah." Nina cracked her neck, anger dispensing any remnant of her tiredness. "It's high time I paid Mickey Boehler a visit."

ACT 2

Ready for my close-up.

Thursday, 5 September 1984

CHAPTER

SEVEN

The 1920s Spanish-style façade was known the world over. In spite of her disdain for the industry that had chewed her up and spat her out, Nina still got a buzz driving through the huge gates of Phoenix Studios.

As Nina rolled up, the gray-haired, buttoned-down security guard in his equally gray uniform greeted her with a bow, and ticked a box on his clipboard.

"Good morning, Ms Maddox."

No matter how many times she'd asked, Reg simply refused to call her by her first name. "It wouldn't be proper," he'd always insisted.

Although it had been years since she'd worked as an actress, Reg treated her like she was turning up for another day on set. He was one of the few good ones in Hollywood, a genuine flesh and blood human being in the land of plastic.

"Hey Reg, how's the family? Those daughters keeping you out of trouble?"

"You know me, always in trouble." He chuckled. The

guy was the straightest individual Nina had ever met. He ran an eye over Nina's ride. "Not your usual... style, Ms Maddox?"

Her car was in the shop. When she'd dropped it off, her mechanic's jaw had dropped. Greasy Steve said he'd call her with the damage once he'd determined how much to fleece her. Tires, glass, and bullet holes weren't going to be cheap. At least she had Trank as a client now, although billing him could be tricky, seeing as he was officially dead.

Phoebe's Toyota was not on the same cool scale as the Charger. In fact, she didn't even know what scale the Corolla would be on. Still, at least it didn't have bullet holes.

"Mine's in the shop," she replied.

Reg handed her a pass to hang from the rear-view mirror. "You know the way."

"Where do they keep the pool cars these days, Reg?"

He pointed. "Hang a right, go down Fairbanks past Chaplin, a smidge after you pass sound stage twenty-two. Can't miss it. Ask for Jimmy. Tell him I sent you."

"Thanks Reg, you're a gem." Before she put the car in gear, she asked, "Hey, I heard you were on duty a few nights back, when Alicia Morrison left the studio?"

Reg's face was solemn. "I was, yes. She just walked out. I asked her if she wanted me to call her a cab, but she waved me off, so I assumed she wasn't going far. Her limo driver came searching for her an hour or so later. I sure hope they find the little thing."

"What was she wearing, can you remember?"

"The mileage might be high, but the noggin's still in good working order." He tapped the side of his head. "She had on her usual red coat, a long one with black buttons— Little Red Riding Hood, I used to call her. Sweet kid. First day she turned up, I thought she was you. Blond hair like you used to have. The two of you could have been sisters, I tell you."

Not sure how to respond, Nina thanked Reg for his time and made her way to visitor parking, keen to extricate herself from Phoebe's "racing red" shitbox. She was reasonably sure her Charger could outpace Phoebe's car even with four slashed tires.

Following Reg's instructions, she came up to a wooden hut in front of a chain-link fence. It was a parking lot, but unlike any other. There were ambulances, army jeeps, school buses, futuristic cars with all kinds of protrusions, and of course, police cars of all descriptions and eras. It represented every kind of movie the studio made—bar Westerns and historic dramas, she assumed, unless they put dune buggies in biblical epics. Nina wasn't up on the latest Hollywood trends.

From a squat shed came an equally squat man with the physique of porridge in a latex glove.

He waved and asked, "Can I help you?"

"Jimmy, is it? Reg sent me over."

"That's right. What can I do for you?"

"The name's Nina. I'm looking for a specific kind of car. A two-door pony, maybe ten to fifteen years old, like a Challenger, Camaro, Barracuda. Has to be black."

The squat man ran his grease-stained hand over graying stubble. "Think I might have somethin' like that. Give me a sec."

He unhooked a clipboard from inside the door and jerked his head, motioning for her to follow. They strode through the lot full of mismatching, exotic, and mundane vehicles. A hand-drawn number was painted at the top of each parking space. After a couple of minutes, Jimmy pointed to a familiar-looking Plymouth Barracuda.

"Got a Camaro too, but that's out with *Dynasty* until the end of the week." He stood back, allowing her space to give it a once-over. "What's this for?"

Nina walked around the Barracuda. "Doing some research."

"Comeback picture, is it?"

Is there anyone in this town who doesn't know me?

The license plate was different, but Nina was sure she'd seen this very same vehicle under very different circumstances only hours before. When she reached the rear of the car she found a hole, about the size of a bullet from a Beretta.

So, the car came from the Phoenix lot. That connected Wagner, Trank, and Phoenix. *Yes, but how?*

"Can you tell me the last time someone took it off the lot?"

Jimmy regarded her suspiciously. "How's that research?"

"I'm thorough," she replied, and left it at that.

The short man frowned, but didn't object further; apparently that was answer enough for him. He checked his clipboard. "Six weeks ago, an episode of *Highway to Heaven*. Reminds me, I should turn her over, can't leave these gas guzzlers too long or they seize up like my wife."

Ignoring the casual misogyny, Nina asked, "Can anyone else book the cars out without you knowing, Jimmy?"

"They do and there'd be hell to pay, let me tell you! I've been on this lot for thirty years and never once have I ever made a mistake, not once. You ask Mr Boehler, he'll tell you. I run a tight ship, I do."

"I have no doubt. Thanks, Jimmy, this is perfect. I'll be in touch."

Pleased to know his reputation remained intact, he gave her a sloppy salute. As she walked away, he shouted, "Good luck with the comeback!"

~

"I HAVE AN APPOINTMENT WITH MICKEY," Nina said to the pencil-thin brunette with cheekbones that could cut cheese.

The reception area outside Mickey's office was sleek, modern, and uncluttered. It was just as Nina remembered it, except for the gorilla in the expensive suit standing awkwardly at the rear door. The thick-necked goon fit the cliched gangster heavy profile so well he should have been chewing on toothpicks, flipping coins, and wearing spats.

Since when did Mickey need a bodyguard?

The secretary tapped on a computer worth more than Nina's car without looking up. "Name?"

"Nina Maddox."

Pursing her thin lips, she said, "*Mister* Boehler will see you now," then stood and skittered toward the office.

Nina hadn't met this particular secretary before. Mickey tended to go through them rather quickly. She opened the rear door to the studio head's office, but before Nina could step through, a meaty arm descended like a boom gate.

Remaining silent, Nina simply cocked a challenging eyebrow at the suited heavy.

"I gotta search you. Orders."

"You can certainly try," Nina folded her arms, "though I wouldn't recommend it."

The thick-jawed heavy's eye twitched. Nina stood her

ground and stared him down. She assumed this kind of intimidation worked on most people, but Nina wasn't most people. If this big lug was waiting for her to relent, he clearly had no idea who he was dealing with.

"No search, no meeting," he grunted.

"I bet your lips move when you read, don't they?"

The secretary leaned between the warring factions. "She's on Mr Boehler's list. A regular. No need to search her, Leonard."

Nina frowned. Bodyguards should be called Alfonso or Knuckles. Not Leonard.

The unfortunately named Leonard did his best to comprehend words, and lifted his meaty arm. He jerked his head as if he alone had determined that Nina would be granted entry. She followed the secretary down the dado-paneled hallway, watching the assistant's hips sway in a manner she assumed most men appreciated. If she were a man, or otherwise inclined, Nina would prefer her own curves, but then, she wasn't the usual type who entered The Steamroller's gladiatorial arena. Nina was still waiting for a woman to be made studio head.

The secretary opened the door and soullessly announced, "Nina Maddox, Mr Boehler."

"That will be all, Kate," Boehler announced in a deep baritone, answering a question she hadn't asked.

The assistant huffed, and growled under her breath, "It's Naomi." Seeing that Nina had heard her, she whispered, "Kate was two secretarys ago."

The big man sat behind the biggest oak desk Nina had ever seen. The room was adorned with Phoenix Studio movie posters (only the hits) and props from Hollywood's heyday, including a pair of signed Stallone boxing gloves and a replica, or at least she assumed it was, of the

Maltese Falcon. Tucked in the corner was a set of gold-plated golf clubs which had apparently never even seen a green.

Mickey "The Steamroller" Boehler wasn't much to look at. Then again, that was the secret to his success. He was like a cliché heavy from an old black-and-white movie. No neck to speak of, features as thick as yoghurt, and a big bald dome that would make an ideal battering ram. His skin was a little too tanned, his teeth a little too bleached. He was also a little too plump for Rodeo Drive, not that anyone would dare say so. Not to his face, anyway. In this town, if a wrong word got back to The Steamroller it was a fast-track to the career cutting room.

Various articles had covered the big man's formulative years. Growing up in Ohio, the now-powerful Mickey had been a shy, friendless, and insecure pimply kid, always picked last for team sports. That, Nina believed, was what drove the fire in his belly. He moved out west and through sheer tenacity alone, rose to become arguably the most powerful man in the industry. Legend had it that Mickey arrived at his fifteen-year high school reunion via helicopter, a Playboy bunny on each arm, waltzed around the stunned room for ten minutes, then took off. If that didn't tell you everything you needed to know about Mickey Boehler, nothing would.

Naomi-not-Kate said, "The mayor's office called confirming your tickets to the fundraiser Sunday evening."

"Ask me later."

The assistant bowed and silently left the room. Mickey gave Nina a sideways glance, as if he didn't want her to know about his social plans. Of course, Nina wasn't about to let him off lightly.

"You sucking up to the mayor, Mickey?"

"Everyone sucks up to someone. Even the great Nina Maddox, I'm sure."

"For the right company."

"You want a ticket? You could be my date?"

"Bow ties and ball gowns ain't my thing, Mickey."

"Can't blame a guy for trying."

Mickey was notorious for refusing to attend black-tie events. He even skipped the Oscars when one of his pictures was miraculously nominated. Before recent incidents, if he'd pressed the invitation to the mayor's event, Nina would have relented. She owed the big guy. Mickey had backed Nina when no one else would. He'd given her fledgling detective agency her first job. And second. And third. In fact, pretty much all her income had resulted from Mickey's belief in her and her abilities as an investigator. Without Mickey, there would be no Scream Queen Detective Agency.

It was another example of Mickey's other, less publicly known side. When no one was looking, Mickey was capable of unspeakable kindness. When a former assistant, who had left Mickey's employ two years earlier, had a son with a life-threatening congenital heart defect, Mickey paid all the boy's medical bills and never told a soul. Not even the former assistant. The woman turned up to the hospital one day and was told all her son's bills had been paid, amounting to nearly fifty grand. Mickey was a walking contradiction encased in an Armani suit.

Nina took a seat before the massive desk and Boehler lit an equally massive stogie, likely Cuban. The phone rang and Mickey held up a finger.

"Speak." He listened for a good twenty seconds, his face growing steadily redder. "You tell that coked-up has-been when he stars in a movie that can make more than fifty mill I'll consider a pay or play deal, but until the day hell freezes over, he either signs the contract as is or I sign Redford." He slammed down the phone before the other party could reply. As if realizing Nina was still there, he said, "You gotta rule with an iron fist, otherwise these fucks will bleed you dry."

"You can't make art with a clenched fist, Mickey."

The head of Phoenix Studios snickered. "Toots, we don't make art here. This business is about renting seats and selling sugar. You want art, go to a museum."

"Art gallery."

"What?"

"Never mind."

The words were one hundred percent Mickey, but lacked his usual conviction.

"Hey," he said in a friendlier tone, "I heard this morning Coppola is bleeding money on *The Cotton Club*. The producer Evans is taking a bath on this one. Man, I could tell you some stories about that guy. The movie is so in the shitter they're calling it The Cleopatra Club."

"Who's calling it that?" Nina asked.

"I am."

"Oh, right."

"Sure, there's no juicy Liz Taylor stories, but apparently it's a nightmare and they're hemorrhaging cash daily. I have an inside guy who's feeding me gossip. They're running a pool on when Coppola will be carted off to the funny farm. Not *if*, when."

Industry gossip was the closest Boehler ever came to small talk. It infused every surface in Hollywood—studio heads to hot dog vendors loved dishing the dirt. The whole town believed if you weren't the one slinging the gossip, someone would be slinging it about you.

"What's with the muscle in reception? You casting for

another *Planet of the Apes* movie out there or did you schtup someone's wife again?"

"You're a laugh riot, Nina, I'll put you in Burt Reynolds' next picture."

"No thanks. Moustaches tickle."

"Good job on Trank. No blowback on that one, thank Christ. Hell of a way to go." He hadn't answered her question about the heavy. Mickey took a drag on his stogie. "We'll take a hit on the show, obviously, but we have enough episodes in the can for syndication, so that's a positive. No big scandal, which it could have been. Think we'll ride it out without too much trouble. That Morrison kid's taken most of the headlines anyway."

"That's why I'm here," Nina mostly lied. "To ask you about her."

For a man who made million dollar deals on a daily basis, Mickey wasn't as adept at hiding his tells as he thought. Nina could have sworn he grew paler. Was it that a teen star had disappeared on his watch, or something else?

"New case, huh?" he asked, his voice less sure now.

"Yep, her agent."

"Ughh, Ross. That turd has been squeezing my balls for years."

Studio heads hated agents. If they ruled the world, it wouldn't be kill all the lawyers, it would be kill all the agents. Though they'd eventually get around to the lawyers too.

"Got any idea where she might have gone?"

"Not a clue." Boehler's fingers inched toward his phone, which was usually surgically attached to his meaty fist. It was clear he wanted to wind the conversation up as soon as possible. Likely because it wasn't making him money, but there could have been another reason, though Nina had no idea what.

"We done, Nina? I have..." He rolled his hand. Nina ignored the gesture. She had no intention of finishing yet.

"What can you tell me about Morrison herself?"

He grunted and took a puff of his cigar, realizing Nina wasn't so easy to get rid of. "Not much. We had her out on loan from Disney. Never met the kid, but everyone knew she was the next big thing. A couple more years of shitty kid-friendly pap then she'll do the breakout adult picture and will be made in the shade. She's making a horse show-jumping coming of age piece of shit for us. The kids'll love it. Ross squeezed my balls on that deal too."

Again, Nina was struck by the lack of conviction in Mickey's delivery, like he didn't believe the words himself. For a man who blustered through every conversation, his tentativeness was a major departure. "Was she at least good?"

"She was totally unreliable, missed more call times than she hit, sometimes didn't show up at all. Director was bustin' my balls to replace her."

Interesting. At least she'd gotten *something* out of the verbose studio head.

"Anything on her last movements?"

Boehler eyed the phone again. "She'd wrapped for the day. Director said she was meant to take a town car, had the standard studio guy booked, but she slipped out another door and fucking walked out the front gate. She told her PA she was meeting someone, but didn't say who."

"What's her PA's name? I'd like to meet them," Nina asked, pencil hovering over her notepad.

"Uh, I wouldn't worry. The kid'll turn up."

The words were right, but they were too rushed, like an actor delivering lines for a part he didn't want.

"Seeing as I'm being paid to investigate, I might as well, you know, investigate," Nina said with more humor than she felt. "Can I get the PA's contact details from Naomi?"

"Who?"

"Your secretary."

"I thought it was Kate?"

"Not that she's aware of."

"Sure." Mickey flicked his hand. "Grab 'em on the way out if you really need to. Kate—uh, Naomi has your cheque for the Trank thing, too."

He motioned to his phone. Mickey desperately wanted the discussion wrapped up. It was a strange conversation in that it was completely bland by Mickey standards. He hadn't dropped any innuendo or tasteless remarks. He hadn't tried to coax her out of retirement or into bed—he usually attempted both at once. The Steamroller seemed nervous. That made Nina nervous.

She hadn't gotten much from Mickey about Alicia. In fact, he'd done his best to give her nothing at all.

The initial reason she'd booked the meeting with Mickey was to get an angle on the Trank case, something she'd thoroughly failed to do. Nina decided to try and catch the big man off guard. She really had nothing to lose.

As he reached for his phone, Nina asked, "Hey Mickey, one more thing. Did you organize to kill Hank Trank?"

There was a moment where it seemed all air had been sucked out of the room. You could hear a pin drop in Palm Springs. Instead of shock, disgust, or offense, Mickey burst into a guffaw and slapped the desk with his big hand.

"Jesus Christ, Nina, you do get to the point." He waved

an appreciative cigar in her direction. "I do love a direct woman. My four ex-wives will tell you the same."

"Did you?"

"Marry four times?"

"Kill Hank?"

The humor dying on his thick lips, Mickey said, "No. Why on earth would I kill TV's number one star?"

"I've seen the Nielsens, he's not number one. Not anymore."

"Did you see last night's numbers? They went through the roof. Number one of the night. And it was a rerun. We've still got half a season to air, he'll be number one again, you watch. That why you're here, Trank? I thought you were snooping for the Morrison kid? Which one is it?"

"Bit of both."

"Hey, listen here," he stubbed out his cigar defensively, "I paid you for yesterday's work on Trank, don't try and squeeze me for more. It was a one-day gig. You want to do more, that's on your clock, not mine. Like I said, check's already written. That's it, kiddo."

"Sure thing, Mickey, I was just asking, all good."

His response wasn't that of someone covering their tracks, more like a studio boss covering the bottom line. Her attempt to shove him off balance hadn't succeeded—if anything, it cast doubt on Mickey knowing anything about Trank at all. She hadn't expected him to drop to his knees and confess, but she had hoped to see more chinks in his armor. *Damn.*

Although The Steamroller seemed edgy, if anything, he became more himself when discussing his former star. So what had him worried? Was it possible he had nothing to do with the murder of Seth Wagner/Hank Trank or Lewis Diehl? If not, who the hell was responsible? Nina rubbed her temples. She had one more bullet in her chamber.

She wanted to know how Mickey was connected to Diehl, and why the mere mention of Mickey's name had the stuntman so scared.

"Hey Mickey, one last thing…"

The big man grunted. "You sure you're not one of my exes? You're breakin' my balls like one. Do I have to start paying you alimony too?"

"Yesterday, on the set of *Lethal Heat*, a stuntman by the name of Lewis Diehl lost his life. That was one of your pictures, what—"

Nina's words tumbled from her lips and trailed off. It wasn't lack of nerve. It was the sight of every sheet of color peeling from Mickey Boehler's face. She'd never seen this burly, assured man stunned, ever. The man before Nina was shaken, terrified even. In an instant he morphed into something far more confrontational.

Planting his huge fists on the desk, The Steamroller lowered his gaze and growled, "What the *fuck* did you ask me?"

"I just heard—"

"Heard? *Heard!* What the hell are you working on, Maddox? First the Morrison kid, now *this!*"

Hurling his chair backward, he rounded the desk, angrier than Nina had ever seen him. He thrust a stubby finger an inch from her face, his other hand a bulky fist, forcing her backward in the chair.

"You come into *my* office, accusing me of fuck knows what. Is that why you're here? Did he hire you to rat me out?"

Raising her hands in faux-surrender, Nina glared at the accusatory finger Mickey had shoved in her face. Like a viper, her right hand darted to his wrist and twisted. At the same time, her left hand grasped his forefinger and bent it backwards, eliciting a satisfying howl. Mickey staggered backward and she relinquished her grasp, giving him a satisfying shove.

Seated serenely, Nina addressed the still-standing Mickey as coolly as a glacial breeze. "Our friendship only goes so far, Mickey. Don't you fucking push it."

Acquiescing with a bow of his head, he cradled his injured finger and slunk back to his desk, tail between his legs. They both took a moment.

What the fuck is going on Mickey?

Inhaling unsteadily, his demeanor suddenly became calm, friendly even. "You don't want to be mixed up in this, Nina. Drop it. Tell Ross to shove his investigation. Stay the fuck away. People are going to get hurt. I like you kid, but even I can't protect you from what's coming. Go on a holiday to Vegas. Hell, I got a suite at the Bellagio, stay there, on me. You don't want to be around. Believe me."

In the space of a seconds, Mickey had morphed from stunned to violent outrage to scared to concerned. He was falling apart before her eyes.

What puzzled Nina more than anything was what had prompted his angry outburst in the first place. He was a bully, yes, but she'd never once heard of him laying a hand on a woman. Businessmen, sure, but despite his long, *long* list of faults, being violent with women was not one of them. The studio mogul was rattled beyond reason. It made him unpredictable. It made him dangerous.

"Vegas? Thought you swore off gambling, Mickey? That's what you told me months ago, when you said you got in over your head."

The big man visibly flinched. "I go to Vegas for the ambiance and sense of calm."

"Right, and I go to Salt Lake City for the benders. Listen, I didn't mean anything when I asked about the stunt accident. I was curious, that's all." She used her best calming voice. Not for the first time, she thanked her Stanislavski training. "Making chitchat."

Mickey accepted the comment with a flick of his head and swallowed hard. Nina had never seen him display weakness before, not once. The mere mention of Diehl had rattled him, far more than news of an employee dying on his watch should. Bringing up Trank had barely garnered a reaction. Even the outright accusation of murdering him had elicited nothing more than a laugh. But discussing Alicia Morrison had made him nervous, and the mention of Diehl had sent him spiraling into anger and fear.

Before Diehl had fallen to his death, the mere mention of Mickey's name had sent the man into a panic. Now, mentioning Diehl had triggered the same reaction in Mickey. *What is going on?*

She wanted to know about the studio car but decided to let it go, at least for now. Further questions would not only get her no answers, they'd likely put her directly in the firing line. She'd learned long ago that discretion was the better part of saving her ass. Instinct told her that with this particular case, she could use all the safety she could get.

She watched as he settled back into being the big studio head behind the big desk, the unflappable Mickey Boehler. They both knew it was a lie. She'd just seen the mighty Steamroller flapped, and they both knew it.

Nina stood. "I think I have everything I need."

She didn't, but she would soon enough.

As she made her way to the door, Nina stopped and

turned to the big man. "Hey Mickey, just so we're clear, you ever come at me again, I'll break every one of your fat little fingers one by one. You understand me?"

He regarded her with what approximated a human expression. "I have a lot going on right now." When Nina refused to say anything in reply, he added, "I do understand, Nina. And I'm sorry."

She'd never heard the big man apologize, ever.

That, more than anything, scared the shit out of her.

CHAPTER

EIGHT

The commissary was thankfully open, so Nina could sit down with a coffee and wait for her hands to stop shaking. She didn't know if it was anger or fright at Mickey's out of character actions. The likely answer was yes.

The studio head had clearly been rattled. He'd threatened her. Then he'd warned her off, tried to convince her to get out of the city. What was it about Lewis Diehl that had him so rattled? He'd also been uncomfortable when she'd mentioned Alicia Morrison, but it was Diehl's name that had really triggered him. *What the hell was going on?*

Whatever she'd embroiled herself in was bigger than Hank Trank, and that was saying something. What had spooked the most powerful man in Hollywood? Maybe she should have taken him up the offer of a holiday in Vegas. She'd certainly had some good times in Sin City.

In the end, did Nina even want to find out what was going on? Whatever it was that had Mickey so terrified wasn't likely to thrill her, either.

Add to that, her tires had been slashed in a none-too-subtle threat. And if the two murders weren't warning enough, someone had taken shot at her. What the hell had she gotten herself into?

She shook her head. *Stop it.* She was working herself up. She'd faced down screaming directors, packs of rabid press—hell, she'd faced down murderers. She was tougher than this. She was going to get to the bottom of whatever this was, no matter what. She was Nina *fucking* Maddox.

Spine straightened by her little pep talk, she downed the awful coffee and steeled herself. She had work to do.

Making her way across the Phoenix lot, she came to a collection of tiny offices, far away from the important ones and that had definitely seen better days. They had once housed staff writers, before the studio system collapsed. Writing was now outsourced, and a select few earned hundreds of thousands for the right project. Maybe Nina should have been a writer instead of a PI, she mused. She assumed there would be less gunplay, though she couldn't be sure.

She knocked on the Dorothy Lamour suite and waited.

A faint, "Who is it?" drifted through the weathered wooden door.

"Ms Write, my name is Nina Maddox and I'm investigating the—"

The door flew open and an early twenty-something beamed at Nina. Dressed in a dress far too conservative for her age, compromising an unnecessary amalgam of lace, chiffon, and shoulder pads you could use to hang glide. Her hair was tied back tightly, and the ensemble was completed with a pair of cat lady glasses far too old for such a young woman.

"*The* Nina Maddox?" The woman's eyes were wide behind the thick glasses. "Janet Write. Oh, crap, you knew that already. Shit, I just swore in front of Nina Maddox. Shit, did it again. Sorry, sorry." She pulled herself together and extended a hand. "A pleasure to meet you. I've seen all your movies."

Nina shook the slight woman's hand. The nervous Janet was pretty, but not quite *movie* pretty. Nina suspected that, like so many in this city, her shoulders were draped in a cloak of failed movie star dreams.

"All my movies?" she asked. "What did you do with the rest of your afternoon?"

An awkward laugh was her only reply. The young woman had the bright-eyed expression of someone not yet jaded by the cynical industry bound to chew her up and spit her out. In an instant, Nina created a role for herself. She stood straight, beamed widely and dialed her voice up a couple of octaves to match the woman's childlike chipper tone.

"Could I come in? It will only be a few minutes. A couple of girls shooting the breeze. That cool with you?"

Nina highly suspected Janet was holding in a squee as she ushered her into her office, which was really a glorified broom closet. The two sat grinning inanely at one another.

"It's a real big pleasure to meet you, Miss Maddox." She shook her head. "My dad's gonna freak when I tell him about this."

Deciding the ignore the latter comment, Nina leaned forward. "Call me Nina, please."

"Oh! Sure," she replied, bouncing in her chair, "Nina."

"How long have you worked at Phoenix Studios, Janet?"

"Eighteen months just gone." She glowed, relishing the opportunity to talk about herself. "I came to LA, like most people, I guess, thinking I'd just walk into Schwab's to buy a sandwich and walk out a movie star." She rubbed the back of her neck. "Doesn't always work out that way, huh?"

It seemed Nina's guess about the cloak of failed dreams was right on the money. *This town.*

"No, it doesn't. So, you got into PA work?"

Janet's brow furrowed. Her face clearly said, *how do you know about little old me?* She didn't verbalize the question, though. "That's right. Us girls have to pay the rent, right?"

"Absolutely. After the movies, I became a private investigator."

"No way!"

For effect, Nina handed her a business card confirming that she was indeed the sole proprietor of the Scream Queen Detective Agency. Janet took the card and cradled it with reverence, as it were the Shroud of Turin.

"You have your own agency? So cool."

"It sounds more impressive than it is," Nina stated honestly, maintaining her peppy tone.

Janet held Nina's business card reverently. "Is this *your* agency? Like, you own it?"

"Again, you might want to pump the brakes on being too impressed. The phone number is for a dive bar, and my office is above said dive bar and sometimes smells of cat vomit, but yes, I am indeed living the dream."

Rapport established, Nina was ready to get down to business. Thankfully, Janet beat her to it.

"What can I do for you... Nina?"

"I'm here about Alicia Morrison."

The carefree, starstruck smile was metaphorically slapped from Janet's face. It took all of a second for her demeanor to collapse in on itself, and the bright bubbly woman was washed away.

"She's so talented. To be so young and to have achieved

so much. You should see her fan mail. Such a tragedy. I hope the little thing turns up safe."

The lines tumbled out without the conviction of her previous delivery. In fact, without any conviction at all.

"Yes, I'm sure you do." Nina did her best to keep the easygoing persona. "I've been asked to look into her disappearance, and I believe you were the last person to speak to her."

"Second last."

"What's that?"

"The old guy at the gate. Reg. He spoke to her last; when she walked past him. He said hi and she said nothing at all."

"Right, second last. Of course." Nina took out her notebook. "How would you describe your relationship with Alicia?"

"Oh, fine." If Janet strained her jaw any more Nina was sure she'd burst something.

"And the chronic lateness?"

"She's still learning about—"

"Janet."

"Hmmm?"

"Tell me about Alicia." She leaned forward. "The real one."

The young woman angled her head toward the cracked ceiling. "She's a fucking bitch and I hate her." Her eyes flared and she covered her mouth in horror.

"There we go." Nina tapped her knee. "Some truth, finally. Feel better letting it out?"

Shoulders slumped, Janet scowled. "I hated the little brat." Realizing what she'd admitted, she quickly added, "But I didn't do it." Under her breath she muttered, "Unless you count stabbing the cow in my dreams."

"Maybe that's enough complete honesty for now." Nina

patted her hand. She wanted to keep the discussion on track, at least for now. "No one is saying you had anything to do with her disappearance. I assure you that's not why I'm here." Nina put her notepad down. "Off the record, okay?" Nina neglected to explain there was no record to begin with and that she wasn't a reporter. It was what people in the movies said in situations like this; she assumed Janet would be familiar with the cliché.

"I'm not here to get you in trouble. I want to find Alicia, and the best way to do that is to know the truth. All the truth. This is a safe space, Janet, only you and me here."

The woman gnawed on her fingernail. "She... she wasn't very pleasant to be around."

"A diva?"

The young woman shook her head. "No. Well, yes, but it came from..." Her voice trailed off.

"Safe space, remember?"

Janet hesitated, then blurted, "Drugs" and immediately pursed her lips.

"Alicia does drugs? What kind?"

An involuntary laugh escaped Janet's lips. "All of them. She parties hard. Amphetamines, grass, coke, uppers, downers, God knows what else." She leaned forward conspiratorially. "Look at her film schedule. There's a standard gap when they dry her out by throwing her back into rehab."

"She's fifteen."

Janet shrugged. *It's Hollywood.*

"So, the kid likes to party and you were her PA?"

Janet dipped her head in agreeance. "Three days into shooting, the director knew the little bitch was high as a kite every day. I did my best to get her on set on time, but she didn't make it easy. Screamed and yelled, threw whatever was handy. She's... not a nice person. The director was already talking about replacing her."

"Where were her parents through all this?"

Janet shrugged. "Only saw them once, they were as hopped up as their kid. They came asking her for more money. I got the impression their little princess was their cash cow. Of course, they were on the news last night, all tears and concern." She sniffed. "Crocodile tears if you ask me."

Nina made a note: *interview parents.*

"So, if her parents weren't looking after her welfare, who was?"

"No one, as far as I could tell. By all accounts she hung out with skeezy types off set. Even though she was a rising star, I get the impression her nose candy and her parents were bleeding her dry. She was always on the phone to her agent asking about the next deal, and if she could get paid in advance." Janet assessed Nina. "You know, she looks a lot like you. The old you, not the cool new one. The movie blond one."

"Yeah, folks have said that. Don't see it myself." Nina needed to stay on topic. "You think she's disappeared because of drugs?"

"Maybe, I don't know. Like I said, she was running with some wild folks."

"Tell me about the last time you saw her."

"She called me a fat dumb cunt and threw a Diet Coke at me."

Even by Hollywood standards, Janet was on the lean side. Nina was forming a none too flattering picture of Alicia Morrison.

"I take it your relationship was... acrimonious?"

Janet tapped her nose. "The studio assigned me when

they figured out she was a mega-bitch. Imagine being that much of a known diva before you even can get a learner's permit." She shook her head. "The day she vanished, she turned up to set two hours late. Once she'd wrapped for the day she screamed at the makeup assistants until she made herself hoarse, then demanded I get her a Diet Coke. When I gave it to her, she threw it in my face. Ice and everything. Apparently, she wanted a Tab even though she asked for a Diet Coke, and I'm a shit assistant because I don't read minds."

"So, after the," Nina dramatically mimed drink throwing, eliciting a giggle from Janet, "then what?"

"I went and got dried off, and by the time I came back she'd already left. She didn't tell anyone where she was going. The driver came in around six to ask when she'd be done, and we went on a hunt for her. Someone checked with the gate and the guard confirmed she'd walked out."

"Did she have any appointments, dinner reservations?"

"No. I told the police the same."

"Mickey mentioned something about her saying she was meeting someone?"

"Yes, but I didn't say anything to the police because it didn't make any sense. She said she was meeting someone at a nightclub called The Crucible. I'd never heard of it, have you?"

This was LA; a new night spot for the young and beautiful opened every other week. "The Crucible? No. Sounds awful."

"I even let my fingers do the walking, looked it up in the Yellow Pages, but nothing. There's no such place. She was obviously off her face. She used to say some wild stuff, claimed she was going to be first lady one day soon. She's *fifteen*. You know," Janet made mime of snorting a particularly long line, "I wouldn't believe a word she said."

Nina made a note, disregarding Janet's caution. "And she left in a red coat? Reg at the gate said that's what he thought she was wearing."

"That's the one. Wore it all the time. I think it was so she could tell everyone she bought it in Milan. Pretentious cow." She looked up at Nina. "I mean, you know, I hope she's safe and well."

No, you don't.

"Thanks, Janet. I'll give you a call if I have anything else for you."

CHAPTER
NINE

Nina entered her upstairs apartment quietly. It was thankfully free of surprise lovers—the only males present were a sleeping Sputnik cuddled up on the couch next to an equally restful Trank. Tiptoeing her way across the floor, she snuck up on Trank, who was snoring quietly with a hardcover copy of *Right Ho, Jeeves* resting on his chest. On the record player, Otis Redding's *Dock of the Bay* rotated with the needle floating in its final groove. Nina frowned approvingly. *Good choice, Hank.*

Picking up his shoes, which had been neatly placed on the floor beside him, Nina quietly dropped them in his lap, causing both him and Sputnik to jump.

"Get your shoes on loser, we're going out."

Shaking off the shock, a bleary Trank asked, "What are you talking about?"

"Clem Kaufman." She held aloft a piece of paper. "Stuntman and known associate of both Seth Wagner and Lewis Diehl. The one who supposedly borrowed his car. The one who could be the third member of Wagner's team who'd apparently found a way out of the stuntman game. Phoebe got me his address. He's all the way out in Moreno Valley, so we've got a drive ahead of us. Pee now or forever hold your piss."

"Wait. Hold on. Why am I going?"

"Same reason I brought you along to Wagner's—you might see something I don't."

Besides, the long drive would give Trank ample time to fill in the numerous gaps in his story.

"Last time I went anywhere with you I was shot at. You're a dangerous woman to be around, Nina Maddox."

"Exciting, isn't it?"

"Not the precise word I would choose, no." Slipping on his shoes, he asked, "How was Mickey? I bet he was distraught."

She didn't have the heart to tell him Mickey was indeed distraught, but not about Trank. He'd been more distressed about Diehl. She was still trying to figure out the angle on that one.

"Did you tell him I'm alive? Was he over the moon?"

"I did not."

Trank shook his head in confusion. "Why not? I make millions for his studio. I still don't believe he'd send thugs to Wagner's apartment to shoot at me."

"But he'd send thugs to shoot at me?"

"Well, he has met you."

Against her better judgment, Nina laughed. She liked Trank, and really hoped he didn't turn out to be a murderer. She'd hate to have to haul him to the closest police station. She'd do it, but she'd hate it.

She gave him the rundown on her chat with Mickey, sandpapering the edges to protect the star's ego.

When she returned to Asta's, she'd called Phoebe from the bar. Her friend had traced Clem Kaufman's address. It was currently sitting in the back pocket of her jeans.

Trank closed the book he'd been reading. "You don't have a television, so I had to pick a book." He motioned to Nina's bookshelves. "PG Wodehouse. HP Lovecraft. HG Wells. JD Salinger. Do you only read authors with initials instead of full names?"

Ignoring him, Nina changed into a heavier leather jacket. By the time they reached Moreno Valley it would be getting late, and the desert gets chilly at night. Picking up Phoebe's car keys, she once again frowned at the thought of her beloved car, sitting in the shop.

Downstairs, they were almost out the door when Titus yelled, "Nina, phone." With his big fist over the mouthpiece, he added, "You know, you could just buy an answering machine. Saw Radio Shack have some on special."

Nina crinkled her nose and gave Titus a kiss on the cheek as she took the handset from him. She rounded the bar as he went to pour a beer.

"Nina speaking."

"This is Andrew Ross." The agent sounded pissed.

"Ah, Mr Ross, I was up at the studio today tracing Alicia's last known movements. I've got a lead on—"

"Don't bother."

"I'm sorry?"

"I said, don't bother."

"I assure you, I've made progress. These things take time, I'm going to—"

"She's dead."

The phone felt heavy in Nina's hands.

"Oh shit. I'm so sorry to hear." She turned to Trank, who regarded her curiously, not privy to her conversation. "What can you tell me about what happened, where she was found?"

"Why does it matter?"

Taken aback by the question, Nina said, "It could lead to the truth."

"I can't buy a Mercedes with ten percent of the truth."

Fucking agents.

"I'd like to know."

"Then call the cops. Needless to say, I'm only paying you for today."

Nina rang off and called a number she knew by heart. When the call was answered, she said, "Birmingham, homicide," and waited.

A gruff voice answered, "Birmingham here."

"It's Nina Maddox, don't hang up!"

"Give me a reason not to." Nina could hear the detective's teeth clenching through the phone.

"I might be able to help you with the Alicia Morrison case."

"Jesus Christ, woman, we just got that."

"So I heard. I might be able to help. You gave the agent Andrew Ross my details, which I appreciate by the way, so I'm on the case. Tell me what you know."

Huffing, he replied, "Her body was found a few hours ago."

"Where?"

"In the trunk of a car at LAX. Long-term parking. Apparently, some Japanese tourist complained about the smell."

That meant she'd been there for days, Nina surmised. "Any details on the car?"

"A '72 Buick Riviera."

Nina turned instantly to Trank. She must have turned white because he asked, "Nina, what's wrong?"

Birmingham went on. "We're running the plates. We were literally just assigned this case, like half an hour ago. How did you know to call?"

"The car," she swallowed hard, "it wouldn't happen to be a deep chestnut color by any chance, would it?"

"It... it is. How the fuck did you know that?"

Nina hung up. Her hand remained on the phone as she stared at the wall of bottles lined up behind the bar, trying to make sense of her jumbled thoughts.

A hand was placed gently on her shoulder. Trank was beside her. "Nina, what is it?"

Down the far end of the bar she saw Titus tense in response to Nina's change in expression. The big man's meaty fists clenched at the ready. Nina's pugnacious guardian angel.

"Alicia Morrison has been found dead."

Trank shook his head sadly. "Oh, that poor child."

"She was found in the trunk of a car." She lowered her voice. "In Seth Wagner's car. The same make and color, everything. The one that was missing from his apartment. The one Clem Kaufman borrowed."

"What?" Trank balked.

Nina bit her nails. "Somehow, the man who was killed in your bed is tied to the death of an up-and-coming star. The deaths of Wagner, Diehl, and Morrison are all connected."

She grabbed a bottle of Bell's whisky from the shelf and poured them two shots. Titus gave her the stink eye but she ignored him. She downed hers, leaned both elbows on the bar and blew out an exaggerated sigh.

"Trank, what the fuck have you gotten me involved in?"

~

Trank and Nina drove in silence down Route 60, their thoughts swirling.

Clenching the steering wheel tightly, Nina fought her mounting anger. This case was doing her head in. There were so many unanswered questions.

Why was Diehl so afraid of Mickey, and why did Mickey freak out at the mere mention of Diehl's name? Was it because Nina had just been talking about Morrison, or something else entirely?

Was Mickey responsible for it all? If so, what could he possibly gain from murdering two stuntmen and a rising star? Why murder Seth Wagner in the bed of his prized TV star? Why did he act like Trank truly was dead? And why send Nina to Trank's house in the first place?

How did the deaths of Diehl and Wagner connect with the death of Alicia Morrison? Why was Clem Kaufman borrowing Diehl's car, and how did the dead starlet end up in the trunk?

Nina saw how white her knuckles were, having virtually strangled the steering wheel. She stared at the three-lane highway before her.

There was so much she didn't know. Every piece of information led to more questions. Nina was pissed at having no answers. But one of the biggest questions had a solution, and he was sitting right next to her.

"Hank." She hadn't realized how much aggravation could be expressed in a single word.

The big man jumped; he'd been lost in his thoughts. "Mmmm?"

"Where the actual fuck were you when Wagner was killed in your bedroom?"

Taken aback by her abruptness, Trank fell silent and shrunk into the door panel. He must have realized there was nowhere to hide now. "What, what? I... I told you."

"No, we established you gave me a bullshit story. I'm sick of being fucking lied to, Hank. I'm sick of knowing fuck all about what the fuck is going on. I'm fucking sick of being in danger when I don't even fucking know why. So, either you fucking tell me where the fuck you were, or I toss you out of this fucking car without even slowing the fuck down. Am I making myself fucking clear?"

"You are clear." He swallowed hard. "Very sweary, but clear."

"Fucking A I am. Now spill."

Trank squirmed in his seat. "Uh, alright, but you must promise, and I mean *promise*, that whatever I tell you will never be repeated outside this car. Can I have your word?"

"I can't believe whatever it is you're keeping secret is more important than your freedom. Than avoiding a murder charge."

"It very much is, I assure you. Now, do I have your word?"

"Sure."

"That wasn't exactly rousing."

Nina changed lanes to overtake a slow-moving delivery van. "You don't pay me for rousing. All you get is 'sure,' and a half-assed promise I won't throw you from a moving vehicle. I'm tired, I'm angry and I'm PMSing like a bitch." She wasn't, but found it usually put men off kilter. "It's time to spill, Hank." She turned and raised a challenging eyebrow.

Even now there was hesitancy in his response. "After I left Seth, a very much alive Seth, I went to a club."

"That's... That's it?" Nina stared at him, only returning her attention to the steering wheel when she realized she'd drifted out of the lane. "A damn *club*? You could have gone to jail for a fucking *club*? I expected something far seedier. Cock fighting. Toddler cage matches to the death. Skeet shooting with live puppies. Anything other than just a dumb club."

"You don't understand." His voice was quiet, as if he expected the people in the cars nearby to overhear his words. "This is a very elite club. Very *very* secret. No one is allowed to speak of it, even if you meet a fellow member in the outside world. Anything goes in this club, and I mean *anything*. Your wildest fantasies are catered for—at a price, of course. The exceptionally select clientele pay an exorbitant membership, and in return they're granted access to anything they want. Once you enter their luxurious walls, it's like the rules of the rest of the world no longer apply. There's no signage, no cute little packet of matches, nothing to give away its existence. Those who enter have pledged to never speak of it, under threat of death." He leaned forward to see her face. "I'm speaking literally here, Nina. You sign a contract that says they will kill you if you divulge the existence of the club to anyone."

Nina laughed, but stopped when she saw the earnestness on his face. He was serious. Deadly serious.

"So, this club of yours, what makes you so sure they'd actually kill you?"

"I have absolutely no doubt in my mind. Their new security manager is this ex-CIA guy. The scariest man I've ever seen. Not strong, he's not physically intimidating. It's his eyes. They're the eyes of death. You know he'd kill you with a swizzle stick if given the order and he wouldn't even ruffle his tuxedo. When I was interviewed, I was told in no uncertain terms that he would destroy me if I ever spoke of the club's existence with anyone. I wholeheartedly believed them."

"They interviewed you?"

"Yes, I was invited to an interview with a selection committee. They could see me; I couldn't see them. They understood I had particular... tastes that could not be met by other venues, and would guarantee my complete freedom—once I paid the excessive membership fee, of course. There was an unambiguous understanding of the consequences should I stray from their very strict rules."

Nina didn't completely buy the story, at least not yet, though she believed that *he* believed what he was saying. A club so debauched and severe members *agreed* to be murdered should they let it slip a mention of the club's mere existence?

"Were Wagner or Diehl members of this club? Is that why they were killed?"

"Oh god, no. They wouldn't be able to afford even a cocktail there. As far as I know, they had no knowledge of the place. I obviously never mentioned it to Seth."

"Who else goes to this place?"

"The elite. The hideously wealthy. Congressmen. Civic leaders. The most senior people you can imagine. You've seen many of them on the television spouting the need for a return to traditional family values. I've seen them coked up to their eyeballs performing acts that would make a porn star blush."

Nina started to imagine what he might mean, but found the exercise distracting. The images weren't helping her driving.

"Care to share what your particular tastes are that can't be met elsewhere?"

"No, I most certainly do not." He folded his arms.

"Well, what can you tell me about the club?"

"I think I've already said too much."

"No, Hank, you haven't said anywhere near enough. The choice is simple. You either give me everything you know or you're likely to end up like Wagner and Diehl. That motivation enough for you?"

The scowl on his face indicated it was. "There's a main bar area. The best cocktails in the world are made there, with the most exclusive ingredients. There's a gambling room with scarily high stakes. I usually avoid it, gambling isn't my forte. There's a buffet, of sorts."

"Of sorts? A buffet sounds a little down-market."

"Perhaps 'buffet' is the wrong word. What would one call a selection of every imaginable drug of the highest possible quality?"

"John Denver's house?"

Nina frowned. Whoever owned this place must pay a fortune to keep the cops away. Prostitution, drug trafficking, gambling, God knew what else. Plus, the CIA-trained security head, the death threats. They'd be heavily connected.

"How do you become a member?"

"They must approach you. That's the only way. When you find what they're offering it's like the hand of God. Part of the draw is that it's so ridiculously exclusive. To have a membership your contemporaries can't have, that they don't even *know exists*—well, that's pretty appealing."

Nina could see his point. For a city so fervently devoted to status, it was quite the drawcard.

Trank went on. "Working girls and boys cruise the dark

spaces, who are frankly the most beautiful human beings you've ever seen in your life—and I work in Hollywood. It's like you're on another planet. There are upstairs rooms where you can go to perform whatever debauchery you can imagine. There's no judgment. No restrictions. It's like no other place on earth."

Nina tried to picture what the place would look like and the decadent activities that might occur there. It wasn't an unpleasant thought experiment.

"The exclusive clientele are kept happy because all their niche desires are catered to. Then there's the added cachet of watching the next big star hit it big and saying to yourself, oh, I fucked him or her a couple of years ago." His face glowed as if reminiscing about doing exactly that. "There's a dirty secret all the powerful people of this town know deep down. Despite all the influence, despite all their power, they ultimately end up empty inside. So, they keep coming back, feeding the machine, trying to fill the void that can never be filled."

Nina had to admit, that was pretty deep for a TV star. "What do they call this den of iniquity?"

"The Crucible."

Nina slammed on the brakes, prompting a cacophony of horns and yells from pissed off Angelinos. The delivery van she'd passed came within inches of slamming into them, horn blaring.

A panicked Trank screamed, "Nina!"

Recovering, she put Phoebe's car into gear and tentatively pulled onto the shoulder of the highway. She pulled on the handbrake and turned the engine off, to the dulcet tones of fading angry horns.

Nina breathed hard. "When I spoke to Alicia Morrison's

PA, she said Alicia had mentioned a club, a club she claimed to be going to the night she went missing."

"Oh god."

"It was called The Crucible. If that's true, she was there a couple of nights before you were."

"What the hell was a child doing in that place? There's no way she should have even known about it. Nina, we're talking about a place where anything can happen. A place of decadence and drugs. A place no fifteen-year-old should ever, *ever* go."

Nina's imagination went down dark paths she didn't want to imagine. She felt sick. She wanted to curl up in her seat and wish the whole stinking case away. She hoped she was wrong.

"Where is this place?"

"Nina. I can't..."

"Tell me now or by god, I swear I will rip out your taint with my bare fucking hands, Hank!"

Blinking at her several times, the rugged action star let out a tiny whimper. "Are you okay? You seem to be falling apart a bit..."

"Falling apart?" She glanced at the skid marks she'd left on the road. "I'm surprised I'm still together. No one is telling me the truth. I've got a studio head who was once at least cordial, if not a friend, now flipping between petrified and intimidating. There are three dead bodies and counting. I've been threatened, had my tires slashed and shot at, and let's not forget the guy who's still playing his cards close when I'm literally the only person on the planet trying to save him. So please enlighten me, Hank, how peachy should I be feeling right about now?"

Hank lowered his head conciliatorily. "Down on the

700 block of South Wall Street, opposite the flower market. It's in an industrial part of town. Quiet at night. Secluded."

Still trying to make sense of what she now knew, Nina started the engine.

"Hank Trank, sometimes I wish I never met you, you know?"

"Oh, I have no doubt."

CHAPTER

TEN

An hour later Nina had calmed down. A little. Well, not a great deal, if she was completely honest.

Finally, some pieces were beginning to fit together, but Nina wasn't sure she was going to like the final picture. Alicia Morrison went missing when she was allegedly headed for The Crucible. Two nights later, Trank frequented the same club. That meant whoever ran the club would have known he wasn't at home. It was pure supposition on her behalf, but if they had followed Wagner there, or somehow knew he was hiding out at Trank's, they also knew he'd be all alone. The police said there was no sign of forced entry at Trank's mansion. If Trank was right about the head of security being an ex-CIA agent, he would have no trouble entering Trank's place undetected.

Nina's fingers, which desperately needed a manicure, tapped the steering wheel. Alicia Morrison couldn't have walked to the club; it would take hours to walk halfway across LA. Nor would she have wanted to. The club wasn't in a pleasant part of town, just next to Skid Row; the great unwashed, and how. So the question was, how did she get from the studio to The Crucible, if indeed she had? How was Wagner, a stuntman Trank was adamant had no connection to the club, suddenly linked to her murder? And how did the dead starlet end up in his trunk at the airport?

It was like she'd woken from a dream and was trying to make sense of the misty jumble of half-memories. She really wished she was in her kitchen right now. She needed the help to think. Plus, she realized how little she'd eaten. Her stomach growled in agreeance.

Further down Route 60, the view from the highway became less suburban and more industrial, until it changed again into semi-desert. Long stretches of flat arid land were framed by the Box Springs Mountains in the distance. Nina took the exit into a sparsely populated area. Clem Kaufman's house stood alone at the end of an undeveloped road.

The sun descended, devouring Los Angeles behind them in a vibrant pink hue. Stars not visible in the city began to shine above the wide-open desert. It must have been by design that light pollution kept most of Hollywood from seeing the stars at night; it wouldn't want the competition.

They turned down a wide-open street suitably named Cactus Avenue; there was nothing in the lifeless desert for miles around. The single-story house was only a few years old. There was a boat under tarps in the driveway, a black Trans Am parked next to it. Past dusk, there were no lights on in the house.

It took a certain type of individual to live this far away from civilization. Kaufman obviously liked his privacy.

Nina exited the car silently and opened the trunk to remove her search warrant. Knowing the drill by now,

Trank followed silently. He'd been mute since the revelation about the club, lost in his own thoughts, just like Nina.

Nina placed her hand on the hood of the Trans Am; cold. She lifted the tarp covering the boat, revealing nothing but rusty tools and empty beer cans.

When she knocked on the front door, the echo carried through the still night. Nina could have sworn a coyote howled in the distance, but she may have imagined it. They waited. No one answered. After two more attempts, Nina extracted her Beretta. Trank didn't hide his surprise.

In a low voice, Nina said, "After our encounter out the front of Wagner's, I think it's best to be cautious, no?"

"Oh, I agree. Do you have one for me?"

"No, but I can give you some cutting remarks if that helps."

"I don't think a scathing remark, no matter how witty, will be much use once they shoot me dead."

Nina raised a forefinger. "Yes, but think of the emotional trauma you'll have inflicted on them for years afterward." Smiling, she took a tire iron from her search warrant and handed it to Trank. "Hold this if it makes you feel better."

Swishing the rusted metal tool through the air, Trank replied, "It does, actually."

"Just don't knock me out unless I ask nicely, okay?"

Removing her lockpicks, Nina went to work. The door opened with a creak. No one protested. No one could.

Trank stepped into the lounge. "Dear mother of god."

With the sun nearly over the horizon, the house was in semi-darkness, but there was enough light to see inside. Like Wagner's apartment, the place had been ransacked. Papers were flung across the floor, cupboards hung open with their doors torn off or hanging, their contents dispensed among the chaos. Cushions had been slashed, their linings adding to the mess. Whoever had searched the place had been thorough, and destructive.

Tellingly, just like at Wagner's, the videotapes had received special attention. Every case had been pried open and the cassettes removed.

Nina moved carefully through the disarray, careful not to trample anything they may need later or that would reveal they'd been there. The ravaged scene was so reminiscent of Wagner's, the link between the two became tighter by the minute. Was this another stuntman who'd met an untimely death?

The house was deathly quiet, no sign of human life. The roof creaked, likely cooling after being beaten by the California sun all day. The house still retained the heat of the day.

Stepping into the kitchen, Nina found what appeared to be the answer to the question of Kaufman's fate. Beneath the contents of the kitchen cupboards strewn about, a large pool of dried deep red liquid had pooled on the tiled floor.

"Is that..." an already startled Trank muttered, "is that blood?"

"Looks like it."

It seemed that, unlike at Wagner's, whoever came to call had found the house occupied. Evidently, the visit didn't end well for Clem Kaufman. There was a lot of blood.

Like the front of the house, the contents of the kitchen were scattered as if the intruder was searching for something in particular. Anything from the fridge had melted, and the milk was rancid after days baking in the desert heat.

Nina leaned down and inspected the floor. In particular,

the pool of dried blood. Leaning forward on her haunches, she inhaled deeply. "Huh."

"Huh, what?" Trank shook his head. "What's huh about someone being murdered?"

Nina leaned forward. "This isn't right."

"No, it isn't. There's been another murder."

She waved a finger at Trank. "No, I mean the blood."

"Yes, there's a lot of it."

"No, it doesn't..." She leaned back. "Look, I did horror movies."

"Yes. I know. I don't see how—"

"Lots of blood in horror movies."

"I hardly..."

Nina lowered her face to an inch above the blood and sniffed deeply. Behind her, Trank made an uncomfortable squeak. But she wasn't done. Nina poked out her tongue and licked the blood on the kitchen floor.

"Nina!" Trank shrieked at a pitch no non-castrated man should be capable of. "What the hell are you..." Trank made a gurgling sound as he fought the urge to vomit.

Nina raised herself back onto her haunches and grinned smugly. "Thought so."

"You thought you were a sicko and wanted to confirm it?" He shook his head. "You really are losing it, aren't you?"

She stood and gave him an indifferent scowl. Trank followed her out of the room, a concerned look on his face, gripping the tire iron tighter. Nina walked back to the lounge and placed her hand on the TV.

She extracted her Beretta and Trank reeled. Before he could protest, she stared him in the eye and fired three times into the roof.

Trank staggered backwards. "What the hell are you—"

Nina cut him off by yelling, "Come down here or I make

this roof one big slice of Swiss cheese. You have ten seconds!"

A series of clunks and scrapes moved speedily across the ceiling until there was a loud *clunk*. A wooden ladder dropped from a hatch in the hallway ceiling and a middle-aged man descended quickly. He stood, wincing, with his hands in the air, sweat patches staining his underarms.

In the semi-darkness, he stammered, "P-p-please don't kill me."

"We're not here to kill you." Nina put the Beretta back in its holster.

He watched the gun as Nina put it away. "How did you know you wouldn't hit me?"

"I didn't. Clem Kaufman, I presume?" When she received a nod, she said, "We have a lot to talk about."

The man stepped into the lounge, and Nina got a better look at him. Up close, Kaufman was older than she expected a stuntman to be. His once-dark hair was gray at the sides, and the wrinkles on his tanned face told the story of a man who'd spent a career exposed to the elements. It could be said he had an athletic physique—if that sport was darts. His midriff told of years of beer and fried food, and he had a complexion to match.

Turning from Nina for the first time, he pivoted to Trank. "Seth! Where the hell have you b—" Taking a step forward, Kaufman man pulled up. "You're not Seth."

"A fact I am grateful for on many levels," Trank replied.

"You're Hank Trank," he gasped. "The news said you were dead."

"Don't believe everything you see on TV," Trank replied charmingly. "I should know."

Kaufman turned to Nina. "You seem familiar."

"My name is Nina Maddox, I'm a private investigator.

I'm investigating... I'm sorry to be the one to tell you this, but Seth Wagner's dead."

"Seth's dead?"

The shock on his face was unmistakable. He'd genuinely believed Trank was Wagner in the half-light, and the devastation on his features now told Nina he was either an extremely accomplished actor or experiencing genuine disbelief.

"Where? How?"

"That's far more complicated than we can get into right now. Why are you hiding out here?"

"I was hoping Seth would turn up. Been waiting days."

"Or call?"

Kaufman screwed his face up. "I can't answer the phone, are you nuts? What if it was them? I had to wait for Seth to turn up in person." He scratched the back of his neck. "I guess that's not happening now."

Kaufman's gaze drifted into the middle distance, lost in his thoughts, his grief.

Trank tugged at Nina's arm. "Please explain to me how the hell you knew he was up there."

"First clue was the blood." Nina didn't care if she sounded self-satisfied. "Props departments use variations of the same recipe for fake blood." She counted off on her fingers. "Corn syrup, red food coloring, and variable levels of blue and green food dyes. It has a sweet smell that real blood doesn't. I know both, and I have to tell you, the stuff all over the kitchen floor was as genuine as a real estate agent's Christmas card."

"Yes, but..."

Nina wasn't done. "The kitchen stuff was thrown all on top of the blood after it had dried. So, I assumed someone wanted to make it look like they'd met an untimely end *then* the place was broken into and ransacked."

Trank raised a finger. "Yes, but—"

Nina interrupted; she wasn't done being smug yet. "Then there the TV." She turned to Kaufman. "You were watching it right up until you saw our headlights, weren't you?"

Kaufman became intensely interested in the filthy carpet.

"And the fake blood?" she asked him. "Who was that for?"

"I knew they'd be coming for me. I hoped the blood would throw them off my trail, make them think I'd already met my end. They still tossed the place," he motioned to the carnage that was once his home, "but I hoped they'd stop looking for me if they thought I was already dead."

"Worked for me," Trank said.

He has a point. Nina turned to Trank, amused, but there was no mirth on his face.

She turned the conversation back to Kaufman. "I take it you wanted them to think you were dead after you heard Diehl died in such mysterious circumstances."

"How did you know about—?"

Nina cut him short. "How many days were you hiding up there?"

"Three." His voice was shaky, shocked at how much Nina knew. "Glad I did, too. Two goons turned up day before yesterday, and, well..." He motioned to the wreckage of his home. "They even searched the roof, but I hid in an old water heater."

"Smart man." Nina thought it best to compliment him, she needed him on side. "But you could have run, especially if you knew people were after you—but you didn't. Why?"

"I... I was waiting for Seth. He has something we need to make this all go away. If I ran, he wouldn't know where to find me, so I stayed."

"You three boys got yourselves into a spot of bother?"

"You think?" Again, his gaze fell to his wrecked house. "When I heard Diehl died I didn't think for one second it was an accident. And now you tell me Seth's gone too..." He looked woozy and put his hand on the back of a chair for stability.

Nina decided to go out on a limb. It was a hunch, but she wasn't going to get anywhere playing it safe. "The thing you originally thought was going to make Wagner, Diehl, and you rich?"

Kaufman gave Nina a cautious nod, like he didn't want to give too much away.

"You were hoping Wagner would turn up with the videotape, weren't you?"

"You know about that?"

"I do now."

Trank held up a hand. "Wait, hold up. What the hell are you talking about here. What videotape?"

She turned to him. "Both Seth Wagner and our new friend here had their places searched. Most of the stuff was tossed about randomly, except the VHS tapes. In both houses, each and every cassette box was taken. Your house was untouched, money left lying around, but the one room they searched was your home cinema. The cops thought it was some super fan, but it wasn't. It's all connected."

"They were looking for some videotape in particular," Trank mused.

"Exactly." Nina tapped her foot. "They tortured Wagner, probably trying to get him to reveal where the tape was. He obviously didn't tell them, because after they tortured him, they tossed your cinema, Wagner's, and here. Whatever they're after, they don't have it. Our friend here said he was hoping Wagner had it." She turned to Kaufman. "What is on that videotape?"

"Oh no. Nope. No way." Kaufman vehemently shook his head in case his words were ambiguous. "I tell you that, I have zero leverage, nothing. No. Until you help me get out of this mess, you get nothing more out of me until I'm safely out of this stinking town, we clear?"

It was the first backbone he'd shown since they'd arrived. Nina wasn't impressed.

"The police found the body, Clem."

"W... what?"

"The body you dumped. In Seth Wagner's car. Eyewitnesses saw a man fitting your description and using your name borrowing Wagner's car from his apartment. The exact same car that was found at LAX today with the decomposing body of one Alicia Morrison inside the trunk."

What remained of Kaufman's backbone dissolved into putty. His face turned white and he collapsed like a marionette with its strings cut. He crouched in a puddle on the floor, weeping into his hands.

Trank turned to her, utterly lost.

"Dark hair, gray at the side." She motioned to the sobbing man. "Matches the description Mrs Bennet gave us at Wagner's place. Said it was like a skunk, remember?"

Trank blinked several times. Nina could have sworn she heard fizzing, like his brain was shorting out.

"So he," Trank pointed to the bawling Kaufman, "Diehl and Wagner were trying to get rich quick with a videotape of some description that somehow led to the deaths of Wagner, Diehl, and Alicia Morrison?"

"Seems that way." Nina leaned over the distraught

Kaufman. "And our mate Clem here is going to tell us exactly what he's fucked around with and found out. Then, and only then, will we consider hauling his ass out of town. Isn't that right, Clem?"

Regaining his composure somewhat, Kaufman wiped at his tears and dipped his head in confirmation.

"Right. First things first. Did you kill Alicia Morrison?"

"No! God no."

"Then how the hell did she end up in the trunk of your friend's car?"

"I didn't kill her. None of us did, not me, Seth, or Lewis. We... we..." He steadied himself. "Seth, he knows a guy, a friend, kind of, who asks him to do things every now and then, on the QT right? They had... an item... they needed to get rid of..." He glanced up guiltily, his shoulders slumped. "The Alicia girl. Seth, he said he couldn't do it alone, so he roped in me and Lewis. We've been best friends for twenty years."

Nina was reminded of the old adage: *friends help you move house, best friends help you move a body.* "Go on."

"So, uh, we picked her up from this place."

"The Crucible."

"Jesus Christ, how the hell did you know that?" Kaufman asked, astonished. Receiving no answer other than a stern glare from Nina, he went on. "We got there about five am. It was closed up but Seth had a set of keys. The place was as fancy as all get-out, like Buckingham Palace, but with a bar and a casino and—"

"Just stick to the story, Clem."

"Right, right, sorry. Seth was told where the body was and we grabbed it and got out of there as fast as we could."

"Where, precisely?"

"What's that?"

"Where in The Crucible? I understand there are many rooms."

"Oh, right. The Arbuckle room. Second floor." Kaufman shuddered. "She was... in a bad way. Like, stuff had been done to her. Bad, bad stuff. No one should ever have to go through what she did, especially not a kid. It was really fucked up. We had to see that shit, right?" If Kaufman was after sympathy, he was looking in the wrong place. Evidently realizing this, he went on.

"We got out of there as soon as we could. Rolled her up in a rug and put her in the trunk and drove off." He scratched the back of his head. "The original plan, my plan, was to drive her out past Hermit Falls. We had the shovels and everything. But as we were driving away Diehl pulled out this video cassette from his jacket. While Seth and I were rolling the body in the rug, he'd found a secret compartment in the wall. There was a video camera hidden behind a mirror; they had the whole place wired."

"Oh, dear lord." Trank had gone whiter than any man should. Video cameras at The Crucible was obviously news to him too. Nina waved him off, not wanting to interrupt the flow of the story. She gestured for Kaufman to continue.

"So," he looked up, shamefaced, "Diehl, he kind of swiped the tape."

"Kind of?"

"We didn't know until he was waving it around in the car. Then he suggested maybe we shouldn't bury her, at least not straight away. Maybe we could make some money out of this. Maybe we could, you know..."

"Blackmail someone?"

His head dipped shamefully. "I wasn't going for it, I really wasn't, but then Diehl starts spinning this story about how we have the body and the videotape and gets all excited, which got Seth excited. In no time the two of them were telling me what a great idea it was. Saying anyone who did what they did to this kid deserved all they got, you know? When you're hopped on adrenalin, that shit kind of makes sense after a while."

Nina recalled Diehl, before he died, insisting that it wasn't his idea at all, that he'd only helped. She chose not to mention that now; she didn't want to interrupt Kaufman. Besides, in the end, it didn't really matter whose bad idea it was, it had cost them all dearly.

"We watched a few seconds of it when we got back to Seth's. It had the Alicia kid wearing this red coat thing, walking up to the John wearing this fluffy white bathrobe like he's at a day spa. She slinks up to him on the bed, all sexy like. Christ, the way she walked you'd swear she was twice her age. We turned it off before anything happened, Seth and I couldn't stomach it. Lewis was keen though."

"Who was the John? Who were you knuckleheads going to blackmail?"

Nina waited to be told it was Mickey. It was the only thing that made sense.

Kaufman shook his head vehemently. "No way. That's all you're getting until you take me away from here, understand? You've gotten way too much already. I want to be far away from this place by dawn. Too many of my friends have died, I ain't going to be the next one. Capisce?"

"First of all, no one outside of a mafia flick uses capisce in a sentence. Secondly, is the videotape here?"

Kaufman shook his head. "I wouldn't be here if it was. I called a neighbor of Diehl's after I heard he died on set, they said his place had been done over like mine. Someone knows the tape went missing, what it's worth, and they're tearing up half the city for it."

Nina scratched her neck. "What I don't—"

She was cut short by the sound of screeching tires. In the still night, the sound was deafening. Racing to the window, Nina saw the doors of a late model Cadillac fly open and two men sprint out. One was tall and lean, the other squat and muscled, both wearing ski masks. They looked like the Laurel and Hardy of crime. The sound of the front door being kicked in demonstrated their intent all too clearly.

Kaufman turned and yelled, "You led them here! You bitch!"

Nina extracted her Beretta and Trank lifted his tire iron. Staying true to form, Kaufman ran. He scrambled to the hallway, no doubt in an attempt to reach the safety of his hiding place. He didn't make it. The tall figure tackled him to the ground, subdued him with a single punch, then stood.

The following seconds were chaos personified. Nina stepped in front of Trank, gun raised. The shouting made it impossible for her to convey a plan to Trank, which was just as well, as she didn't have one.

The two hooded figures flooded into the lounge, pointing guns and shouting incomprehensible orders. Nina fired, illuminating the stark black house in a flash of deadly light. Bodies moved, and more shots were fired.

Shouting at Trank to stay behind her as she was flanked by the rushing men, Nina felt an excruciating sting to the back of her head. A new, unwelcome blackness enveloped her, and she felt her body tilt and fall. She fell for a very long time, perhaps years, perhaps decades, she wasn't sure.

Everything went sideways and the world went black.

~

Nina woke with a jolt.

She wished she hadn't.

The pain from the back of her head was piercing. Her fingers felt the base of her skull, finding an egg-shaped mound. There was no blood, but the terrible agony more than made up for it.

"Haaank."

Her dry mouth made it hard to form words. *How long was I unconscious?*

Outside, it was much darker than when they'd first arrived. Using every ounce of strength she could muster, she used her fists to prop herself up. Managing to get onto all fours, she felt no better at this altitude than she had on the floor. She waited for the nausea to dispel, but it clung to her like wet spandex. Sucking in a few lungfuls of air, she staggered unsteadily to her feet.

Holding an armchair for support, she called out again. "Hank!"

No reply.

Panic gripped her. Where the hell was he?

"Hank!" She coughed. "Kaufman?"

Silence was her only answer. She made a cautious slow lap of the house, finally coming back to the lounge and slumping in an armchair next to the phone. There was no Trank, but she'd found something else.

Nina picked up the cordless handset and dialed a number.

"Homicide."

"Put me through to Birmingham."

"He's at home."

"Then put me through to his home. He'll want to take my call. It's Nina Maddox."

A series of clicks and beeps followed. Eventually the line was connected.

"You hung up on me."

"Believe me, that's the least of my issues."

Noise in the background suddenly cut out; it sounded like Birmingham had turned off the TV. "You got information on the Morrison murder?"

"That murder? No." Nina rubbed the lump on the back of her head.

"Well, then, Trank's murder?"

"Uh, not that one either."

"Maddox," a hint of trepidation filtered into the homicide cop's voice, "don't tell me..."

Nina's gaze drifted to the hallway, where Clem Kaufman lay slumped on the floor with multiple gunshot wounds to the chest. He stared back at Nina with cold, lifeless eyes.

"Birmingham, you're not gonna believe this..."

ELEVEN

Hours later, Nina sat outside Kaufman's house, on the bonnet of Phoebe's Toyota Shitbox. The Riverside County Sherriff Department and Moreno Valley PD cops were arguing over jurisdiction, while the local county coroner's team did their thing. Nina was too tired to care.

The desert night was cool, and she shivered in her leather jacket. No one had offered her a blanket and a hot cocoa like they did in the movies. The best she got was half a Babe Ruth from a traffic cop and a sneer from everyone else. Nowhere near as warming.

There was no trace of Trank in the house. While waiting for the first cops to arrive, she'd found the strength to go into the roof and check Kaufman's hidey hole. No Trank. The only minor consolation was that there was no blood, either—genuine blood, that was—other than Kaufman's. That didn't mean they couldn't have hauled Trank away and murdered him elsewhere. But why kill Kaufman where he stood and take Trank away?

Birmingham eventually rocked up two hours after she'd

called him. It was the first time Nina had seen him wearing anything other than a cheap polyester suit. The ensemble of an oversized Lakers T-shirt, worn jeans, and stained runners wasn't exactly an improvement. His veneer of world-weary cop put the other officers at ease as he approached. They knew their own on sight.

After a brief chat with the two officers vying for supremacy, Birmingham made his way over to Nina.

"The locals are allowing me here as a professional courtesy because I was the one to call it in. I can't be part of the investigation."

"And yet, here you are."

Nina was tired. She couldn't remember the last time she'd had a decent night's sleep. Tonight wasn't going to be the night either. Her head still pounded from the blow to the back of her head, but she was careful not to rub it. If the cops discovered she had a recent injury that would only lead to questions she didn't want to answer.

"What can you tell me?" Birmingham asked as the coroner's assistants wheeled the mortuary cot through Kaufman's front door.

Nina rubbed her tired face. "I've already been through this, like, five times."

"Then I'll be number six. Look, Maddox, I'm missing the Dodgers Padres game for whatever you're mixed up in. The least you can do is clue me in."

Luckily Nina had had hours to perfect her story. It contained as many elements of the truth as she could stuff in, along with some necessary obfuscation.

"Parties I'm not at liberty at divulge the identify of were concerned their colleague Seth Wagner hadn't shown up to work. He's a stuntman. I visited his place, at..."

She raised an eyebrow, as if Birmingham should be

taking notes. In response, he theatrically patted down his jeans, as if he carried his police notebook with him at all times. He held up a finger, darted to his car and returned with a pencil and a packet of Marlboros.

"Okay, go."

"11916 West Pico Boulevard, apartment 1A. Wagner didn't answer his door, but I could see through a gap in the curtains that the place was a mess. Potentially ransacked."

"You didn't call it in?"

"I didn't know for sure. He could have just kept a messy house."

In response, Birmingham grunted and nodded for her to continue.

"Receiving no answer to my knocks, I walked around the apartment building and noted that his vehicle was missing from his parking space."

"Right, the Buick Riviera. When you called me after you found out about the Morrison killing you could have told me you knew who it belonged to. We hadn't run the plates yet."

"Sorry about that. But we're getting ahead of ourselves. I spoke to Wagner's neighbor." Nina hoped he didn't ask which neighbor—she didn't want him following up and finding out that she—and Trank—had claimed to be cousins from Louisiana. "The neighbor advised that a man had borrowed Wagner's car a few days before. He had gray hair on the side of his head and called himself Kaufman. I didn't think much of it at the time, it was just another lead in a non-urgent case. Looked like a dead end, no real leads on Wagner's whereabouts."

Nina had known exactly where Wagner was, but telling Birmingham to check the LA morgue would raise more questions than she was prepared to answer. She went on.

"Then, quite separately, I was engaged to investigate the Alicia Morrison disappearance. Believe me, the intersection with her murder was completely unexpected."

She didn't even have to lie about that.

"Once you confirmed the make and model of the car Morrison was found in, finding Kaufman took on a whole different level of urgency. So, I hustled out here. When I arrived, the door was wide open. I peered through the front door and saw Kaufman lying in the hallway. I went in to render aid, but he was dead already. That's when I called you."

"Any idea where Mr Seth Wagner is?" Birmingham's gaze turned to the mortuary cot being wheeled to the awaiting van. "I might have some questions for him."

"If I did, would I be here?"

The childhood taunt of *liar, liar, pants on fire* echoed in Nina's ears.

Her story was a labyrinthian maze of truths, half-truths and blatant deceit. For Birmingham to buy it, he'd have to believe Nina was some sort of super PI with an uncanny analytical and exploratory mind displaying hitherto unheard-of detective capabilities. She hoped he bought it.

"That story's horseshit and you know it."

So much for hope.

Nina folded her tired arms. "It's my story, Birmingham. Unless you've got a charge for me, I'm going home. I'm dead tired." She watched Kaufman being loaded into the back of the coroner's van. "Tired. Just tired."

Somehow the homicide cop's face turned even more world-weary. Quite the feat. With a scowl that could curdle yogurt, Birmingham huffed and stuffed the packet of cigarettes in his jeans pocket. He gave a jerk of his head that said, *get out of here.*

Nina didn't need to be told twice. She might have a concussion, but she knew asking Birmingham for a lift home would lead to an uncomfortable couple of hours. She'd rather chance blacking out on the highway than spend that long with a skeptical cop.

As she headed off in Phoebe's loaner, she came back to one recurring thought. What the hell had she gotten herself involved in?

She was no closer to finding out who had killed Wagner, Diehl, Morrison, and now Kaufman. And she'd lost Trank. She'd strung a series of lies for the cops, who would no doubt start pulling at those threads soon enough. She had no leads, no evidence, and no time.

Was Trank dead in a ditch somewhere? Was he being tortured? She didn't know. But she was already formulating a plan for how to find out. As Nina turned onto Route 60, she knew she had two hours to bash that plan into shape. That, or black out and crash into a ditch somewhere. She'd chance it, to get away from yet another murder scene.

"ARE YOU KIDDING ME?" Phoebe asked in her usual reserved way. "They killed him dead?"

"Is there another way?" Nina asked as she chopped the green chillis.

From across the kitchen bench, Phoebe watched Nina work while bringing her up to speed with her latest adventures. Nina's best friend valued her life too much to enter Nina's kitchen when she was cooking.

Without asking, Phoebe grabbed two Samuel Adams from the fridge and handed one to Nina. The two clinked bottles.

As she returned to her seat, a waft of steam enveloped Phoebe. "What are you even making?"

"Gaeng Keow Wan Gai."

With a scowl, Phoebe replied, "So glad I asked."

"Thai green curry. The secret is getting the curry paste right before you begin cooking. That creates the aromatic base, then it's the fresh ingredients that make it pop; the eggplant, the peppers."

Phoebe leaned over the bench and peered into the steaming wok. "That's a lot of food for two people."

Nina didn't respond as she tossed in the chicken. Cooking was clearing her head. The lump on the back of it had practically disappeared. No concussion, just a mild headache dispensed with by an aspirin. She'd worked out the core of her plan on the drive back from the Moreno Valley. Instead of falling into bed, she'd been energized by her idea. Now she needed the mindful activity of cooking to finesse the finer points. She was practically there, though questions still remained.

Where was Trank? If they wanted him dead, why hadn't they killed him at the scene? If he was kidnapped, to what end?

If Wagner was killed because of whatever he, Diehl, and Kaufman had gotten themselves mixed up in, what connection was there to Trank? If there was one at all.

Nina flipped the wok, hoping the answers would manifest themselves. Nothing yet.

"You can't do all this yourself, you know." Phoebe took a sip of her beer. "Even *we* can't do this alone. We're going to need some help."

She was right. They couldn't. As if on cue, there was a knock at the door.

Phoebe turned to Nina curiously. "Who's that?"

"Help."

Nina wiped her hands on a dish towel and strode to the door to greet a smiling Lang. The forensics photographer was dressed casually in jeans and a light sweater. He gave Nina a kiss as he entered.

"Did you bring the stuff?" Nina asked.

He held up a bag stamped with the seal of the Los Angeles County Department of Medical Examiner.

From the kitchen, Phoebe yelled, "Is this a drug deal? Because I'll tell you right now, I'm down with that."

"Not this time." Nina jerked her head for Lang to come in. "Phoebe Jones, Armin Lang. Armin Lang, Phoebe Jones."

Phoebe gave Lang a bow as she assessed him, from gelled hair to comfortable loafers. "This the one you're having heterosexual sex with?"

"You can just say sex, Phoebs."

"Is it?"

"Yes."

Phoebe frowned approvingly. "Not bad, if you're into that kind of thing."

Lang laughed as Nina handed him a beer. Sputnik leaped off the armchair he'd been lounging in and strode over to Lang. He rubbed himself against Lang's leg and purred loudly. Lang bent down to give the ginger cat a pat.

"Little bastard never does that for me." Phoebe scowled at the cat. "Nina, I think your cat is racist."

Chuckling, Nina said, "He likes your dad."

"Nina, your cat is sexist."

"He loves me."

"Nina, your cat is a homophobe."

"He likes Trank."

"Nina..."

"Yes, Phoebs?"

"I don't think your cat likes me."

"We know, hon."

Nina fried up some naan bread and served up their meals. They exchanged small talk while devouring Nina's sumptuous food. Within minutes, Lang was sweating profusely.

Noticing, Nina said, "I made it pretty mild."

"I guess I'm not used to the Nina Maddox level of intensity."

Phoebe kicked Nina under the table. Nina ignored her.

Wiping his brow with his handkerchief, Lang asked, "So, what's your plan?"

Nina outlined the plan she'd been formulating. When she was done, there was even more sweat than before.

"You're... going to break into a super-secret club by yourself, where the security guy is ex-CIA and they hunt down anyone they take exception to and murder them. And you're doing that alone. That's your plan?"

"I wouldn't have worded it quite like that, but essentially, yes."

"I'm coming too," Phoebe said steadfastly.

"No, you're not. I'm only telling you about this in case something happens." She paused. "And because I need to borrow your car."

"I'm coming too." The words seemed to surprise Lang as much as they did Nina.

"*You're* not going either. I just needed the bag. Guys, I'm not trying to form a gang here. This is way too dangerous to get you involved in. I just wanted someone to know what I'm doing in case I don't make it out."

"Which is why you need us! You need us to have your back. You don't know what security they have. This isn't a one-person job."

"Phoebs, no."

"But I'm an associate member of this detective agency."

"You know that's a made-up title, right?"

"I'm still coming. And that's final. I'm an accountant, right? So anything that brings some excitement to my humdrum little world, I'm down for."

Lang gulped. "I'm in too." His words were more convincing than his delivery.

Nina spent the next five minutes trying to talk them out of it, but eventually gave up, especially when Phoebe started singing "Eye of the Tiger" to drown out Nina's protests. Lang wasn't as enthused, but steadfastly refused to back down. Nina was equal parts frustrated and warmed by her friend's loyalty.

Nina had to revise her plan to account for three people. She resolved to do whatever it took to keep them safe.

"Kaufman's untimely demise means we don't know who called them in to dispose of Alicia Morrison's body, or even why. Was it the same person who killed her, or someone different? I don't know if Mickey is one of these people, the sole person, or none of them. He's mixed up in it somehow, that's for sure, but we don't know how. And the only way we're going to find out is to go to the one place that ties all of this together."

"What are you expecting to find, exactly?" Lang asked.

"Ideally, the name of the person who booked the room where Morrison died. Or at the very least, a list of members, so we have a list of suspects to whittle down. If we can identify who owns the club, we could interview them. Something, anything. The answers are in that club somewhere. We just have to find them."

"You're the private dick." Phoebe sniggered at her turn of phrase. "But I would have thought you'd be out searching for Trank. He's the one who got you involved in all this in the first place."

"I absolutely want to find him, and I will, but right now I have zero leads on where he could be. Like, literally none. As far as I can figure out, the best chance I have of finding Hank Trank is to find out more about Alicia Morrison and the people who killed the blackmailing knuckleheads."

The other two nodded.

"See, you need me to come along—I can help if they have paperwork and ledgers." Phoebe placed her hand on Lang's arm. "I'm not trying to be offensive here..."

"I highly doubt that."

"...but what's Mr Loveboat here bringing to the table?"

Nina sloshed a beer in Lang's direction. "Forensics photographer. As in, murder scenes. That enough of a qualification?"

"I mean, it's no accountancy degree." Lang smirked.

Phoebe had the faintest hint of a smile. "Don't make me like you, dude."

"Sorry."

Nina had to admit, seeing these two disparate parts of her world interacting and getting along wasn't as terrible as she'd thought. "Kaufman said The Crucible was empty at 5 am, so that's when we'll go in. We'll obviously do some surveillance before then, so let's leave here, say, 3 am. Now, I'm going to ask one last time, are you sure you want to do this?"

"Yes."

"Yes, absolutely."

Nina's shoulders slumped. She knew there was no talking them out of it. "Fine. We should get some sleep while we can."

Phoebe thrust a finger in Lang's direction. "And that means sleep. None of this heterosexual sex business."

"Yes, ma'am."

"Damn straight."

Lang's humor evaporated and he shifted uncomfortably in his seat. Nina noticed and asked, "What is it?"

Phoebe turned, her gaze shifting between Nina and Lang, but she said nothing.

"Well," Lang started, "I have a question."

"Out with it."

"How do you know Trank isn't the murderer? Wagner was at his house, murdered in his own bed. He was a member of the club where Morrison died, he could have killed her too."

"I know for a fact he didn't throw Diehl off the roof."

"What about Kaufman? You said he was murdered after you were knocked out. Is it at least *possible* Trank was responsible?"

Phoebe was watching the discussion like a tennis match. Nina was tempted to ask if she wanted some popcorn.

Nina rubbed the back of her head where the lump had been. Everything had happened so quickly. The two men had rushed in and the place erupted into chaos. She tried to remember where everyone was.

Trank was right behind to her.

Holding a tire iron.

She shook her head. "No. I don't believe it. The shock on his face when I first saw him outside his place. I've gotten to know him."

Lang's expression reeked of skepticism. "He's an actor."

"Not that good of an actor."

"Remember, there were no signs of forced entry at

Trank's. Can you even be sure his story about being at The Crucible the night of Wagner's murder is true? Did he really have an alibi he couldn't use under fear of death? What if he's more mixed up in The Crucible than you think?"

Nina leaned back and folded her arms. "Why do you want Trank to be the bad guy so much?"

"Why are you defending him so much?"

"Okay." Phoebe raised her voice. "I'm calling time-out on this. Neither of you know the truth, you're just throwing spitballs at each other, and that sounds kind of disgusting now I've said it out loud. So why don't we take a deep breath and finish this delicious meal?"

The other two made grunting noises of agreement. Nina elbowed her friend and mouthed, "Thank you."

"You know me. Always the peacemaker."

"You going to make peace with Sputnik?"

"That little jerk can go to hell."

Sputnik raised his sleepy head, somehow knowing he was being talked about. He yawned, stretched, and went back to his mid-evening nap.

The three finished dinner in a far more pleasant manner, managing to eke out a few laughs along the way. Lang and Phoebe cleared the table, did the dishes, and dried up.

When they were done, Nina said, "Okay. We're about to go break into a secret underground club where a child star was brutally murdered, where Trank was allegedly last seen before someone was murdered in his bed, and where an ex-CIA agent will kill you if you even acknowledge the club's existence. Sound like fun?"

"No," Lang said flatly.

"Absolutely not," Phoebe agreed.

"Great. Let's get ready."

TWELVE

The three sat huddled in Phoebe's little Toyota Shitbox, watching for any movement on the 700 block of South Wall Street. It hadn't taken long. Within the first half hour they'd seen a limousine pull up out the front of the nondescript beige industrial building. It honked its horn and the roller door opened. An elegant woman in a jade green evening gown slid rather lubricatedly into the back seat and the limo took off toward the hills. She wasn't the only one. Soon, a succession of elegantly dressed patrons filed out and were deposited into the back of another limo.

It was an industrial part of town, not prone to many limousines, and especially not at four in the morning. The location, the seclusion, the exclusivity. It all fit Trank's description of The Crucible.

"That has to be it, surely?" Nina asked, more to herself than the other two.

In the front seat, Lang grunted agreement. From the back seat, light snoring was Phoebe's only reply.

The third and fourth limos pretty much sealed the deal.

It must have been closing time. That meant there were at least some staff still inside, possibly straggling customers, too. It was too early to break in. All they had to do was wait.

Half an hour later, several private cars exited in a convoy, likely staff. Finally, a black van rolled out, idling in the drive as a tuxedoed man closed the roller door and secured it with three padlocks.

Even from this distance, the man with a severe crew cut made Nina uneasy. It wasn't the fact that he was physically muscled, though even through the suit she could see that he spent hours crafting his physique. It was more that he was perpetually coiled, ready to strike.

Mr Crew Cut carried himself with a self-assurance that wasn't arrogance, but rather, a confidence that he could kill you seven times with a paperclip before you got your hand to your gun. The way he carried himself had Nina thinking perhaps this was The Crucible's head of security. She had no trouble believing he could be ex-CIA. There was a vague familiarity about him, but Nina couldn't place it. If one was to put a ski mask on him, he might match one of the men who'd raided Kaufman's. *Possibly.*

Nina slunk down in her seat, knowing she wanted to never be near Mr Crew Cut if at all possible. Thankfully, he didn't so much as glance in their direction before he jumped in the driver's seat and took off, heading north.

Nina bit her nails for a good fifteen minutes, enough to have nothing left. The scene was deathly quiet, other than Phoebe's snoring. Nina gave her friend a less than friendly poke. "It's time."

Nina's gaze strafed the three-story building. "Are you completely sure we want to do this? You can still pull out."

In unison, Lang and Phoebe answered, "We're in."

Nina was happy they were there, though it did add

extra pressure to keep them both safe. After going through what could generously be classified as a plan, they exited the car. Nina extracted her search warrant from the trunk and Lang picked up his work bag containing the items he'd brought to Nina's.

Phoebe noticed the bag and whispered, "What is that, anyway?"

Nina replied, "Something I hope we don't need."

Without further discussion, the three slunk across the street. The Yale padlocks were high quality and took longer than Nina wanted to get past, but twenty minutes later they slipped under the roller door.

Inside was as industrial as the exterior: the large parking bay of yet another rundown commercial building in a sea of rundown commercial buildings. The concrete yard provided just enough space for an experienced limousine driver to perform a three-point turn. The red carpet at the main doors, flanked by two pot plants filled with lush gardenias, was the only sign this was anything other than an everyday industrial building.

The lack of security cameras surprised Nina at first, but then she remembered the clientele. Anonymity was key. No one who entered this particular club would want evidence they'd ever attended. Career suicide was so gauche.

Making her way through the front door more quickly than the roller door, the three entered. The interior was in shocking contrast to the stark industrial exterior.

Nina's unease grew. *This is too easy.*

The first small room was a classy foyer that wouldn't be out of place in an upmarket Parisian hotel. There was a coat room off to the left. Reception was classy without being gaudy, a rarity for Los Angeles.

The imposing reception desk was no doubt usually

manned by some stunning lovely charged with keeping the riff raff out and glad handing those who belonged. Passing it, they approached a door that undoubtedly led to the club proper. It was fastened shut with a large slide bolt.

"Um…" Phoebe said. "Anyone think it weird that the lock for this door is on the outside?"

Nina did. But they'd come this far. Cautiously, she unbolted the door and it swung silently open. Inside was breathtaking, almost literally. The massive bar had real leather booths and banquettes, antique beveled mirrors, oak wainscoting, and brass lamps. It reminded Nina of Ma Maison's, an infamous industry watering hole on Melrose where she'd once gotten riotously drunk with Jack Nicholson. The darkened interior of The Crucible was nowhere near as friendly and inviting as Ma Maison's, though. In the intense light of their flashlights, the space became altogether sinister. Classy, sure, but sinister all the same.

Nina reminded herself that Trank was a member here. Perhaps they weren't friends quite yet, but she'd grown fond of the big lug. Then she remembered what Lang had said. Perhaps Trank wasn't as innocent as he first appeared? She still wanted him to be safe, no matter where he was.

She felt the back of her head. Could he have knocked her out? If he was mixed up with the killers, then why not kill her? *Where was he? Was he even alive?*

Their flashlights swept the opulent space.

"I feel like my mortgage just doubled while standing here." Phoebe whispered.

"How much do you think a drink costs?" Lang asked.

Nina stepped forward. "Your soul."

They'd agreed to stick together for a pass of the two floors to ensure there was no nightshift guard or straggling

A-lister. Or rabid German shepherd; Nina's main fear after seeing the bolt on the front door.

So far, it seemed they were alone in the club. They got to work.

Off the main bar was a room with huge wide open double doors. Nina prowled over and saw that they led to an intimate gambling room, complete with tables set up for roulette, blackjack, and poker. She recalled Trank mentioning he'd steered clear of the gambling room as his interests lay elsewhere.

About to suggest they start their search, Nina froze. At the far end of the bar she saw motion, low, predatory motion.

This was no rabid German shepherd.

This was worse.

Much worse.

Grabbing Lang and Phoebe, who hadn't yet seen the interloper, Nina said in a barely audible whisper, "Nobody make any sudden movements. We're going into the gambling room and closing the doors behind us."

"What, why?" Lang said in what sounded to Nina like a thunderous yell.

With a shaky hand, Nina pointed. They both gasped.

In the dark recesses of the bar, they were being stalked. The enormous head of a tiger hovered an inch off the polished floor, crouched low, dark eyes reflecting the light back at them, its rear end poised to attack.

It seemed the exotic nature of the club extended to their nighttime security. Of course, a guard dog would be far too pedestrian. Why have a German shepherd when you could have an exotic beast instead?

The three backed slowly toward the gambling room. When they were within feet of it, the enormous tiger pounced. Its giant, murderous paws struck the parquet floor as it sprang forward, jaw open wide, its glistening teeth stark white and razor sharp. The air filled with a guttural roar as it closed the distance in a blur of orange and black. The sheer force and precision of the attack was both awe-inspiring and bowel-loosening. The tiger raced at them with raw power and lethal grace.

Nina pushed the other two behind the right double door as the tiger leaped through the breach. It skidded on the polished wooden floor, propelled by its immense speed, and Nina seized he opportunity. Pushing her friends out the door they'd just rushed through, she pulled the doors shut behind her, trapping the ferocious beast inside.

The door bucked as the beast crashed against it, but the heavy doors held firm.

"Do tigers know how to use door knobs?" Lang asked breathlessly.

"Let's not chance it."

Nina motioned for Phoebe to pass her a poker from the nearby fireplace and threaded it through the polished brass door handles. Satisfied the predator was contained, she finally allowed herself to breathe.

They took a moment to come to terms with the fact they'd just been attacked by a wild animal in a Los Angeles club. Lang was the first to speak.

"Someone's going to be surprised when they open those doors tomorrow. They won't be expecting a tiger in the gambling room."

"No, they'd usually be on the lookout for cheetahs." Receiving nothing but blank stares, Phoebe flung her hands in the air. "Oh, come on, that was fucking gold."

Nina was thankful for the break in tension. It was just

what they needed, although she wasn't sure her exterior conveyed that as well as she'd hoped.

Once everyone calmed down, with the help of several shots from the bar, they did a sweep of The Crucible, floor by floor, Nina's gun at the ready in case of any further surprises. Thankfully, there were no lions, tigers, or bears. Throughout the elegantly appointed hallways they encountered not a single soul, wild or otherwise. They finally relaxed, as much as they could.

Phoebe split off to the room marked "Office," situated in the far corner behind the bar. Nina and Lang headed reluctantly to the room on the second floor. The room where Kaufman said Alicia Morrison had gasped her last breath.

Nina wondered, not for the first time, if it was wise to have brought Lang along. Using people wasn't in her nature, another reason she didn't really fit in with the Hollywood crowd. It had genuinely surprised her when he'd volunteered. Outwardly, he came across as a rugged, self-confident outdoorsy type, but in reality, he was a softie.

Her best friend was virtually the opposite. For an accountant, Phoebe was surprisingly gung-ho. While her appearance suggested she was conservative, Phoebe was certainly her father's daughter. Tough, even violent when required, she could look after herself. Nina suspected that was why they were best friends; Nina gave Phoebe ample excuse to let her crazy out. Breaking into a top-secret club in the middle of the night certainly qualified as crazy.

Climbing the wide, burgundy-carpeted staircase, Nina said, "The Crucible mustn't have known about the body."

She spoke in part to break the awkward silence, but also to talk through the thoughts swirling around her mind.

"Why do you say that?"

"If they did, they wouldn't have hired amateurs who

would seize the opportunity to blackmail their members. Not the best business model."

"Good point."

"Plus, they would have been the first to grab the video-tape; they wouldn't have risked it falling into the hands of the aforementioned knuckleheads."

Lang accepted the logic. "So...?"

"So, someone called in these guys because that's all they had. And for whatever reason, they wanted to bypass the security guy who locked up outside. That guy would know how to dispose of a body, I'm sure, so whoever called in the knuckleheads must have been—"

"Desperate?"

"And then some." Nina thought more. "But someone with keys, knowledge of when the place would be empty. It had to be someone on the inside."

"Who didn't trust or feared the security?"

"Exactly."

Lang mulled it over silently. They reached the landing and strode down the wide elegant hallway, lit only by the glow of their flashlights. Each doorway had a stylishly engraved brass plaque designating the room's name: The Swanson, The Pickford. In no time they came across The Arbuckle.

Not peering in Lang's direction for fear she'd lose her nerve, Nina inhaled deeply and turned the doorknob. The room was as she'd imagined it, only more so. It was generous, ridiculously so. Like everything in The Crucible, it was tastefully appointed. There was a small bar, a couch, several armchairs, and numerous mirrors—including one on the ceiling. Underneath that very large mirror was an equally large and circular bed. Nina would bet her car it rotated.

"Classy."

Lang didn't answer, whether due to nervousness, disdain at her flippancy, or the fact he was currently engaged in a career-ending break-and-enter, she wasn't sure. She thought it best not to ask.

Nina strode to the closest mirror, a floor to ceiling number with fancy beveled edges, and placed the tip of her finger on the glass. It was a simple test to determine which side the reflective coating was on. The glass on a two-way mirror is one-directional, meaning there would be no visible gap between Nina's finger and the mirror. Nina's finger was tip to tip. The mirror was as real as a wooden leg.

It took a few seconds to find the latch, well concealed at the top right. When she slid it to the left, the mirror swung silently open. Behind was a video camera, sitting on a tripod, plugged into the wall power. Behind her, Lang let out a low whistle.

"Imagine the blackmail this baby would be used for."

Nina was. A lot.

She pressed a button on the Sony camcorder and the cassette compartment sprung open. Empty.

On closer inspection, Nina saw another wall behind the first one. The wall with the mirror was fake. The carpet in the small alcove didn't seem any different to the room proper, nor was it dusty from lack of use. If she were to hazard a guess, the fake wall and mirror had been a recent addition, perhaps within months. *Curiouser and curiouser.*

Lang put his bag on the ground and took out two self-pump spray bottles, latex gloves, and a bulky camera. As he placed the items on the lush carpet, he kept his face turned away from Nina in a way she knew was deliberate. He held himself like he wanted to say something but was hesitant to do so. Once again, Nina was willing to bet her car on a hunch, this time about was what was going to happen next.

"Nina..."

"Yes?" She did her best to replicate his steady tone.

"I've been thinking..."

She really wished she'd placed that bet.

"About?"

"Did you wonder why I agreed to come along tonight?"

"If I recall, you volunteered."

"You know what I mean."

"Is justice the wrong answer?" Seeing the attempt at humor flitter to the floor unappreciated, Nina added, "We've been through this."

He didn't meet her gaze, as if knowing he'd lose his nerve if he did. "I love you, Nina."

It was then Nina knew, really knew, what she had to do. She liked Lang, and in her quieter moments would even add "a lot" to the end of that sentence. But it wasn't enough. It never would be. Nina honestly believed she was broken. Past trauma had shattered her, rendering her heart incapable of accepting or providing love. Nina was damaged goods, and no amount of well-meaning words could mend her.

She had to end his misjudged love for her before it was too late. She'd hinted, and when that hadn't worked, she'd outright told him, but it still hadn't taken. She needed to break up with him. It wasn't heartlessness that propelled her to end the relationship—in fact, it was the opposite. Lang deserved so much better. The only way for him to find love was to seek it elsewhere, and the only way he would do that was if she ended it.

"I absolutely want to have this conversation with you, I do. But not now." She motioned around the room. "We have more pressing matters. The last thing I want is for you to get caught and have to explain to your boss why you were embroiled in a break-in with a no-good, dirty private investigator. Let's crack on with it, hey?"

Lang's dejected look told her he didn't agree, but he knew Nina well enough that arguing would get him nowhere.

They slid on latex gloves and spent the next ten minutes methodically spraying the walls, headboard, couches and chairs—any available surface. The spray had to be evenly applied in a defined pattern to ensure all surfaces were correctly coated. Nina was thankful for the disciplined task. It meant revisiting Lang's conversation would be impossible, and it prevented her thoughts from drifting to that very subject.

When they were nearly finished, Phoebe stuck her head around the door.

"How's everyone going in here?" Seeing the spray bottles and assailed by the strong odor, she screwed up her nose. "What in the Kentucky fried fuck are you two doing?"

"Spraying luminol," Lang replied.

"I come back to the same question."

"This stuff will glow blue if there's any blood present."

Phoebe bit her nails, visibly unsure.

Lang picked up on her confusion. "The process is called chemiluminescence—it's when objects use chemical energy to produce light, like when you break a glow stick and start the chemical reaction. What we're doing here will make any blood visible, even if they've washed it already. The iron present in blood catalyzes the chemical reaction, which leads to the luminescence, revealing the location of the blood. It will show up as soon as we turn out the lights." He held up his camera. "And on a long exposure we'll have an even better idea if there's been any blood present recently."

Nina removed her gloves and turned to her friend. "How'd you go?"

"Thankfully these bastards have money and everything is computerized. I didn't have to photograph a whole heap of ledgers like I thought I would." She waved a five and a quarter inch floppy disk in her hand. "They have takeout."

Removing his gloves, Lang picked up his camera and removed the lens cap. "We ready?"

Nina gave him a confident nod, concealing how she truly felt. She strode to the light switch, took a deep sigh and killed the lights.

It took a moment for her eyes to adjust, and when they did, Nina wished they hadn't. The room glowed a bright, cool blue. All surfaces in the room shone in an eerie glimmering sapphire light. The carpet, the headboard, the walls —especially the walls. Streaks of blue light were in fact streaks of blood. That wasn't the most disturbing part. Savage, visceral handprints that scraped along the walls told a sickening story, as if the prints themselves were desperately trying to escape the bed. Those prints had been made by bloodied hands, the size of a woman's, or in this case, a teenager's. The entire room glowed an unsettling blue, revealing the horrors that had taken place within its luxuriously appointed walls.

In the darkness, Phoebe's voice was soft and frightened. "I don't think we're going to need that long exposure after all."

Nina slouched onto her haunches, fighting the urge to throw up. "What the fuck did they do to that poor girl?"

～

NONE of them spoke on the drive home. There was nothing to say.

All three were consumed by dark, swirling thoughts. Or, as Nina classified them, nightmares. They now had evidence corroborating Kaufman's account of what happened in The Arbuckle room. Alicia Morrison had met a bloody, violent end. She'd been horrifically murdered, and it hadn't been quick. She'd been alive enough to attempt to escape, but she hadn't made it out of the torture chamber alive.

Somewhere, a videotape of those horrific events existed. There was very real evidence showing the final moments of this poor defenseless victim. But where was it? Whoever was after the tape had searched Trank's, Wagner's, Diehl's and Kaufman's homes. The fact they were still searching meant no one had found it yet. It was the one thing that could end this whole murderous story.

Nina had to find the tape.

Instead of going back to Nina's, the three drove to Phoebe's place, by the canals off South Venice Boulevard. The sun was rising and it reflected off the calm, beautiful canal, but Nina wasn't in the mood to appreciate beauty; she'd seen too much of the ugliness of the human soul. She wasn't sure she would appreciate it ever again.

They'd decided on Phoebe's place because she owned a personal computer. Nina couldn't conceive of a reason she'd ever need a computer in her home. She wasn't George Jetson. After brewing them all a tea, Phoebe turned on the clunking machine. Bathed in the glow of the black and green screen, she typed away.

Nina couldn't sleep, afraid of what her closed eyes would show her. Instead, she took a shower, trying to cleanse the putrid stench of the case off her skin. It didn't work. When she emerged from the steamy bathroom, hair wrapped in a towel, Lang handed her a plate with freshly buttered toast. She politely took it, knowing she couldn't keep it down if she tried.

Phoebe was hunched over her clanking keyboard, harrumphing as she furiously wrote notes on the legal pad beside her. She leaned back, shaking her head. That was when Nina noticed the large book on the floor beside her. It resembled a phone book, but was organized wrong.

"What's this?" Nina asked.

"It's actually your birthday present for next month. A reverse telephone book. Ordered by phone number, not name. Includes unlisted." Phoebe regarded her sheepishly. "It's not exactly legal, but dad knows some nefarious types who had one to sell."

"That's what you consider a suitable gift?" Lang asked dubiously.

"It's awesome!" Nina gave her friend a hug. "But why do you need it now?"

Phoebe pointed a bright pink nail toward the monochrome screen. "Whoever does their books thinks they're so clever. There are no names here, but there's phone numbers."

Nina gave her friend a gentle punch on the arm. "Hence the reverse phone book."

Her friend gave her an air kiss. "It's going to take some time to work through this, but I have some information already." Phoebe turned to face Nina. "You're not going to like it, I'm afraid. Like, at all."

Nina ignored the warning and bent down to investigate the columns of numbers. One was clearly a long list of Los Angeles phone numbers, while another column was some sort of computer filing code. The others showed dollar amounts, in positives or negatives.

"What am I looking at here?" Nina asked.

"My worst nightmare," Lang offered. "Nothing but columns of soulless numbers and math."

"I love it." Phoebe beamed. "Give me this stuff over human beings any day." She spun in her chair to face them. "These books are a gold mine. Seriously. A-list actors and actresses, congressmen, senators, studio heads. Even the goddamn mayor. This list alone is dynamite."

"That's fine, I guess. Does it say who booked The Arbuckle room the night of the murder?"

"It doesn't seem to have that in the computer system, no."

"But you can tell me who was there that night?"

"I think so. I'm still learning their system, but I should be able to once I figure out how everything fits together."

Nina narrowed her eyes. "What?"

"What, what?"

"Phoebe Elizabeth Jones, don't pretend to be all coy and shit. You've found something, what is it?"

"You're not going to like it."

"There's so much I don't like about this case already."

"No, I mean, you're *really* not going to like it."

"Jesus, Phoebs, spill."

"I have the owner of the club." She tilted her head toward the screen. "The financials state who set up the club, signed the initial deed and so forth."

"I don't see how that's relevant, or even why it made you—"

Phoebe pointed to the screen, her face suddenly somber. Nina followed her finger, first to the phone number on the screen, then to the underlined entry in the reverse phone book. It was a Laurel Canyon address. Then Nina read the name.

She dropped the plate, which shattered on the floor, toast flying in all directions.

Nina reeled back. "Motherfucker."

CHAPTER

THIRTEEN

Nina performed a loose approximation of sleep for a few restless hours, but somehow felt even more tired when she finally dragged herself out of bed. She'd given Lang a lift home; thankfully, he'd been too exhausted to ask if she wanted to go steady or whatever regular people called dating these days. She'd kissed him goodnight, but it felt more like a goodbye. Once this was all sorted, she'd get him good and drunk, rock his world and then break up with him as nicely as she could manage. But that wasn't her priority right now.

Phoebe promised to dive into The Crucible's books and see what else she could shake loose. What she'd discovered already was dynamite. And scary.

It was afternoon, but Nina was too tired to read the clock. She poured some food into Sputnik's bowl and went for a shower. It didn't help. Still troubled, she dialed a number she'd memorized long ago.

"Mr Boehler's office, how may I help you?"

"Hi Naomi, Nina Maddox here. I need to get a meeting with Mickey ASAP, please."

"Oh, good afternoon, Ms Maddox. I'm afraid it will have to be tomorrow at the earliest. Mr Boehler had to leave the office rather urgently."

"When did he leave? Do you know where he went?"

The pause in the secretary's response told Nina she'd been too abrupt. "I'm sure I don't know, I'm afraid."

"I get it, that's the standard line, but on the small chance you do actually know, please understand I'm trying to save Mickey. There's... stuff going on and I need to talk to him before it gets any worse." Nina knew the next part would get her attention, but it was also the truth. "And before anyone else has to die."

"Die...?"

"I'm afraid so. Look, I'm real sorry to lay this on you. You cop enough from Mickey already, but please know I urgently need to talk to him, so if you have any idea at all where he could be, you could be saving lives by telling me. And I don't mean passing a tampon under a restroom door saving a life either—I mean literally."

There was another pause, but this one was laced with unease. "Home. When he raced out the door he said he was heading home and not to tell anyone."

"Thank you, Naomi. Now," Nina took a deep inhale to calm her impatience, "can you tell me what happened right before he left? Was he in a meeting, did someone call?"

"He... yes, he received a call. The other party stated it was extremely urgent. The voice sounded vaguely familiar."

"Who was the caller?"

"He said his name was Mr Smith." She let that little non-fact dangle in the air for a moment.

"Thanks Naomi, I owe you one."

"I hope you can help him."

"That remains to be seen."

By the time Nina reached Laurel Canyon, dusk was painting the city below a reddish orange. The winding streets she'd once considered quaint were now frustrating in Nina's haste. Why couldn't Mickey live in an oversized mansion in Pacific Palisades or Beverly Hills like everyone else? Nina knew the answer, of course: because Mickey Boehler didn't do anything that was expected of him.

His mansion in the hills had once been owned by a member of The Eagles or Led Zeppelin or The Beach Boys, Nina couldn't recall which. Whoever it was, Mickey had overpaid by a significant amount so he could brag about the former owner. Clearly, it hadn't paid off, as Nina couldn't remember who it was.

She still had a hard time believing Mickey Boehler, her almost-friend and semi-steady employer, was the secret owner of The Crucible. It wasn't uncommon for actors, producers, and studio heads to own restaurants or bars. Clint Eastwood had Hog's Breath Inn up in Carmel. Sonny Bono had Bono's in West Hollywood. Lana Turner had The Luau on Rodeo Drive. Preston Sturges used to have The Players on Sunset. But this was different. A secret gambling and sex club with prevalent drug use and enough debauchery for a thousand lifetimes? That was excessive even for a man famed for excess. But Phoebe had shown Nina the evidence in electric green and black. Mickey Boehler was the legal owner of an illicit club where gambling, prostitution, and drug trafficking took place. He'd be going away for as long as if he'd been charged with every one of the crimes committed in his movies.

The main and practically only question Nina had was, *why?* Why would Mickey risk everything he'd built to own a club whose mere existence could ruin him forever? There was only one way to find out—ask. What she did with the answer would depend on Mickey.

Nina felt the weight of her Beretta in her shoulder holster. Mickey may have given her work in this town when no one else had, but that didn't mean she wasn't going to protect herself.

The cab wheezed up the final steep incline. With her car still in the shop, and not wanting to push Phoebe's friendship any more than she already had, she'd hailed a cab on the street and had it drop her off a block and a half from Mickey's clifftop mansion. She cased the street. Quiet. Very quiet. That was a natural state for Laurel Canyon, unless there was some depraved rock and roll party with groupies and the like. No wild parties could be heard, but the night was young.

Nina decided to traipse through a neighbor's yard and come in via Mickey's back door. There was a good chance the neighbor was away on tour, shooting somewhere exotic, or hadn't gotten out of bed yet. She knocked on their door, ready to pretend she had the wrong address—she didn't want to be arrested for stalking in the exclusive enclave. When no one answered the front door, Nina slipped down the side of their house, leaped over the low wooden fence and into Mickey's backyard.

Mickey didn't do anything by halves. A huge garage led to marble steps, which ascended to a large terrace. Nina traipsed up the steep incline. Manicured vines wrapped around faux-Greek columns, next to matching statues and more terracotta planters with bountiful flowers. It was exactly like an ancient Grecian garden, if the ancient Grecian garden had been dreamed up by a coked-up production designer.

The terrace overlooked the sparkling city below. Despite her cynicism and disdain for the city, it was a hell of a view. There was nothing quite like LA during magic hour.

The back end of the house appeared unoccupied. One could even classify it as ominously dark, if one was so inclined. Nina wondered what she was getting into. What if Mickey had the new goon she'd spotted in his office with him? Maybe she should have brought some kind of backup. Like a Sherman tank.

Approaching the large patio doors, Nina checked for security cameras, alarm systems, or doggy doors. She couldn't recall Mickey having any, but she'd only been to his place once, for a New Year's Eve party, and her recollection of that night was patchy at best. Though she did remember the three porn actresses and the tapioca pudding. That sort of thing, you're going to remember no matter what state you're in.

Setting down her search warrant, she went to work on the lock. Considering how much people spent on their front door and window security, Nina found it remarkable that patio doors normally had the cheapest locks imaginable. She was inside the house in less than twenty seconds. If Mickey was somehow innocent in all this, she'd be sure to recommend a security upgrade. If he was an illegal purveyor of gambling, a pimp, a drug dealer, and responsible for the deaths of at least four people, she'd probably keep quiet on the matter.

Inside the house was dark, and eerily quiet. Treading lightly, she made her way up to the main floor. Nina suspected the vast majority of the noises made in Mickey's house were courtesy of either a blaring TV showing *Entertainment Tonight*, Mickey shouting into the phone making a multi-million-dollar deal, a grandiose party, or a noisy orgy. She could hear none of these. The house was deathly silent.

Reaching the first landing, she turned toward the hallway leading to main living area. Like the outside, the main motif of the interior was ostentatiousness at the expense of taste. Superfluous Greek columns and statues of vaguely Greek, overly well-endowed naked women lined the hallway. It looked exactly like Athens of old would if it were run by Benny Hill.

Halfway down the darkened hallway, she stopped dead. Footsteps were coming from somewhere, but sound bounced off the walls in the cavernous tiled house, making it hard to pinpoint. Distant laughs echoed. Laughs, plural. Male. Boisterous. And, to Nina's wary ears, menacing.

Gripping her trusty Beretta, Nina prowled down the gloomy hallway. Nearing the living area, she heard muffled chatter, then the sound of smashing glass, a scream, and more menacing laughter. She couldn't see into the room yet, but wasn't sure she wanted to.

A hulk of a man staggered into the hallway before Nina. It was Leonard, the shaved gorilla bodyguard from Mickey's office. Eyes wide, he clutched his throat as cascades of blood pumped through his desperate stumpy fingers. Gurgling in terror, he tried in vain to stem the torrent of blood draining from his slashed throat. With a few teetering steps he stumbled forward, collapsing on the white tiles, a sea of blood pooling beneath the dying man.

Nina froze. Taking his final, blood-drenched frantic gurgle, the bodyguard silently reached for her. Fingers outstretched, he stared desperately at Nina with the panic of a man who knew with absolute certainty he was going to die. His body convulsed and, after a final death rattle, he stopped moving altogether, eyes wide, staring at nothing at all. The gruesome death was om stark contrast to the bois-terous laughter that echoed from the main living area.

Standing rigidly still, Nina aimed her gun at the entrance, ready to blow the head off whoever came through the breach. No one did. She stood motionless, doing her best to not even breathe. Whatever was happening in that room was clearly more important than the death of the man who'd just bled out in front of her. No one came to collect the body, or even to check if he was truly dead.

After what felt like hours, Nina crept toward the living area, drawing ever closer to the open-eyed corpse. As she got nearer, the voices became more distinct. At least one person talking, maybe more.

Unwilling to poke her head around the doorway, for obvious reasons, Nina crouched behind a tall Greek urn with white sticks poking out of it, protecting her from view. She didn't know if someone had left the sticks in the urn or if it was meant to be art. She didn't know much about art apart, although she liked that painting of the dogs playing pool.

She was thankful Mickey had installed a wall of mirrors at the far end of the living area, no doubt due to the afore-mentioned orgies. From her vantage point behind the urn, the mirrors gave her a clear view of what was going on. She had to cover her mouth to remain silent.

At the center of the spacious and mostly white room, a man was strapped to a dining chair. Sitting rigidly straight and apparently exceptionally angry was Mickey "The Steamroller" Boehler. He sported a red welt on the left side of his face, but otherwise appeared unharmed. He was pissed and he was scared, though from this distance Nina couldn't guess the ratio of those sentiments.

Nina's mind raced. What all did this mean? She'd

stormed over to Mickey's mansion because Phoebe had discovered he was the owner of The Crucible, which put him at the top of the suspect list. But why was he tied up and being tortured? Was he the bad guy or not?

Who had the balls to take on The Steamroller? In his own home?

There were two other people in the room, both standing, each the polar opposite of the other. They made an odd pair. One was a lean, straight cut, crew-cutted killing machine. The other was a squat, slightly rotund, sleazy gangster type. They weren't the kind of men you'd expect to hang out together, but here they were, towering over a tied-up titan of the movie industry. It was a strange kind of world.

Both had their jackets off, and both were packing. The taller one had dual guns strapped to his chest holsters. Nina recognized him as Mr Crew Cut, the one who had locked up The Crucible before Nina and her team had broken in.

Instinct had told Nina to be wary of this man, and in this predatory city, instinct was everything. He brandished a flick knife in front of Mickey, not in a threatening way, more like it was a fairly pedestrian implement, a pen or a salad fork. His casualness cloaked his vulturine stalking. He was an apex predator, a coiled weapon.

In contrast, his squat companion had the deportment of someone who was elementarily bored. Nina hadn't seen the pudgy, middle-aged man with the Mediterranean complexion before. He was no less threatening, however. If he were an actor, the only roles he'd land would be gangster types. He was more your quintessential menacing type. The way he held himself suggested that if he chose to threaten you, you'd know for damn sure he meant business.

Whoever these two were, instinct told Nina they were

both killers. The dead body before her in the hallway suggested she should trust that instinct. There was no way she could take both men down at the same time. She'd have to wait for an opportunity, and pray they didn't suddenly head toward the hall.

Seeing the two together made Nina think back to when Kaufman was killed and Trank disappeared. The two men standing before her fit the physical appearance of the two ski-mask wearing attackers perfectly.

"Now that annoyance is out of the way," the squat man said, "let's get back to the matter at hand, yeah? Before we were rudely interrupted by your—let's be generous and call him a bodyguard—you were about to advise us of the whereabouts of an item we want to reclaim."

His offsider Mr Crew Cut calmly as he wiped the bloody flick knife on Mickey's three-thousand-dollar suit jacket.

"You killed Leonard," Mickey said, dumbfounded.

"Yes, yes. We've moved past that, please keep up, Mr Boehler." Mr Crew Cut's delivery was unhurried, and as smooth as Japanese silk.

As her gaze drifted back to the dead body, Nina was sorry she'd made that crack about Leonard moving his lips when he read. It was probably true, but she still felt bad about it.

Mr Crew Cut went on. "Let's get back on track. Mickey, where is it?"

"Where's what?" Mickey asked, managing to tear his eyes from Leonard's corpse.

"The videotape, Mr Boehler."

"You want a video? Shit. I have hundreds of 'em downstairs. Help yourself."

Mr Crew Cut gave a humorless chuckle. His squat companion's facial features didn't change.

Shaking his head slowly, the man stabbed the bloody flick knife into an antique side table. Mickey winced. Nina didn't know if it was the threatening manner or what he'd paid for it.

"Now, we know you engaged the three stunt performers to dispose of the body of Miss Alicia Morrison after a member became, shall we say, carried away. Logic would dictate those who stole the tape in question would eventually come to you for assistance. Therefore, you would be most qualified to advise us where the tape in question can be found."

"What fucking tape?" Mickey shook his head in genuine confusion. "What the hell are you on about? Tape of what?" Mickey turned to the shorter man. "And I didn't engage three stuntmen, I engaged one. Seth Wagner. He's done delicate jobs for me in the past, he's always been reliable. I didn't know he was going to bring in others."

"We have our own security, Mickey." The short man pointed to Mr Crew Cut. "Bringing in outsiders was a stupid move."

"No, *you* have your own security, Pellicano." Mickey turned from the gangster and glared at Mr. Crew Cut. "And I don't trust him."

"You're going to have to get used to the new arrangements, Mickey," the gangster said. "I own you now, and you do things my way. That includes using *our* security for security matters. You've royally screwed things up by bringing in amateurs."

"I've screwed up? Jesus Christ, Pellicano, your boy here is going around murdering half the fucken' city and *I'm* the one who screwed up? You've lost it, you really have. He's a psychopath. I could have talked to Seth and straightened this whole thing out, but you've scared him off and now I can't find the guy. He's disappeared."

Mickey glared at Mr Crew Cut pointedly, as if he suspected what had truly happened to Seth Wagner. *Clever boy, Mickey,* Nina thought.

Mr Crew Cut took a sip from a heavy crystal glass containing a dark liquid. It was highly likely it wasn't the first and from the way he downed it, it was equally likely it wouldn't be his last.

Mickey went on. "What does your security guy do to calm things down? Boom, he murders Diehl on one of my sets. You know what my insurance premiums are going to be now? Then this clown kills Kaufman. All of which could have been avoided if you'd just told me what was going on."

"The situation was already out of hand." Mr Crew Cut's voice was measured, if a little slurred by the booze, Nina realized. "Once you engaged the stunt performers to remove the body, the security of the club was compromised. That was a reckless move, Mr Boehler, very reckless. And because of this, the tape went missing."

"What fucking tape?!"

"This isn't going anywhere." Pellicano groaned and turned to his security manager. "Bring him in."

"Is that wise?" Mr Crew Cut asked.

"Nothing about this is wise, but I'm sick of Mickey's whining. We may as well show him what's at stake."

Giving a shrug, Mr Crew Cut pivoted and walked to the opposite side of the room and out a large double door.

Mickey turned to his squat host. "This where I get a lap dance?"

"This isn't one of your shitty movies, Mickey. Wise-cracks count for nothin' here."

"What the hell have you gotten me mixed up in, Pellicano? This was meant to be a pure business relationship, not whatever the hell this shitshow is."

"Then maybe you shouldn't have gambled yourself into the shitter in the first place, huh? Rule one of running a casino, Mickey: if the house can't cover bets, the house folds. I'm not the one who repeatedly doubled down trying to chase his losses. But I *am* the one who bailed you out. No one forced you to sign the contract, you're a big boy who signed it all the same."

Lowering his head, Mickey mumbled, "I never should have made the deal."

"Yeah, but you did, didn't you?" Pellicano said, growing more animated. "And now I own you. The great mega successful studio mogul. *I. Own. You.* Didn't your mom ever tell you not to fuck around with the Vegas mob, Mickey? I bailed you out and took the heat when I didn't have to," a serpentine leer crossed his thin lips, "for certain concessions, of course. If I hadn't, you'd be lying in a grave somewhere next to Jimmy Hoffa. The least you could do is be grateful, you prick."

"Fuck you, Pellicano."

"You need to work on your gratitude, Mickey."

Nina's mind reeled. So many fragments were falling into place she was having trouble keeping up. Mickey was the owner of The Crucible, and had borrowed from the Vegas mob to cover the club's gambling debts. That hadn't gone well, and this Pellicano guy had bailed him out.

A member of the club had murdered Alicia Morrison. When Mickey found out, he'd bypassed the new security Pellicano had put in place, namely Mr Crew Cut, and called in Seth Wagner instead. Wagner brought in his fellow stunt professionals, Diehl and Kaufman. It hadn't ended well for any of them, though Mickey didn't have the full story—he still thought Wagner was out there somewhere.

It hadn't answered everything, but Nina was far closer to the truth than she had been. She still had no idea who'd murdered Alicia Morrison, but was thankful Mickey had nothing to do with it. He was merely an incompetent business owner who made incredibly dubious financial decisions. Nina would be lying if she said she wasn't relieved.

Now all she had to do was figure out how to extract the big idiot without getting either of them killed in the process. *Easy.* She really could use that Sherman tank right about now.

Nina was distracted by a loud scraping sound. It sounded like someone was dragging a fridge across the marble floor. As the thing he was dragging came into view, she realized she hadn't been far off.

Pellicano's security man unceremoniously righted the chair with a thump, and the figure he'd deposited next to Mickey slumped forward. Mr Crew Cut removed the gag from the newcomer's mouth. Like Mickey, he had his hands tied behind his back, but unlike the studio head, he was far more beat up and defeated. His face was a purple mélange of bruises, his left eye was completely swollen shut, and his entire body sagged like a man who had been through too much and had nothing left.

Hank "The Tank" Trank was not in a good way.

Nina gasped. She wasn't the only one. Mickey's mouth dropped open.

"What the hell is this? Hank! You're alive! How the hell are you alive?" Mickey bucked in his chair. "My god, man, what the fuck is going on? You're alive? You're alive!"

Mickey's head flicked between Trank, Pellicano, and Mr

Crew Cut. It was the first time Nina had ever seen him lost for words. He was literally dumbstruck.

At a glacial pace, Trank raised his head. "Hey Mickey, how have you been?"

"Can someone tell me what the hell is going on!"

Pellicano wiped his nose with the back of his hand. "It's very simple—so simple, even you might be able to follow, Mickey. The Wagner guy was staying at your star's house. Side note, your prize all-American heartthrob is a closet pillow-biter, but hey, each to their own, right? It's the eighties, I've even got a couple of fags working for me. Anyways, we knew your boy Trank was going to be at the club, so we sent Valentine here to extract the videotape in question, but the little cretin wasn't forthcoming and then he, you know, died. But before the fag breathed his last, he gave up his two accomplices. Everyone assumed it was Trank, even you. You can blame the Maddox broad for keeping it from you, Mickey. Hank here said it was all her idea."

Well, that answered another one of Nina's questions. Mickey had sent her to investigate Trank's death in good faith. He'd really thought his star was dead.

Mr. Crew Cut's name was Valentine. Nina didn't like the name. She liked the man even less. She also wished she had her notebook with her to get all this down.

"I...I..." was all Mickey could manage.

"Sorry, Mickey," Trank slurred, "we didn't know how much you were into all this."

Realization swept across Mickey's big bald bullet-head. "Yeah, okay, yeah. I'm piecing this together. So, when Nina came to see me, she was trying to figure out if I was the one going around knocking people off." He tilted his head skyward. "Oh Nina, wherever you are, I apologize for getting you into this shitstorm. I tried to get Leonard to scare you off."

Thanks, Mickey, Nina thought, not knowing if she meant it or not. Nina took a moment to regard the dead man lying on the floor. Neither Pellicano nor Valentine matched the physical parameters of the driver who'd shot up her beautiful car outside Wagner's place. It must have been Leonard, trying to scare her off. Same with the slashed tires. She felt slightly less bad about her general lack of sympathy for Leonard now.

Valentine helped himself to Mickey's drinks cabinet and poured himself a sizable whiskey, no ice. He took an equally sizable swig from the cut crystal glass.

"I told you to lay off that stuff." Pellicano scowled.

Valentine frowned. "You also told me this'd be a cushy gig, not all..." He waved at Trank and Mickey before taking another gulp.

Mickey leaned over to Trank. "I'm glad you are alive, buddy."

Trank raised a beaten head. "The club." His voice was groggy and slurred. "He's been taping members of the club. Seth and the others got hold of a video of Alicia Morrison's murder. That's what they're after."

"What? What!" Mickey's head darted to Pellicano. "You've been recording... Those renovations you ordered, is what they were? You've been spying on my members? Jesus Christ, Pellicano!"

That meshed with Nina's observation about the fake wall, which had been a relatively new addition. Pellicano wasn't merely interested in the videotape, he was obsessed with it. He'd killed four men so far to obtain it. Nina could only surmise that was because of the explosive blackmail it would enable. A Hollywood star could have money, sure, but politicians had influence, too. Imagine the power Pellicano could wield with a congressman, police chief, or studio head in his pocket? The same question resonated in her skull: *who the hell was on that tape killing Alicia Morrison?*

The squat gangster tried to act coy; it was unconvincing. "You have a powerful clientele at that little club of yours, Mickey. Sorry, my club now, with my big 'ole fifty-one percent. Big stars, powerful industry leaders, politicians. I would be a fool not to take advantage of that."

"I never agreed to any of this!"

"I helped you get out of a fix, Mickey. It's only right I get some advantage from it."

"But I didn't know you were going to blackmail everyone. If this gets out I'm ruined."

"But it won't get out, Mickey, that's the beauty of it. No one will bring this to the authorities. If they do, they would be hoisted themselves on their own petard, their debauchery laid bare for the world to see. It's the perfect arrangement." The gangster sniffed. "We'd barely even got started on this thing. The other night was the first time we started recording and bam, right out of the gate, we strike gold. Then you had to go and screw it up by bringing in amateurs who stole the one piece of gold we'd mined so far."

Mickey Boehler had the good sense, given his current situation, not to verbalize what was on his mind. His facial expression, however, gave a clear indication as to what those thoughts may be. In particular, what he would very much like to do to Pellicano should the circumstances be reversed.

"Mickey, Mickey," Pellicano paced, "we've spent hours trying to get anything out of your star boy here and he's given us nothing about the tape. *You're* giving us nothing about the tape. You can understand how frustrating this whole situation has become?"

Trank's battered head flopped toward Mickey. "They killed Seth in my bed with my Oscar. I'm not giving them shit."

Nina had never been prouder of the ex-footballer. Trank knew he was going to die, but he wasn't giving them the satisfaction of groveling. Neither Trank nor Mickey were the cowering type, and that would have angered the hell out of the gangster.

Every fiber of Nina's soul told her to act, but still she hesitated. Pellicano and Valentine were armed, guns strapped to their chests, readily accessible. The two men she had to save were between them, and the distance she'd have to cover was too great.

Was she waiting for the right moment, protecting her people, or was she just scared? The answer, she knew, was yes. Though she didn't know which of those things was driving her actions, or lack thereof.

Pellicano ran a palm down his weaselly face. "All we want is the fucken' tape. There's no one else left. One of you idiots knows where it is. You both make million dollar deals all the time, right? So, I'm going to make a deal so simple even you two boneheads can understand it. Either one of you tells us exactly where the videotape is or you both die, here and now."

"You won't kill us, we're too valuable to you."

Pellicano's shoulders slumped. "Mickey, when are you going to get it through your thick, bald-as-fuck skull? You're just a front for the club. A figurehead. Like a little emblem on a cocktail napkin, nothing more. The club will go on without you. You're nowhere near as important as you think you are. Have we not shown you how important this tape is? We've been forced to kill your three stunt idiots over it, what makes you think you're any different?"

And Leonard, Nina thought. *Won't someone think of poor Leonard?* Nina turned to the dead man in the pool of his own blood. She was certainly thinking of poor Leonard.

Pellicano clicked his fingers at Valentine, who extracted a pistol. "Now, who wants to live and who wants to die? You have one minute."

Nina knew Mickey had the weakest hand of the two. He'd just admitted he didn't know about the tape, or that Pellicano had been taping members at all. As far as the heavies were concerned, Trank may have been stoically holding out, but Nina knew he had no more idea than Mickey did. Neither man could save themselves, as neither had the information Pellicano needed.

Nina had to act, and she needed to act soon.

She was a reasonable shot, but not good enough to run into a room cold, fire from twenty yards and hit Valentine without hitting Trank or Mickey. And she'd have to do exactly the same with Pellicano before he shot her. Even Dirty Harry would find that impossible.

Think, Nina's mind screamed. *Get them the hell out of here!,* her internal monologue screamed back. *Fine, how?* She asked herself. She didn't have an answer.

She needed a distraction, and she needed it fast. She'd been too consumed with working out what had been going on, instead of focusing on saving the two men before her. Nina's mind raced.

Marching toward Mickey, Pellicano extracted his pistol and screamed in his face, "Tell me where the goddamn tape is or I'm going to kill you!"

Instead of reeling in fear, Mickey Boehler smiled. It was a generous, warm smile. It was the same warm and generous smile he'd given thousands of times across desks all over the city. Even from this distance, Nina could see Mickey was finally morphing into the studio mogul he was known and feared to be. Even tied to a chair, Mickey was still a commanding presence.

"You listen to me, you greasy little slime merchant." Mickey's voice was as smooth as a glass ocean. "First of all, in a negotiation, you don't get anywhere by yelling. That's pure amateur stuff. You yell, you lose. It shows you have the weaker hand, and son, in a negotiation you never let the other guy know you don't hold all the cards. Second, and this is an important one," he leaned forward, "we've already told you we don't know about any damn tape, so we're never going to tell you where it is because *we don't know*. As a result, and I mean this with all due respect, you can go fuck yourself."

Nina had to concede The Steamroller had some cojones on him. Not many men could stare down two gunmen and still be the biggest badass in the room.

"Pellicano, I've faced tougher punks than you every single day of my professional career. I rose from nothing to be the most powerful man in this stinking town. You may have muscled into my business, but you don't own me. Now, stop your little power play and untie me. This has gone on long enough. You need to remember who you're dealing with. I'm Mickey fucking Boehler!"

Pellicano stepped forward, placed the gun to Mickey Boehler's head and shot him right between the eyes.

ACT 3

Fix it in post

Friday, 6 September 1984

FOURTEEN

Nina's slapped her hand across her mouth to stop herself from screaming. Her ears rung from the reverberation of the gunshot in the tiled room.

Pellicano had murdered Mickey Boehler brutally, his brains exploding from the back of his skull and across the white marble. The chair teetered backwards and the limp body hung in midair like someone had hit pause on a VCR. Gravity soon took over and he slammed onto the floor with a sickening thud.

Nina was numb. When it came down to it, she'd frozen, and it had cost Mickey everything. She'd failed her friend. She wasn't a crier, but the tears were forming now.

"What the fuck, man!" Valentine cried, stabbing a finger toward the bloody corpse. "You just killed our meal ticket!"

Hank Trank had descended into some form of shock. His one good eye was open in fright, lips parted, but he didn't make a sound. He stared blankly at the body of his benefactor and friend. It was as if his brain had shorted out and all sense of reality had been blown away along with Mickey's brain.

Sliding his pistol into its holster, Pellicano waved a dismissive hand. "The club is mine now, more or less. In the case of accidental death, my fifty one percent becomes a hundred. So, we'll need to make this," he gestured to Mickey's motionless form, "look like a robbery gone bad. Get a crowbar and shit to make it like burglars were trying to get into his safe in the study, attempted to torture the combination out of him and fucked up or something."

"Fucked up is right." Valentine stood over the body. "I'm going to have to spend hours in here to cover our tracks. This has to be completely clean, it's not going to be an easy job."

"You told me when you worked for the Agency you staged coups and shit. Surely one little murder of a fat fuck movie douche shouldn't be too taxing?"

Valentine squared his jaw, and his intense gaze told Nina all she needed to know about what he thought of the gangster. "I'll do my job."

"That's what I pay you for." Pellicano sniffed, and scratched his crotch. "I gotta take a leak. Do what you need to. We're out of here by midnight."

"Sure. I'm going to need some cleaning gear from the car." There was an edge to the man's tone that bordered on hatred. He downed the remainder of his drink. "What about him?" He nodded in Trank's direction.

The two turned to the comatose Trank. His head was slanted to the left, his eyes vacant black pools.

"We could..." Pellicano mimed shooting Trank in the head, like he had Mickey.

Valentine rubbed the back of his neck. "We haven't finished the interrogation, but I'm pretty sure he doesn't know shit about where the tape is at." He mulled it over. "No… let's take him when we're done. Executing him here is going to complicate matters. Besides, I'd like to try one last time to see what he knows because thanks to our itchy trigger finger we have no one left to ask."

"Fine. Leave him for now, go get your cleaning shit," Pellicano said, holding his crotch like a five-year-old. He really had to go. "Look at this lump, he ain't going nowhere."

Valentine leaned down and waved a hand before Trank's unblinking face. "Yeah, we're good."

To be sure, he tugged at the ropes binding Hank, then he and Pellicano sped off through different doors. Nina was thankful neither was hers.

Racing to Hank's side, Nina did her best to look away from Mickey's prone body. The blood splatter covered a wide area, and the deep red was vibrant against the stark white tiles. It was hard to look anywhere without catching a glimpse. Mickey's orgy mirrors didn't help.

Guilt pushed down on her, making her movements sluggish. *I should have acted sooner!* Though she knew deep down that if she'd come in earlier, guns blazing, she'd be lying there next to Mickey. Still, she still felt remorse weighing her down on her. It always would.

"Hank, can you walk?"

The big man took a glacial period of time to lift his heavy head. When he did, his dark, sunken features were glazed and unfocused.

"Alicia? Am I dead?"

"It's Nina." She placed a hand to his cheek. "We're getting you out of here, but I can't carry you. Can you walk?"

Nina's gaze darted around the room, looking for something sharp enough to cut the ropes. Her attention fell on Valentine's flick knife, still sticking out of the antique side table. She raced over and extracted it.

"What?" Crevices of confusion crisscrossed Hank's face. "What did you say?"

"Hank, can you walk?" Nina's hand was a blur as she furiously sawed at the rope. "Because you need to. Right now. They could be back any second."

"I... I don't..." His gaze drifted to the corpse beside him. "Mickey... Oh hell, Mickey..."

Cutting through the ropes was taking way longer than she'd hoped. "We'll give the big guy the wildest wake this town has ever seen, but right now we need to get you out of here. Mickey would be the first to tell you to drop the sentimental crap and run. He was a smart man. He'd want you to live, Hank, can you do that for him?"

A tear trickled down the exhausted man's face. "For Mickey?"

"For Mickey."

The knife cleaved through the last of the rope. Hank was free, but still he sat, unmoving. Nina grasped his arm and pushed the unsteady man to his feet, searching anxiously for any sign of the murderers' return.

"Time to haul ass, Hank."

Standing on wobbly legs, Trank gritted his teeth and focused on the simple act of taking one step, then the next. The strain was obvious, but to his credit he made no sound. He concentrated on staying upright and propelling himself forward, albeit far too slowly for Nina's liking.

Guiding him back the way she'd come, Hank shuffled his heavy feet as she continually checked over her shoulder. They rounded the large entrance into the hallway. A minor accomplishment.

Hank pulled up hard when he saw the bodyguard face down in a pool of his own blood.

"That's Leonard. No one cares about him, apparently. Come on."

As she dragged him forward, Trank glanced back at the prone corpse. Nina tugged him onward. They had a long way to go.

Hiding wasn't an option. The mansion was vast, but finite. The two murderers and whoever else they called in could take their time hunting them down in the confines of Mickey's place. No, they had to run, and running was the one thing Hank wasn't doing.

"You need to pick up the pace, Hank."

"I'm trying... I... I don't want to fall."

Instead of answering, she half lifted, half dragged him down the immense hallway. No noise came from the room behind them, but Nina knew Pellicano or Valentine would return any second. She pushed them both on.

As they reached the rear balcony, an explosion of rage and smashing erupted from inside the house. Their head start was over.

Nina had no car, no easy means of escape. She had to improvise. And by improvise, she meant steal.

Mickey had an enormous garage of classic cars that put Nina's Charger to shame. It was located down the cliff and off to the right of the balcony. The walk down to the garage was steep, but every step afforded a stunning view of the city below. It was situated so Mickey could dazzle any strumpet he brought home with the alluring view before ensnaring her in his lair. All she and Trank had to do was get down there before they got shot in the head.

Descending the steps, Nina heard pounding footsteps headed her way.

Itching to take two steps at a time, Nina had to slow to assist the shuffling Hank. She was amazed he could move at all after the beating he'd endured, but equally frustrated he couldn't move faster.

We're not going to make it.

As an apparent full stop to her alarmist thoughts, a gunshot rang out, and a pot plant exploded beside her head. They both ducked, but didn't stop. *Stop and you're dead.*

Suddenly Trank picked up the pace, taking three steps at a time, and Nina matched his stride. At a turn in the path, Nina halted, extracted her Beretta and fired two shots back. Valentine dove out of sight. She caught up with Trank in no time. They were only halfway down the cliff path, and at the bottom there was an open stretch of pathway between the end of the stairs and the garage. If Valentine made it to the edge of the balcony before they made it to the garage, they'd have no chance. She started taking three steps at a time.

Gunshots rang out and echoed around the canyon. Lights came on in the surrounding houses. The white railing exploded just behind Nina's hand, but her pace didn't slow. Trank was keeping up, but visibly struggling.

When they finally reached the bottom of the stairs Trank doubled over and wheezed. His legs gave out and he collapsed on the ground. Nina scanned the balcony above and fired two rounds to let Valentine know she wasn't going without a fight. She clasped the gun between her hands, vigilant and ready.

Trank and Nina assessed the open ground between their cover and the garage. The thirty yards may as well have been three hundred.

Trank struggled for air. "I can't do it, Nina, I can't. I've got nothing left."

"Sure you can, Hank." She pointed at the garage door. "We jog over there and take a ride in one of Mickey's prize sports cars. They're nice and comfy. It's not that far. Though," she paused, "the door's going to be locked, so I'm going to need you to crash through it." Seeing the doubt on his exhausted bruised face, she pulled him to his feet. Stuffing her search warrant bag under his left arm, she said, "Pretend you're in the play-offs for the thing. It's first down and five and you've got to bum rush the endzone for a touchdown goal."

A weak smirk creased the corners of his mouth. "You don't know a lot about football, do you?"

"Not a thing. But I do know if you don't reach that end zone goal—"

"You can just say end zone."

"—you'll never win the world series."

"Superbowl."

"Sure."

"Sometimes I forget you're Australian."

"That's okay, sometimes you forget you're a badass too. You ready?"

"No."

"That's the spirit."

Nina crouched into a running stance. Trank followed suit, but with a wince.

"When I give the signal, you run. Don't look back, don't stop for anything, that includes me. The door's cheap plywood, it'll give way, just keep going. The keys are on a rack to your right. Pick whatever car is parked closest to the garage door. Ready?"

"What's the signal?"

Nina winked, turned and fired. Trank ran. He made it halfway to the door before the grass at his feet exploded in a hail of bullets. True to his word, he didn't stop. He rammed into the flimsy door and the frame splintered into shards. Nina followed him through the destroyed door, her arm contorted upward, firing blindly behind her until the clip was empty.

Bullets pummeled the whitewashed brickwork surrounding the obliterated doorframe. Safely behind the solid walls, Nina loaded a new magazine. They were out of the line of fire.

Trank held up two sets of keys. "Shelby Cobra or Rolls?"

"Cobra."

"Why?"

Nina snatched the keys. "Style, baby, style."

Hitting the garage door opener, Nina and Trank ran toward the sapphire blue 1967 Shelby Cobra 427 and leaped in. Trank was too big for the sleek car, but didn't complain. Nina gunned the engine and spun the wheels before Trank had even found the racing harness. Rocketing up the steep incline, Nina kept one eye on the tree-lined driveway and the other on the house.

"This thing has 355 horsepower and can go 0–60 in under 4 seconds, although not up a forty-five-degree drive-way." Spotting movement on a balcony high on her right, near the summit of the drive, Nina yelled to be heard over the roaring engine.

"Take the wheel."

"What... what?" Trank's fear was evident.

Nina didn't have time to discuss the matter. She let go of the steering wheel, hoping Trank would take the hint. He did.

As Trank scrambled for control, Nina aimed her pistol at

the balcony and waited. She didn't have to wait long. The engine whined in protest, needing a gear change, but she ignored it as Pellicano's pudgy little head popped up over the parapet. Nina peppered it with rapid shots. Beside her, Trank whimpered. The succession of bullets sprayed the brickwork and Pellicano had no chance to return fire.

Reaching the apex of the drive, the Cobra was airborne for a split-second, making Nina's stomach lurch. The car landed on an angle, and Nina had to grapple with the wheel to keep them from hitting a wall or careening off the driveway and down the steep hill.

"Nina, slow down!"

Her foot was flat on the floor. The end of the driveway came hurtling toward them. She dropped the gun in Trank's lap, turned the wheel sharply and hit the brakes. The old disk brakes did as well as they could, given their ludicrous speed, but not enough. Nina pulled the wheel sharply and the rear end slid out, smashing into a trashcan.

The engine stalled. Nina restarted it and hit the gas, then fishtailed the sports car down the winding street. She had no idea how long it would take the men to begin their pursuit and wanted to put as much distance between them as possible.

"Are you going to slow down?" Trank yelled over the rushing wind. "These streets are awfully windy!"

"I've been high as fuck on mushrooms with Kieth Richards while driving a Maserati around the cliffs of Gorges du Dades in Marrakech, I can handle this," Nina took a turn too wide and strayed into the path of an oncoming Porsche before correcting, "Probably."

"It's that last word that has me worried."

Laurel Canyon's geography meant it was a labyrinth of

serpentine streets, most of them dead ends. The main way out was Laurel Canyon Boulevard, which carved down the middle of the suburb. It was framed by Ventura Boulevard to the north and Hollywood Boulevard to the south. Nina went north, as it was away from all the places Pellicano and Valentine would expect her to go into hiding. She used every ounce of horsepower the Cobra could give her to widen the gap.

Mickey Boehler was dead. Her friend, her benefactor. Could she have acted sooner? She'd never know, and she'd never have to chance to find out. She knew the guilt would gnaw at her for the rest of her life. No doubt she'd have dreams in which she made a different choice, but for now, she had to live with the one she'd made. And that choice meant she'd lost Mickey.

Scream Queen Detective Agency wouldn't have made it six months if it hadn't been for him. Hell, Phoenix Pictures had plucked her out of obscurity and served her stardom on a plate. It didn't matter that she hadn't cared for the taste, Mickey had given her the rare gift of fame and changed her life. And now he was gone. She would find the time to mourn her friend, but first she had to bring down his killers.

Mickey had gotten in way over his head. Adding to his pain, one of his members had killed Morrison and called Mickey to get him out of trouble. Not trusting Valentine and his scary security team, Mickey called in Wagner and his fellow knuckleheads. It hadn't ended well for any of them, including Leonard.

As Nina turned onto Mulholland, wind tossing her hair in all directions, she assessed her next steps. She needed evidence to nail Pellicano and Valentine. Going to the cops wasn't going to be enough. These guys were smart and, above all, powerful. In this town, truth withered and died before power.

She still had no idea who had killed Alicia Morrison. Whoever the murderous son of a bitch was who sliced that poor girl up was going to pay for what they did. There was a videotape out there somewhere; all they had to do was find it before Pellicano and his cronies did.

Nina pressed the accelerator harder, making Trank whine. Nina's work wasn't done yet, not even close.

CHAPTER
FIFTEEN

Nina drove the Cobra down Ventura Boulevard, wind whipping her raven hair. Before she realized it was happening, she laughed out loud. Even in Trank's bewildered stupor, his one good eye regarded her with concern.

"I don't know where I'm going." Nina took both hands off the wheel and flung them in the air momentarily. "And I mean that in every possible sense."

They slunk around the back streets of Sherman Oaks, keeping off the main thoroughfares. The back streets meant slower speeds, and they could hear one another. The Cobra wasn't exactly the stealthiest of vehicles.

Nina needed to think. She really wanted to cook, but going back to her apartment would be tantamount to suicide. That was the first place they'd try. She needed to talk to Titus. The big man wouldn't be concerned for himself, but would appreciate the heads up, even if he wouldn't say it in so many words.

Where could they go? For a moment she thought of Phoebe's, but she'd put her friend though so much already.

Same went for Lang. Also, the idea of asking for refuge when she was planning to break up with him soon didn't sit well with her. If he were alive, she could have asked Mickey for a spare room, but even though he'd brought her into this mess, she couldn't bring herself to be mad at him. The image of him lying on the floor of his mansion, brains splattered across the white marble, made her vision blur. Nina realized it was tears and wiped them away.

This isn't helping, she chastised herself. Her palm struck the wheel in frustration. *Focus.* She needed to get off the streets.

Then a thought crossed her mind. An absurd and frankly ridiculous thought. Nina shook her head at herself, amused, and turned down North Beverly Glen Boulevard.

Trank noted the sudden change in direction. "Where are we going?"

"How many days have you been wearing those clothes, Hank?"

"I can't even remember now. Two days, three? Seems like years."

"How about we get you a change of clothes, take a shower, and I can cook in peace."

"Sounds marvelous, where is this magical place?" He started to sound slightly more human. Escaping murderous torturers will do that to a man.

"Your place."

Nina was concerned Trank's open mouth would catch bugs. "Are you insane?"

"You'd be surprised how often I'm asked that question."

"No. I wouldn't."

∽

They ditched the Cobra in the open garage of a hilltop mansion. It was up a long drive and shielded from view from the street. On the way over to Bel Air, Nina quizzed Trank about his neighbors and who would likely be out of town. As they walked away from the bright yellow mansion and down the cobbled driveway, she turned to him.

"Whose house is this?"

"Zsa Zsa's."

"As in Zsa Zsa Gabor?"

"You know many other Zsa Zsa's?"

He had a point.

Trank continued. "She's in Mexico filming some god-awful horror thing." He thumbed behind him to the mansion. "The Beatles have stayed there. Ava Gardner and Katherine Hepburn used to live here. Elvis, too."

Nina didn't reply. Nearly everywhere in this town had a smear of celebrity on it. Mickey Rooney once got slapped in the face here. Charlie Chaplin got a hand job over there. Julie Garland once took a dump in that toilet. The city was absorbed with its own self-importance.

Zsa Zsa would no doubt be confused about the collector's sports car in her garage, but she'd get over it. It was just that kind of town.

They walked past a few houses and then down a gap between homes, a path Trank had said would lead to his mansion. Unlike working class suburbs, the rich had less need for things like fences to protect them from one another. It was only the poor who had to worry about things like that.

When they reached the rear of Trank's place, they sat in the dark, under the cover of trees, and staked it out for thirty minutes. No lights, no movement. When she was sure there was no sign of human activity, Nina stood, ready to move in.

Trank grasped her arm and regarded her with his single good eye. "Are we sure no one is in there? It's a crime scene, what if someone's—" His gaze wandered off, searching for the right words.

"Preserving the scene? A crime scene is maintained until the forensic examination has been completed. But preserving doesn't mean just stringing up some tape, police officers need to guard the scene to keep anyone from tampering with evidence. No department wants a cop, no matter how useless, guarding an empty house." She waved at the house. "No cops present, they've got all they need. We can go in."

Nina took off confidently with Trank following close behind.

"I keep forgetting you're good at this."

She turned. "At what?"

"This private investigator work, you're good, Nina." He gave her the first genuine smile she'd seen on him since Kaufman's. "If we... *when* we get out of this, I'll be recommending you to all my friends. I'll do what I can to help your business thrive, Nina."

She gave him a friendly wave of thanks, but focused her attention on the mansion, just in case she was wrong.

Nina entered through the rear porch, tearing the police tape off the back door and making light work of the lock, once again reinforcing her opinion on the quality of patio door locks.

The house was eerily quiet. They kept the lights off and made two sweeps of the building. Even after a couple of days, the place carried the distinct stale smell unoccupied houses get.

They finished their reconnoiter in Trank's private downstairs cinema, the space ransacked by Valentine. Videotapes and covers were strewn across the floor, cupboard doors ripped from their hinges. It brought Nina's thoughts back to one of the main unanswered questions: *where was the tape?* Did anyone alive actually know?

Nina scratched the back of her head, finding the tender spot from when she'd been knocked out at Kaufman's. That triggered a memory. "Hey, Hank."

"Hmmm?"

"Back at Kaufman's, when Valentine and Pellicano stormed in. You were behind me—"

"I'm so sorry. It was all I could think of."

"All you could... Sorry for what exactly?"

Trank seemed to shrink a little. "For knocking you out."

Nina didn't answer. Not immediately.

"You... knocked me out? What the hell?"

"I didn't know what else to do. It all happened so quickly. They wore masks, you didn't know who they were, you had plausible deniability. When they were kidnapping me they were debating whether to take you too. Valentine said he'd killed too much already, and Pellicano admitted he liked your movies, so they left you. It... it was all I could think of."

Nina ran that through her mind. Trank may have saved her life with a simple act of violence. She placed her hand on his shoulder.

"Thanks. Just don't make a habit of it, okay?"

"Deal."

Nina motioned to the ransacked room. "We'll search your place later."

Trank shook his exhausted head. "For?"

"Wagner's house wasn't being fumigated, but he knew

they'd be after him. By then, the knuckleheads had already stashed the car with Morrison's body at the airport, so where would Wagner stash a videotape? It wasn't at his place. It wasn't at Diehl's or Kaufman's either, they've all been searched." Nina pointed at the debris of Trank's cinema room. "And it wasn't here. So where would he hide it? He'd want it accessible, but not obvious."

Trank gave her a vacant stare, and Nina realized she was pushing a man who had too little left in the tank.

"Go have a shower, man, you need it."

Trank glowered. "Are you accusing me of having a less-than-perfumed bouquet?"

Matching his amused tone, Nina replied, "I don't care who you are, anyone would stink after what you've been through. Shower, put on a change of clothes and come down so I can patch you up." Nina motioned to Trank's multiple cuts and abrasions. "I need to make some calls, then maybe we could grab a bite? Go take a long shower, keep the light off."

Trank nodded and wandered off. Nina found a phone in the den and was glad when there was a dial tone. She called Titus.

He answered in his usual gruff manner. "Asta's."

Nina gave a brief rundown of the situation. Titus took in all in without comment. "Basically, expect company."

"I'll be ready."

"I'm so sorry, Titus, I didn't mean to bring this down on you."

"Don't be sorry, just be better than them."

"That's my plan."

"Alright then. Anything else?"

"Tell Phoebe to find a hotel, just to be on the safe side."

"She'll stay at mine, safer."

If Nina was in a different situation, she may have lamented her short list of close friends. She wasn't, so she didn't. "Can you please feed Sputnik?"

"Sure. I'll even give the little rascal a scratch or two."

"You old softie."

"Don't you tell a soul."

"Wouldn't dare."

There was a pause, then the gruff man asked quietly, "What have you gotten yourself mixed up in, Nina?"

"Some heavy shit."

The big man grunted. "You need me, you call, you hear?"

From Titus, that was tantamount to a declaration of love. *In fact, it's exactly that,* Nina thought.

"I will, big guy, thank you."

Nina called Lang and had an even briefer conversation, but the sentiment was the same: don't stay at home, you could be in danger. She rang off before he got too sentimental; Nina couldn't deal with that right now.

Half an hour later Trank emerged from the guesthouse bathroom next to the pool, looking cleaner but not necessarily better. For obvious reasons, he hadn't wanted to shower in the en suite off the main bedroom.

His black eye was still that: black. There were cuts and abrasions across every piece of exposed skin, but he held himself straighter. His hair was no longer matted with blood, and she even detected a minute spring in his step.

Nina treated his wounds with a kit she found in the medicine cabinet. Antiseptic cream, Band-Aids and bandages. He looked like a boxer the day after a world title fight, but he'd heal. Physically, at least.

Neither of them mentioned Mickey. There was no need. They both knew speaking his name aloud would only make it hurt more. Nina found it incredible she was still function-ing, driving, breaking in, strategizing. Right now they were experiencing the numbness of grief. Tomorrow would be worse. She wondered if getting drunk now would be benefi-cial. She wasn't sure. She wasn't sure about a lot of things.

"I wonder when they'll find Mickey?"

Trank's words surprised her more than the break in silence did. His thoughts were obviously wandering down the same miserable path as hers.

She rubbed her upper arm absentmindedly, then sat up rigidly. "Oh shit. I'm going to be a suspect in Mickey's murder."

"Why?"

"I called his secretary and asked where he was. Badgered her into saying he was home because I had to see him. Very urgently."

"As in ...?"

"Going right over."

"Oh dear. That *is* incriminating."

Nina picked up Trank's cordless phone. "I need to get ahead of it."

"Is that wise?"

"Absolutely not." She dialed the number. "Birmingham, please."

"Oh lord." Trank wrung his battered hands.

The line connected. "Yes?"

"Oh hey, Birmingham. How's it going?"

"Oh god, it's you. Please don't tell me you've used your clairvoyant powers and discovered yet another body? I'll be your manager, and you can have one of those late-night psychic 1-800 hotlines. We'll make a fortune."

"You might want to draw up a contract then."

"Wait, you don't mean..."

"Mickey Boehler. He's dead. He was murdered in his home in Laurel Canyon a few hours ago. I saw it happen and ran. Barely made it out. If you talk to the neighbors they'll tell you they heard gunfire and a car screeching out of there. That was me escaping. The two men firing at me were the murderers."

There was a long pause. So long, Nina wondered if they'd been disconnected. Finally, he spoke again, his tone icy. "I'll need you to come to the station."

"Oh hell no, cowboy. The people who did this want me deader than corduroy flares. I'm not dangling my sweet ass anywhere they can take a shot at it. At the moment I'm not sure they know it was me as they saw me from a distance, but I'm sure as hell not going to let them know for sure."

"Who did this?"

Nina debated telling him. He didn't have the facts that she did, but he could attack it from another angle. It was tempting, but in the end, she didn't know if she could trust him, and she sure as hell couldn't trust the department. If word got out, Pellicano would know for sure it was her. Then no one she loved would be safe. She needed evidence against Pellicano first. It was the only way.

"Not yet. But when I have solid evidence against them, I'll contact you."

"Or you find another body."

"That too." Nina inhaled deeply. "Uh..."

"What now?"

"That body in the morgue, Trank."

Nina glanced at Trank; he didn't appear to be disturbed by the topic. She corrected herself; he didn't seem any more disturbed than he'd already been. He squeezed her hand to let her know it was okay to proceed.

"What about it?" Birmingham asked with obvious trepidation.

"Maybe have a chat with the coroner's office and advise them not to rush the medical examiner's report."

"What does that mean?"

"Just saving some people some face is all."

"I'll repeat the question, Maddox. What does that even mean?"

"Yeah, I hear you," she replied sympathetically, "but, I have to go."

"You can't! I need to understand what in god's name is going on!"

"You and me both, buddy. You and me both."

She hung up and pushed in the aerial.

Trank shook his head. "That poor man is going to going to have a heart attack before the week is out." He rubbed his stomach. "I don't know about you, but I'm famished."

At Trank's words, Nina's stomach growled. She couldn't even remember the last time she'd eaten.

"You got anything in that big kitchen of yours?"

Trank's brow furrowed. "I... I... guess so."

"Do you even know where the kitchen is?"

"Yes," he replied confidently. "That's where they keep the champagne."

"Funny man."

"I wasn't actually being funny." He walked toward the rear of the mansion, motioning for Nina to follow.

It still amused Nina that how the famous TV and movie star was so out of touch he'd forgotten how to cook—if he'd even learned in the first place. He led her to his vast, well-appointed kitchen and Nina rummaged around. There wasn't much in the fridge to speak of, besides some butter and bendable carrots. The cupboard had a few bits and pieces, but hardly enough to make a meal. The freezer held more of a bounty.

"We have options."

"I love options!"

This was more like the Trank she remembered.

"There's a couple of frozen steaks, some frozen fries too. I could also—"

Nina stopped short at Trank's raised hand. "Steak and fries sounds like a meal made in heaven. That would be perfect, thank you, Nina." He gripped her hand tight and his voice lowered. "And thank you, Nina." Tears formed. "You saved me, again. They would have..."

He didn't finish, and Nina was thankful. Neither one of them wanted to talk about what would have happened. They both knew.

"You're welcome, Hank. Now, let's get some grub."

Nina turned on the oven and ran hot water in the sink. Finding a cast iron skillet, she turned on a burner on low to heat it up. Placing the plastic-wrapped steaks in the hot water to thaw, she rummaged around in the fridge and pantry. She'd be able to make a nice rosemary and garlic butter for the steaks.

While she'd been preparing the meal, Trank had wandered into his back garden. The lush green of the court-yard would give the kitchen a homely, calm feel in the morning sun.

Trank stood in the center of the patio. He didn't turn as she approached.

"I used to feel so safe here. This place was my oasis from the madness of the city." He sighed. "Once this is all over, I'll sell up. I can't live here anymore," he motioned to the house. "I don't even know if I want to live in LA."

"I hear Albuquerque's nice."

"I'm depressed, Nina, no need to make me suicidal."

The weak humor was a good sign. She didn't want to push him too hard yet, he'd been through a hell of a lot. Moving house wasn't the only thing he'd need once this was all over; he'd need a very expensive shrink, too. Lucky he was in the right town for that.

She put her arm around him. The night was mild; the Santa Ana winds kept the temperature warmer. They also blew the day's smog out to sea, leaving the night sky as clear as it ever got. There was a faint scent of smoke in the air. It was too late in the year for a forest fire. Bel Air wasn't known for its burnt-out car bodies, but something was definitely burning somewhere. The smoke became visible.

Trank noticed too, and turned to Nina. As he did, he pointed back to the kitchen. "Fire!"

Nina pivoted and saw smoke billowing from the kitchen. She ran inside and saw the source. The oven. Plumes of toxic fumes poured from the glass door. She yanked it open and was immediately engulfed by black, toxic smoke.

Choking, she used an oven glove to extract a baking pan with a smoldering black lump at its center. She ran outside and flung it onto the porch bricks, and Trank doused it with the hose.

After coughing herself hoarse, she finally managed to return to regular breathing, though her lungs felt like they were coated in tar.

"What the hell was that?" she asked, sounding more like a drag queen than a scream queen.

"I have absolutely no idea."

They stepped tentatively toward the smoking remains. The stench of burnt plastic was unmistakable. Nina leaned forward to get a closer look before reeling back.

"You've got to be kidding me!" She stomped around in circles, each step angrier than the last. "You have to be fucking kidding me!"

"What? What is it?"

"Oh, you stupid motherfucker. You stupid, stupid motherfucker."

"I don't understand, what..."

Trank leaned down to investigate, then straightened up. He saw it now. The smoldering burnt black plastic mass was roughly book sized. The outer edges were melted. On top were melted pieces that had once been clear. Elsewhere were shriveled threads of black melted plastic, like molten string.

"Oh, dear, you don't think this was..."

Nina continued her furious pacing. "What sort of idiot puts plastic in a device designed to heat things? Oh, look, here's a catapult, I better put a puppy in it. Oh no, they launched the puppy into fucking space! Who saw that coming? Everyone! Everyone saw that coming!"

"Do you think this is the videotape they stole from The Crucible?"

"Unless you have a habit of putting videotapes in your fucking oven then yes, Hank, I fucking think this is the fucking Crucible videotape!"

"I think you should calm down, Nina."

"No, you should calm down, Nina!"

Trank laughed. Against her better judgement, Nina laughed at Trank laughing. The tension dissipated. The smoke didn't.

Nina stopped pacing. "I better open a window."

Half an hour later, they sat outside eating steak and fries. It was still too noxious to stay inside for too long. They'd found some beers and ate in silence for a while, occasionally casting a glance at the melted modern art piece sitting on a baking pan on the patio.

"There goes our best hope of finding who killed Alicia Morrison."

Nina took a swig of the Heineken. Of course, Trank didn't have domestic beer.

He stared into the middle distance. "So, that's it then?"

Nina watched the twinkling stars hovering over the city of stars. "No, Hank. We're not done. I saw what happened to that girl. I saw the desperate hand prints, the streaks of blood. He tortured her, mutilated her. Whoever *he* is. I don't care what it takes, I don't care what we need to do, we're going to find the son of a bitch and we're going to take him down. Then we're going after Pellicano and Valentine and all the bastards responsible for Mickey, Wagner and all the others. We're going to take them all down."

"Alright." Trank sat up, enlivened by Nina's words. "How do we do that?"

Nina took another swig of her beer and stared into the night sky. "I have absolutely no idea."

CHAPTER
SIXTEEN

Just after dawn, Nina raided the neighbors' driveways for newspapers. Every one of them had *Variety*, of course, but she had to hunt for a selection of actual newspapers. She and Trank pored over them over coffee (black, as the milk had spoiled) and scrambled eggs (out of date, but they risked it).

So far, the media had thoroughly failed to connect the disparate murders. Even the obvious link between Wagner, Diehl, and Kaufman all being stuntmen hadn't been picked up on. A memorial for Trank was being planned at the Hollywood Bowl, of all places, a week from Sunday. Barry White was headlining. LA was a weird town.

Nina hadn't been lying when she said she didn't know what their next move was. There was no immediate evidence to nail Pellicano and Valentine to the wall. It would be her word against theirs, and she was sure they already had watertight alibis and had expertly covered their tracks at Mickey's. As for Morrison's murderer, she was even further from discovering the truth.

She missed Mickey already. The hard-headed studio

boss hadn't exactly been a close confidant, but she'd grown accustomed to the big gruff idiot. He was also the only person in this town who'd given her work when no one else would.

Nina was once again suffocated by the thought that she should have tried to save him, even though logic screamed at her that she'd likely be dead too. When they'd shot Mickey, they'd shot her only meal ticket. Nina knew it was selfish to think of herself at a time like this, but the moroseness of their situation made it easy to slip into an egocentric downward spiral. She pushed her eggs around her plate without enthusiasm. Plus, she'd burnt the last of the toast.

"Are we going to get out of this alive, Nina?"

Trank's thoughts seemed to mirror hers. The swelling on his busted-up face had begun to ease, but his battered appearance encapsulated their plight succinctly.

"I'm not going to lie to you, Hank. Right now, I'm not seeing a lot of options." Seeing his face drop even more, she realized she needed to be slightly more upbeat. After all, the man had been thoroughly beaten down. "But I don't know about you, but I'm going to make those bastards pay for what they did to Mickey. And Leonard, even after what he did to my car. We know who they are, we know what they've done. All we need to do is gather solid enough evidence and go to the cops. We've got this, Hank. We've got this."

Trank was buoyed, if not enthused. Nina wished she'd inspired herself, but she hadn't. She felt like she'd lied to Hank. Perhaps she had.

To break her out of her malaise, Nina called Asta's and was surprised when Phoebe answered.

"Uh, shouldn't you be at work, Phoebs?"

"Nah, took a few days off to work on these books of yours."

Nina was taken aback and heartened by Phoebe's altruism. "I can't ask you to do that."

"You didn't, but I did anyway. Brett owed me because I worked a few weekends to get some projects over the line, it's all good." Phoebe's tone became less chipper. "Where are you?"

"I'd rather not say, in case, you know?" The silence at the other end of the line confirmed that she did. "How about we meet at that place we always said we'd meet at if we needed a place to meet?"

Nina looked over to a confused Trank and gave him an amused wrinkle of her nose.

"Oh, I love that place. Noon?"

"Done."

Nina rang off and made some mental calculations on how long it would take to get to Watts. That was when she remembered they didn't have a car. Hers was in the shop and they'd abandoned Mickey's Cobra at Zsa Zsa Gabor's.

"Hey Hank, how good are you at hot-wiring cars?"

"At what?"

NINA WAS ONLY MESSING with Trank. They didn't have to hot-wire anything. They hailed a cab a block away from Hank's. The cab driver hadn't recognized either of them, though he did have a script for a science fiction movie he tried to convince them to read. It was apparently about an alien invasion where they plan to steal all the Earth's water but are thwarted by the hero cab driver and his band of sexy vampire lesbians. They politely passed.

Watts Towers was one of Nina's favorite Los Angeles attractions, partly because it was one of the lesser-known ones. Located in the Watts district, it was a collection of seventeen interconnected structures, some over a hundred feet tall. Built by an Italian immigrant and construction worker, Sabato, it was a non-traditional form of architecture, made of armatures from steel pipes and rods, wrapped with wire mesh and coated with mortar, decorated with pieces of porcelain, tile, and glass. For a non-art lover, Nina dug the aesthetic of the place. Plus, it was one of the few landmarks in the city not overrun by celebrities or tourists. It had its own vibe going on.

Walking among the twisted colorful sculptures, Nina asked, "You been here before?"

"Uh, no."

The first thing most people thought of when Watts was mentioned was the riots. In 1965, fueled by desperate downtrodden people subjected to years of discriminatory police harassment and a lack of basic public services, the Watts riots raged for six days. The only other time Watts was on the news was due to the mounting body count from the ongoing feud between the Crips and the Bloods. Nina wasn't surprised Hank wasn't a frequent visitor to the neighborhood. It was a shame though, as it had the best Soul Food in the city.

They found Phoebe hunched over a thick wad of perforated computer paper. As they approached, her thousand-watt smile beamed. When she saw Trank's mangled face she did her best not to stare.

"Hey losers."

"Hey Phoebs."

They hugged, Nina holding on for a tiny bit longer than necessary. She was surprised when Trank received a hug too. As Phoebe sat down, Nina gave him a look that she hoped conveyed, *you've made it now*. It took time to gain the trust of Ms Phoebe Elizabeth Jones.

They all sat on a mosaic encrusted park bench and in a short amount of time, Nina caught her friend up on recent events. Each part of the story propelled Phoebe's jaw closer to the ground. The story about the videotape baking made her shriek.

"So," Nina tapped the computer paper with the back of her knuckle, "we kind of need a break in either nailing Pellicano to the wall or finding out who the occupant of the Arbuckle Room was the night Morrison was killed."

Nina noticed she'd started to refer to Alicia as Morrison. It wasn't a conscious decision, but likely a subliminal attempt to disassociate the young woman from the horrors Nina had seen in that room. It couldn't be personal, not now.

Phoebe's face contorted into something that wasn't quite a grimace, but wasn't exactly a grin either. "I don't have a smoking gun, if that's what you're hoping for, but I do have some info I think you'll find useful. It was Mickey's club, alright—at least, he built it. I've been over the books four times now. There's no doubt. There are deeds, seed money, everything, going back years. Mickey started the club four years ago, but there's more to it. You were right, he took a huge hit about a year ago. The coffers were gutted, and he topped it up with money from his own accounts, but it was nowhere near enough."

"That's when he couldn't cover the bets of his own casino?"

"Seems that way. Then there's a big payment from a Citicorp bank in Vegas, I'm assuming that was the gangsters you mentioned. Things tick on for a while, big payments going back to Vegas on the regular. I mean, big weekly payments. Then, a few months later, one huge one to Vegas, way more than they sent originally. He paid the mobsters off, with what I'm assuming was sizable interest."

"Sounds like that was Pellicano's money. That's when he took a controlling interest and started messing with Mickey's club. Putting in his own security guy, hidden cameras and the like."

That last comment made Trank wince. There was a high chance he'd been caught on tape performing all sorts of career-ending acts.

Phoebe continued. "It's not a stretch to think Pellicano planned to make a huge return on his investment by running a blackmail scheme. Reputation is everything in this town."

Nina dared not look in Trank's direction. "But then someone went and killed a starlet, and the knuckleheads uncovered the video camera and planned some blackmail of their own."

The sun beat down and Nina squinted, wishing she'd brought her sunglasses. It was good to have confirmation, but this was information she already knew. There was nothing new in Phoebe's discoveries. She didn't expect to find evidence that tied everything up in a nice bow, but she needed *something*. She hadn't been lying when she'd told Trank she didn't know what to do next. She was floundering, and it was only a matter of time before Pellicano and his goon found Nina and those closest to her and put a bullet in their brains, like they had with so many others.

"You know I love you and all that?"

"But where's the killer blow?" Phoebe raised her index finger knowingly. "It's all boring business stuff, really. Pellicano bought the controlling interest, fifty one percent, and apparently has the final say on all business decisions. It's all compliant under Californian business law. He might be a sleazy gangster, but he's a smart sleazy gangster. The security guy," Phoebe flipped several pages, "Valentine. He's on the payroll, same as every other employee, though he gets paid a shit ton more." Her shoulders sagged. "But it doesn't look like there's any sort of booking system on the computer files, so we don't know who was in that room when shit went down."

Nina's despondency didn't evaporate under the sweltering California sun. In fact, it doubled down. Phoebe held up a finger, cutting Nina off before she could articulate as much.

"But I have the members list—well, most of them. Took a hell of a long time matching phone numbers to actual people. Spent most of yesterday and this morning cross-referencing numbers, civic listings—hell, for a few I even went to the microfiche dungeon at the library to see who was in a particular family."

Not even trying to hide her smugness, she handed Nina the list. Her friend squeezed her tight with gratitude.

"It's not one hundred percent, but if I have a doubt I've noted it in column D, giving the reasoning."

"Phoebs, you're a marvel."

"I am, aren't I?" There was no doubt Nina's words were appreciated. "But I have more. I'm on it, but it's not done yet. It's a huge chunk of work, but I'm going through each of these eighty-seven names to determine where each person was the night Alicia Morrison died."

Nina's face was blank. "How the hell did you do that?"

"I'm glad you asked, my little chickadee." Phoebe hefted a huge notebook from her bag. "I've started to call everyone on the list."

"You what?" Nina was stunned.

"I pretend to be a lawyer for GEICO Insurance. That usually gets their attention. I say a car matching theirs was spotted in a series of gas station hold-ups and could they account for their whereabouts. Then I ask where they were over three particular nights, so I didn't give away exactly what we're after."

"That's genius."

"Oh, I know. Most of the people I've been able to contact so far have verifiable alibis, like being out on location, holidays, business trips, and the like. They're in green." She tilted the list for Nina and Trank to see. "Some told me they were at restaurants or parties. Less verifiable, but I have names of witnesses should we need them, as well as the estimated time they left festivities. There's a few who said they were home, most of which I assume will have family or servants to confirm. Again, not airtight, but something."

This wasn't exactly how Nina expected the chat with Phoebe to go. She'd had unrealistic hopes, sure, but suspected there would have been more evidence pointing to Pellicano and his manipulation of Mickey than to Morrison's murderer. Regardless, Nina was thankful she had real detective work to get her teeth stuck into. Waiting passively was not her forte. With this new information, she doubted they'd find the murderer on the first try, but every step they took would bring them closer to the killer.

"Phoebe, we'll make a detective out of you yet."

"You mean give up the glamor of being an associate member? I don't know if I'm ready for that."

Nina knew Phoebe was joking, but she did hope that one day her friend would join her agency for real. In order for that to happen, the first thing she needed was to earn a steady income. Well, the second. She had to not die first, then make a profit.

"Ms Jones, you're an incredible human being."

"Can you tell your cat that?"

Nina scanned the list. There were senators, congressmen, studio executives, and above the line actors and actresses. Several had circles around them. "How come these two are circled so many times?"

"Good eye," Phoebe replied. "This one was the first that stood out to me. Absolutely zero alibi. Loch Thompson."

"I know him," Trank said, seemingly surprised he'd spoken. "From the club, I mean."

"Isn't he in that awful teen exploitation comedy series..." Nina racked her brain for the title. "Panty Raid something? They churn out that shit once a year. He can't be older than—"

"He's twenty-eight." Trank was amused at Nina's reaction. "We chatted at the club a month or two back. I was interested until I realized he was straight."

"I hate when that happens," Phoebe observed.

"He's a pretty level-headed kid, despite what the trailers for the *Panty Raid Club* movies would have you believe—though we were both pretty drunk. He wants to do Hamlet, which might be a stretch." Trank turned to them both. "He didn't strike me as the violent murderer type."

"If recent days have shown us anything, it's that not everyone is as they're perceived." Nina gestured in Trank's direction.

"Point taken." He leaned over the list. "Who else?"

"Tod Bailey."

"The goddamn mayor?" Nina realized she'd raised her voice. Luckily there was no one nearby.

"Him, I haven't spoken to." Trank pointed to the name on the page. "I've seen him at the club a few times, but he gravitated to the political types, not the industry ones. We exchanged polite nods but that was it."

"Isn't he making a senate run?" Nina asked.

"Don't know." Phoebe lifted her notes. "He pays higher dues than most, not sure why. I checked with his office; he had no official engagements the night of the murder. Same as Thompson—he wasn't filming, his assistant claimed he was home alone that night." She hefted her notes. "I haven't called everyone on the list, but these two are the most likely candidates so far."

Grasping her friend's face with both hands, Nina said, "You're amazing, you know that? I woke up this morning depressed as hell because I had no leads and here you go and do the best detective work I've seen in a long time."

They'd made progress. And by they, Nina meant Phoebe. None of it was indictable, but it was progress nonetheless. The question was, would they find the answers they sought before Pellicano and his CIA thug caught up with them? She suddenly felt claustrophobic in the wide-open space.

Refusing to let her encroaching downheartedness win, Nina reviewed what she'd learned, revisiting the conversation. There was something Phoebe had mentioned that was a splinter in her mind, festering until she pulled it out.

"You mentioned payroll information?"

Phoebe moved a wad of computer paper to the top of the pile. "I have the last three months printed, but it goes back a few years. Here."

Nina took the paper and scanned the detail. It wasn't long before a particular employee caught her attention. "What does DNF mean?"

"Where?"

"Here, here, here." Nina's finger pointed out the three letters randomly in the columns of numbers.

"Did not finish?" Phoebe suggested, then shook her head. "That doesn't make sense, not from an accounting perspective. You'd still pay them for a partial shift."

"Did not front?" Trank suggested. "As in, turn up?"

The two women frowned in agreeance. It was the most logical answer, as it was applicable for various employees at different times. Plus, there was no payment information for those dates.

"Why would that matter?" Phoebe asked Nina.

"Because of this one. No DNFs in the preceding months, but three after the murder, one the very next night. They've never come back. What's this payment, TC?"

"Termination costs," Phoebe stated definitively. "Different code type than wages. Severance pay, any benefits owed and other ancillary costs as dictated by the FASB Statement No. 162 of The Hierarchy of Generally Accepted Accounting Principles."

"You're such a nerd." Nina chuckled.

"And damn proud of it."

"So, they didn't show up for assigned shifts and then were paid out what they were owed?"

"Apparently."

"And this is their phone number?"

Phoebe checked where Nina was pointing and said, "Uh-huh."

Nina felt energized. In the space of twenty minutes, her morning melancholy had morphed into a faint optimism. This was nothing she could take to the cops, but it felt like a step in the right direction. Her claustrophobia had given way to hope. They still had to find the true identity of

Morrison's killer, all the while avoiding Pellicano and his death squad, but for the first time that day, Nina felt like she was in control again. She had a mission, she had a goal.

"Looks like we have a few leads here." Nina beamed at her friend. "I don't know how I can repay you, Phoebs."

"Nail these sons of bitches."

"Deal."

SEVENTEEN

As the automatic doors opened, Nina felt like she was the butt of some kind of cosmic joke. Located between Terminals 3 and 4, the brand new LAX International Terminal B was known by a different name. Opened only months before, just in time for the summer Olympics, the terminal was known as the Tod Bailey Terminal, named after the mayor. Nina knew it was some sort of sign, she just didn't know what kind.

She checked the departures board, passed through the metal detector with its indifferent security, and made her way to the North Concourse and gate 137. Thanks to Phoebe's reverse phone book, they had the details of The Crucible's employee. Now Nina had to find her before she left the country.

Nina approached the sparsely populated gate. There was only one member of staff at the service desk, a portly woman whose uniform strained at the seams. She didn't raise her head when Nina arrived.

"Hi," Nina said in her chirpiest tone. "Can you please page Rachael Sanderson? She's on flight 12."

Lackadaisically raising her large head, the woman asked, "May I ask the reason?"

"She works at my company and forgot some important documents she needs." Nina lifted a manila folder to emphasize the point.

"You can go find her." The woman waved to the gate, her tone soaked in disdain.

"I don't know what she looks like."

The woman squinted suspiciously. "Didn't you say she worked for your company?"

"It's a big company."

With a disgruntled grunt, the woman pressed down on the talk button. "Can Ms Rachael Sanderson flying Qantas Airlines flight QF12 please report to the service desk at gate 137. Repeating, can Ms. Rachael Sanderson flying Qantas Airlines flight QF12 please report to the service desk at gate 137. Thank you."

Depressing the button, the woman gave a sassy, pursed-lip sneer, as if to say, *that's all you get* and returned to her crossword puzzle.

Nina waited. Rachael Sanderson probably thought she was going to get bumped up to first class. Nina hoped she wouldn't be too annoyed.

"I'm Rachael Sanderson."

Nina turned to see a woman who was nothing short of breathtaking. Model skinny and tall, she had an androgynous face with high cheekbones, faultless eyebrows, and an all-knowing pouty mouth. Nina thought this queen should be front and center on movie posters, not slinging drinks for the stupidly rich and fatuous. Dressed in a Chanel boucle suit and carrying a Louis Vuitton carry-on, she held a first-class ticket in her well-manicured hand. Clearly she wouldn't be needing that upgrade. Phoebe's records stated she was senior waitress at the club, but obviously one far smarter and better paid than Nina ever was.

"Hi. My name is Nina Maddox, I'm a private investigator. Can I talk to you a moment?"

Defensively folding her arms, Rachael asked, "About what?"

"The Crucible."

Face instantly dropping, her exquisite features recovered quickly. "I'm sure I don't know what you—"

"I'm not here for you. I'm only after some information. I'm not the police and I have no intention of ever contacting you again. I won't pass your information on to anyone else —we never had this conversation. Does that sound fair?"

It was an old lawyer trick, asking a question you'll most likely receive a positive answer to in the hope of building rapport.

"No, it doesn't."

But not always, Nina cursed. "Listen," she guided Rachael a few steps away from the prying ears of the woman on the service desk, who was craning her neck, clearly eavesdropping on their conversation. Out of earshot, she continued. "It's a guess, but this," she pointed to the luggage and ticket, "is because you saw or heard something you didn't like at The Crucible. And I highly suspect I know what it was. Whether it was the last straw or so horrible you couldn't go back, I don't know. Either way, it was enough to stop you from stepping foot in that place, even though you were rostered on, and you're now fleeing the country." Nina took a breath. She knew what she was about to say was a risk, but she had to try. "I think you know what happened inside the Arbuckle Room."

The plump painted lips parted ever so slightly, and her

eyes fought valiantly not to flare. The woman was well trained to conceal her surprise.

"I wish you luck with whatever it is you're doing, but I'm afraid I can't help you." She lifted her bag and unleashed a dazzling customer service smile that would work on any straight male with a pulse.

"Mickey Boehler's dead."

It turned out there were limits to this woman's well-practiced façade; it crumbled to the floor.

"What!" There was no quick recovery this time. "You're lying."

There was genuine fear in her expression now. Her gaze darted to every corner of the departure lounge.

"No, I'm not. I was there. I saw it. I barely made it out alive. Believe me, I understand your caution, applaud it even, but in order to bring down those responsible, I need to talk to you, and I need to do it now."

Perhaps it wasn't an all-out lie, but it wasn't exactly the truth either. Finding Morrison's killer may not bring down Pellicano and Valentine. While connected by tendons, the two limbs had conflicting motives and drives. Bringing one to justice did not guarantee the same for the other. One took over the club, intent on blackmailing guests, and when things went south murdered Mickey and a slew of stunt-men. And Leonard. The other, as far as she knew, was a Crucible member whose particular appetites extended to young girls and murder. Nina was fighting on two fronts and needed a break in either. Her best bet for the latter was standing right in front of her.

"We should sit." Rachael motioned to a seat in front of a closed-down sandwich shop on the concourse.

"How did you find me?" Rachael's cool unflustered demeanor had returned.

"Your roommate advised you were flying out, and if it was as urgent as I said, I could catch you at the airport." Nina motioned to the gate. "So here I am."

"And you say you're a private investigator?"

Nina pulled out a card and handed it over.

"Scream Queen Detective Agency?" She squinted, somehow without wrinkling her golden features. "You're *that* Nina Maddox?"

"The very same." Nina glanced at the board and realized the flight would be called soon enough. "Where you headed?"

"As far away as I can possibly get." Nina remained silent until Rachael added, "Sydney."

"That'll do it. I'm Australian. Born in Melbourne. I have two pieces of advice for you. One, never go to Canberra under any circumstances."

"And the second?"

"Avoid drop bears. Now, I have some questions before you disappear. I know the club recently changed management, how did you feel about that?"

Nina considered the question a softball pitch—unlikely to generate much, but it would hopefully warm Rachael into answering questions on reflex.

"At first it didn't make any difference at all. We saw Mickey every now and then, usually schmoozing someone, acting like he owned the place, because, well, he did. Always tipped well, so we never minded. Then one day there was a new boss—"

"Pellicano?"

Rachael tilted her head, as if saying, *you are well informed*. "Right. Then he was there every night, brings in his new security guy, which kind of unsettled the members, didn't sit well with the staff either. Then there were all the renovations. For weeks on end we didn't know what room would be available and what wouldn't. Then that all died down and the staff, well, we just did what we always did. Apart from Pellicano in the office, it was all fine."

"Until it wasn't."

Rachael nodded in silent agreement.

The gate was filling fast. Nina didn't have much time.

"I'm trying to determine who was in The Arbuckle room the night Alicia Morrison went missing."

She'd chosen her words carefully, not using the word "murder" in case Rachael wasn't aware, though fleeing the country suggested she was.

"I'm not sure I can say. I can tell you there was one person who booked that room only. Called it his lucky charm."

Nina didn't have time to be coy. "Was it Loch Thompson?"

For the first time, Rachael laughed. "The *Panty Raid* kid? He can hardly afford the dues. The guy was only at the club to try and make industry connections, but they could smell the desperation dripping from him a mile off. He drank too much, gambled too much, maybe mouthed off a few times, but he was harmless. Beneath the bravado he's actually a sweet kid. He won't last. The industry he so desperately clings to is going to spit him out, he just doesn't know it yet."

For a brief moment Nina reminisced about her own brief career and how easily she could have succumbed to The Beast. She could have spiraled into drugs and self-loathing and wound up dead before thirty. She chose to get out. She chose to not be a victim of the system, a victim of The Beast.

There was more than one addiction in this town. Drugs

were the most obvious, but fame was so much more potent, and insidious. The Beast made you believe the hype, hunger for the high of adoration. Some could never shake the habit. They lived in the periphery, a face in the corner of every party in the city of parties with whispers of, "Where do I know them from?" Always believing a comeback was just over the horizon, they clung to a hope they should have abandoned long ago. But how do you abandon your dreams when the whole city is built on them? Rachael believed Hollywood would consume Loch, while he probably thought he'd be riding the high forever. The law of averages said in ten years he'd be nothing more than a trivia question. Just like Nina.

Rachael didn't see Loch Thomson as a murderer, only a sad, good-time boy who didn't know the party was over. That left one more name on Nina's list.

"Then perhaps it was Tod Bai—"

"Don't you dare say that name out loud."

Nina thought it ironic that they were in a terminal named after the man. Rachael's renewed panic confirmed Nina had a name to go with the horror.

"Tell me about him." Leaning forward, she added, "The real him."

Swallowing hard, Rachael seemed to fight her better instincts to keep talking. "He's a big tipper, always quick with a joke or a compliment. Remembers all the staff by name." Her gaze swept the concourse in case there was anyone else listening. She lowered her voice. "But all the girls knew."

"Knew what?"

"Behind the genial persona, behind the big tips and big compliments you... you made sure no matter what you did, you were never in a room alone with him. You know?"

Nina knew. All women knew.

Often, women couldn't articulate exactly what it was—a gesture, a leer that lasted a fraction of a second too long, body language, or all or none of it—but they just *knew*. Women understood when certain men were dangerous. Primal instinct kicked in, and either they listened, or they paid the price.

Alicia Morrison was too young to have developed that instinct, and she'd paid the price.

Nina was reminded of the offhand comment Janet Write, Alicia's PA, had made about Alicia saying she was going to be first lady one day soon. Bailey was making a senate run. He was wildly popular in the state after the success of the Olympics, and capturing the California vote would go a long way toward securing the Presidency. Hell, it worked for Reagan.

"Did you see it happen?"

With a blank, emotionless stare, Rachael took her time to slowly shake her head. She swallowed hard, horror in those jade green eyes. "During, no. He called down, asked for me personally. He did that sometimes. He usually ordered the same thing, so I came up with his preferred Cuban cigar and a bottle of Bollinger. It was usually safe when he had company, and after, you know. When I got there the door was locked. He usually unlocked it so I could serve him and his guest in bed. He unlocked it and, my god, he actually said these words." She gulped. "He said, 'I've done something silly.'" Her sculptured features hardened. "Silly. That's what the bastard said to me. There was blood... everywhere. He... he..." She was working herself up now, the trauma bubbling to the surface. "He told me I had to call Mickey, not Pellicano. Mickey, because he'd make it all okay. He slapped a grand in my hand and shut the door."

"And that's when you called Mickey?"

She nodded. "I didn't know what else to do. The club isn't exactly legal. Calling the cops would put everyone in more hot water. I've worked with these people for years, they're family, I couldn't just—"

"It's okay. So, you called Mickey."

"Yes. He told me he'd take care of it." Tears stained her faultlessly applied mascara. "I... I couldn't go back, not after... I have to get out. He knows I know. You haven't seen him when he's... I can't be here." Her gaze turned to the gate and, as if by sheer will, an announcement stated that boarding had commenced and first-class passengers were able to board first. A sense of relief washed over her; salvation was calling.

"Thank you." Nina placed her hand over Rachael's. "I know that wouldn't have been easy."

Rachael squeezed Nina's hand. "I'm sorry I'm not brave enough to do more."

"I think you're brave enough for all of us. Do me a favor. Write me when you're settled. Mainly to tell me you're okay, but in case I need to contact you." She held up a finger before Rachael could protest. "I don't want to know where you are, that could be dangerous for you, I understand. A post office box, a hotel you're not staying at, something like that. I want to keep you safe, okay?"

Both women knew there was more to it. Should this ever get to court, Rachael would be a key witness. But there was no point discussing whether she'd be willing to testify now. So much had to fall in place before that could even be contemplated.

Mulling the idea over, Rachael tucked Nina's card into her pocket. "I'll do that." She lifted her designer bag. "Do you think you're going to get him?"

"I won't lie to you, it's going to be tough, but I am going to do absolutely everything I can to bury that son of a bitch."

Satisfied with the answer, Rachael stood. She straightened her expensive suit and took a step toward the gate, then stopped and turned to Nina. "What's next for you?"

"I guess I'm going to go meet the mayor."

EIGHTEEN

Nina emerged from Titus's spare room and gave a twirl.

"Hot damn," Lang exclaimed.

Lang had been staying with his sister in Encino in case Pellicano and Valentine came after him. He'd claimed he was using the time to catch up with his sister and stated more than once that he was very happy with the arrangement. Nina wasn't sure how much of the positive spin was for her benefit.

Phoebe turned and gave Nina a wolf whistle. "If I weren't so proper, I'd ask if you were sure you're straight."

"Heaven forbid you'd ever say anything inappropriate, Phoebs," Nina chuckled.

The green velvet dress clung to Nina's every curve, its plunging neckline accentuating certain curves in particular, and the dress's trail swished satisfyingly behind her. Phoebe had outdone herself, securing the dress from a Rodeo Drive boutique with less than two hours' notice. It was as far away from Nina's preferred jeans, T-shirt and leather jacket combo as you possibly get, but she had to admit, she felt decadent, slinky, and sexy as hell.

"What do you think, Hank?" Nina asked, giving a wiggle of her hips.

Thankfully, Trank's black eye had begun to heal, and was no longer an angry purple. Titus had applied an "ancient Cajun remedy" that Nina suspected came from Walgreens. Hank was beginning to resemble his old self.

"It's nice," he replied.

Lang and Phoebe turned to him incredulously.

"Nice?" Lang exclaimed, splaying his hands in Nina's direction. "The woman is a goddess."

Trank looked alarmed, realizing he may have undersold his opinion. "Very nice." He gave Nina a knowing wink. "If you like that sort of thing."

Sputnik, who was curled up on Trank's lap, didn't share his opinion. Titus had picked him up, as well as all the cat food he could find, and set him up in the laundry. The ginger furball had grown accustomed to his surroundings and carried himself like he'd always been there.

The gang was all here.

They were huddled outside Phoebe's childhood bedroom at Titus's house in Inglewood. Following Nina's warning to Titus, Phoebe had moved in with her father, which both had said was fine. As soon as Nina stepped inside the house, however, she'd detected an undercurrent of simmering tension. Titus had raised Phoebe single-handedly when her mother abandoned her at three years of age. He was a stern but loving father who'd worked hard to ensure Phoebe wanted for nothing growing up. Their relationship had matured and blossomed once she'd moved out. Nina hadn't had the chance to ask Phoebe what was behind this new conflict, but suspected it was something to do with reverting to and rebelling against past condition-ing. Fathers and daughters were complicated.

Nina straightened Lang's bow tie. His tuxedo wasn't a rental, it was his, and it fit him well. Nina was reminded what attracted her to the chiseled jawed photographer in the first place. The manly stubble gave him a rougher edge, and his aftershave set her mind wandering to less pure thoughts. *Down girl. Focus, Nina.*

Lang and Nina were off to a black-tie event raising money for Bailey's senate campaign. Two months out and the polls had Reagan winning the Presidential race by a landslide. That boded well for Bailey's senate run, but democracy demanded greenbacks to feed the ravenous machine. That's what had secured Nina a ticket—a hefty donation to Tod Bailey's campaign. She hoped the money would allow her the opportunity to get a measure of the man.

"Are you sure this is completely necessary?" Trank asked, obvious concern in his tone.

"The waitress Rachael Sanderson says Bailey killed Morrison and that he was the sole occupant of the Arbuckle Room on the night in question. She saw the blood, and Bailey had her contact Mickey to organize the disposal of the body. Any court in the land would convict. But we're not cops, we have nothing concrete to give them, just half stories told by dead men and a woman who's just flown out of the country. We need more. The only way to get that is to go to the source."

"I still think it's dangerous." Trank folded his arms.

"I didn't say it wasn't."

Lang's swagger sagged. "How dangerous, exactly?"

Phoebe's brow furrowed. "You saw the murder room, what he did to her."

"Yes, but..." There was dread in his demeanor now. "It's a public space. He wouldn't try anything there... would he? That would be insane."

"Sane and this guy aren't firm friends," Phoebe said, fixing Nina's hair. "He's in charge of the best city in the world, has taken credit for the most successful Olympic games ever held, he's about to lock up a senate seat and instead of being happy with all that, he fucks, mutilates, and murders a fifteen-year-old kid. Sane isn't even in this zip code."

"We don't know one hundred percent that he did it," Trank offered, then immediately held up a defensive hand. "I know everything points to him, but like you said, we don't have that, excuse the phrase, killer blow. Without the tape, we don't know for sure. We have no leverage."

"He doesn't know we don't have the tape." They all turned to Nina, who had spoken without even thinking. She waved her hand. "Sorry, idle thought." She turned to Lang, concerned. "You don't have to go to this thing. I shouldn't have even gotten you involved in the first place. It was stupid and selfish, I'm so sorry. I can go to this thing by myself, it's okay."

"Like hell." Lang's back straightened.

"I can go," Phoebe suggested.

"Thanks, love, but I need you working on all the back-end stuff. We may need it sooner than later."

"I'd love to go, but," Trank's upward facing palm motioned to his body, "I'm dead."

Lang squeezed Nina's arm. "I'll be fine."

Once again, Nina felt like a heartless heel asking Lang to be involved, especially when she knew their relationship didn't have legs. If there was another option, she would have taken it, but she needed someone to have her back when she confronted Bailey.

She stuffed her Beretta into her Glomesh handbag. "Okay then. Let's go meet a murderer."

~

MAYBE IT WAS MORE a reflection on her than on the architectural design, but the Los Angeles City Hall always reminded Nina of a giant white dick and balls imposing itself on downtown LA. Freud would surely have an opinion on the building, with its neoclassical base and phallic art deco tower.

She and Lang ascended the Main Street steps at the front of the building in their finery. Nina had to admit, regardless of why they were here, she felt fancy as fuck. It wasn't every day she was able to get dressed up. It reminded her of the days of movie premieres and lavish industry parties. She didn't exactly miss those days, but an occasional sprinkling of glamor gave her a pang of nostalgia sometimes.

She shook her head, reminding herself she wasn't here to have fun. Best case scenario, they would discover in no uncertain terms who'd triggered the events they were all embroiled in and obtain confirmation on who'd murdered a teen starlet. There was too much at stake for Nina to have anything resembling fun. This was business.

They took the elevator to the 27th floor. The doors slid open, revealing a large meeting space with a high art deco ceiling, and they were bombarded with a gush of warm, alcohol-scented air and revelry. The fundraiser was already in full swing. There were tall windows on each side of the space, and an exterior wraparound walkway offering 360-degree views of the surrounding city. The room was decked out in the requisite red, white, and blue bunting, and the mayor's smiling face was plastered everywhere, on posters, fliers, and buttons.

A perky young woman greeted them as they stepped out of the elevator. "Oh, good evening! So glad you could make it. May have your name, please?" She hefted her clipboard expectantly.

Lang peered over the list. "Lang, Armin and plus one."

Normally Nina would loathe being referred to as plus one, but in this instance, she'd grin and bear it.

"Yes, Mr Lang. Thank you so much for your contribution," said the woman, whose name tag read *Cindy!*, with a dazzling assault of white teeth. "The future senator's team appreciates your substantial contribution. And on a forensics photographer's salary, it's particularly generous of you."

"Huh," Lang replied. "When I booked the tickets I didn't mention what I do for a living."

The thousand-watt smile didn't dip a volt. "We here at the future senator's team ensure we know all about our amazing constituents. Now, please help yourself to the champagne and canapés. The future senator is expected any minute now. He'll be sure to want to thank you personally for your generous contribution to his election campaign."

Before they could reply, Cindy with the exclamation point and her red, white, and blue clipboard turned to greet the next arrival in an equally chipper manner. Nina availed herself of the aforementioned champagne and handed Lang a glass, too. After dropping two thousand dollars of her hard-earned money for the privilege, Nina wasn't going to pass up a free drink.

Lang grabbed a plate and offered one to Nina, who shook her head. The buffet had been well and truly picked over. They'd deliberately waited until later in the evening, and the remainders weren't exactly enticing.

"Dude, I'm not sure how long that food's been out."

Piling his plate high, Lang shook his head. "I'm starving. For what they're charging at this thing, they're probably not planning on giving everyone food poising." He took a bite of a brown smear on a tiny piece of toast before making a face, then stuffed the rest in his mouth.

The two made their way to a quiet corner and surveyed the room. They were situated next to one of the floor-to-ceiling windows, which afforded a glittering view. It was a rare clear night, and the city lights dazzled all the way out to the San Gabriel Mountain range. When it wasn't trying, LA could really be beautiful.

"She was... creepy," Lang said, dipping his head toward the air-kissing Cindy with the exclamation point. "I wonder if they did background checks on everyone."

Nina suddenly felt conspicuous among the black-tie set. "I certainly hope not."

The two were quiet for a time, lost in their own thoughts, watching the mostly grey-haired and well-fed attendees gladhand and backslap one another. Other than the attentive staff, Nina and Lang were the youngest people in the room.

Nina realized they were alone and had to engage in that most dreaded pastime the city reveled in, small talk. "So, how's work?"

"It's good. Been flat out but hoping to take a vacation sometime soon."

Being busy in Lang's profession wasn't exactly a benefi-cial aspect for society, Nina thought. Nobody really wanted a busy forensics photographer.

In her mind, Nina chanted, *Don't ask me, don't ask me.* Thankfully he moved on.

"How about you? Besides current circumstances," Lang's hand swept the room, "I imagine you'd be pretty busy."

Nina snorted and then, realizing Lang was serious, answered, "No. I'm not and I don't expect that to change anytime soon. Mickey was the only one who ever gave me regular jobs. And even with that, I can barely cover car costs and groceries."

"But you own your place though?"

Nina snorted. "I don't own it. Titus does, and he doesn't even charge me rent."

"Why not?"

Letting out a long, slow breath, Nina took a sip of champagne. "That's a long and complicated story." She cast her gaze skyward, remembering a past she'd prefer would stay buried, quite literally. "But needless to say, I don't know how long this agency will last without Mickey sending me charity jobs. I think it'll be over before it really got going. I might have to get a real job. You see me as a flipping burgers or calling people about their extended warranties kind of gal?"

"Neither of those are cool enough for Nina Maddox."

"Either of those will pay for Nina Maddox's cat food. Sputnik won't dine out on cool, I've tried. I'm serious, I don't think this private investigator thing is going to work out. I'm up against ex-cops, guys with twenty years' experience in this shit. It's tough. Way tougher than I thought it was going to be."

"You have something they don't."

Nina raised an eyebrow. "Tits?"

"No. Well, yes, especially in that dress, but no. Brains. You've figured all this Trank, Mickey, mayor stuff out on your own."

"I had help."

"But you drove it all, put it all together. None of this would have come to light if not for you. You're amazing, Nina. By all accounts, Mickey Boehler was a lot of things, but throwing money at charity for the hell of it wasn't one of them. He wouldn't have kept giving you those jobs unless you delivered. Mickey believed in you." He leaned closer to make sure he had her attention. "Maybe you should try to do the same."

Nina didn't respond, mainly because she didn't know how to. Compliments always made her uncomfortable. Coming from Lang, it only amplified her unease. Instead, she surveyed the room, doing her best to remind herself why she was here.

The two were quiet for a while, their attention drawn to an elderly couple who drifted to the center of an empty dance floor and began to dance. They held one another close and danced as if gray hair and wrinkles no longer existed. They moved as thought they were the only ones in the room. For the few in the crowd who weren't occupied with schmoozing and social climbing, it was a sweet and tender moment. The song finished and they left the dance floor to a smattering of applause.

"This is nice," Lang said after a while.

Nina shook her head slightly. "Waiting for a murderer is nice?"

"No, uh, I mean, um..."

"I'm only messing with you." She matched his cheerfulness. "I found myself getting caught up in it too, until I remembered why we're here."

"I meant it's nice to be out with you. In public. It's like a—"

"Don't. Please."

"—date." He took a sip of champagne for courage and added, "I know you have a lot going on and you probably don't want to talk about it, but Nina, we're great together, surely you can see that? The fact you're having fun despite the reason we're here means we should give this dating thing a go, surely?"

Lang was right about one thing: Nina didn't want to talk about it. Not now, at least.

She shifted uncomfortably from one high heel to the other. "This isn't the time..."

"It's never the time." There was an edge to his voice, like this had been festering for some time. "I'm going to lay it all out there. I love you, Nina. I do. I know you don't feel the same way, but you don't know me, the real me. But if we could date, see each other outside your bedroom walls, you could get to know that side of me. I'm not asking for your soul, I'm just asking for a chance."

For Nina, the conversation had gotten very heavy very fast, just when she needed the opposite. The earnestness of his delivery made her chest hurt. In his tuxedo, he more closely resembled a sad Labrador than a human.

In a city of phonies, Lang was the real deal.

And it was breaking Nina's heart.

Because she had to break his.

"I don't think this is the time..."

"No, Nina, it has to be now."

Lang's firm voice garnered a few glances. The two of them were now a sideshow, a couple having a relationship "discussion" in public. It was always a popular pastime for other couples, if for no other reason than to distract from their own tedious existence. Attention was something Nina had wanted to avoid at all costs.

"Armin," Nina rolled the champagne glass in her hands, choosing her words carefully.

"I don't remember you ever using my first name." He held up his hand. "The next words are going to be 'you're a nice guy' followed by a 'but,' right?"

"I was trying not to be as cliched as that," she sighed sadly, "but yep, something along those lines. I think you're an incredible human, amazing in fact, which is why I have to stop seeing you. It's not because I don't see your worth—the exact opposite, in fact. You deserve to be happy, you deserve to be with someone who can return the mountains of love you have to give."

Before the deflated Lang could reply, the mood in the room shifted. The lift doors opened to thunderous applause and Fleetwood Mac's 'Don't Stop' echoed through the room. Nina thought it was an odd choice; she'd always thought it was a break-up song. Mayor Bailey entered and pointed gleefully to supporters he might or might not know, shook hands, and waved to the crowd like a man taking a victory lap on election night.

When she turned her attention back to Lang, it was like she was watching the breaking of his heart in real time. He'd stepped up to the plate and taken a swing hoping for a home run, but had ended up striking out. If he didn't know it before, he certainly did now. They were done.

Nina felt like a heel for having to tell him in a public place like this, for not having chosen better words, but most of all for having dragged him along in the first place. She'd felt guilty enough to begin with, but after being cornered into confessing her feelings, or lack thereof, she felt she'd shattered his soul. Lang must have wanted to get as far away from her as possible. Instead, he was forced to stand beside her and play a part. It must have been hell.

As they stood there, side by side, Nina had never felt more alone. Everything about this night was wrong. She wanted to leave, perhaps not as much as Lang, but close. Thankfully, the mayor was glad-handing his way to their corner.

Cindy with the exclamation point guided the mayor in their direction.

"And this is Mr Armin Lang, and…?" She motioned to Nina.

Nina had developed a character for this very moment. Being herself would leave her the opportunity to lash out, but playing a role meant she'd need to stay within the parameters of the character. At least, that was the idea.

"Tangerine Cocks. A big fan." Nina extended a hand. "A big fan, sir. Big fan. That new airport terminal, wow. So terminaly."

"Why, thank you, Tangerine." Tod Bailey's forehead crinkled in confusion, but it didn't affect his crisp white smile.

He shook hands in the firm way politicians like, firm and decisive, though he did add a minor, virtually imperceptible caress to Nina's thumb. It was so quick, Nina would have missed it had she not been hyperaware.

"I have to tell you, I almost didn't make it here tonight." He leaned in conspiratorially. "The garage door wouldn't open—well, the clicker wouldn't open it, so I had to open it manually. You know, using the lever right up the top? Well, I'm no Michael Jordan, as you can tell."

Michael Jordan had just made a substantial debut at the

Olympics and had secured a shoe deal with Nike before he'd played a single NBA game. The kid was going places.

"So, I get this tiny little step ladder, reach up, but my jacket sleeve gets caught in the lever and slides open, and I'm like this." He held one arm up and balanced on one leg. "I can't reach up, I can't step down. I start calling out to Margarette, but the only one who came to my rescue was Scruffy, our Jack Russell Terrier. Unfortunately, he thought it was a game and started biting my ankle. The same ankle, I might add, that was stopping me from falling flat on my ass." He mimed waving off the dog while still attached to the door opener. "Needless to say, I was rescued by my good lady wife or I would have been stuck like that until after the election."

Lang and Nina both laughed, though due to her training, hers sounded more genuine than the forced one of Lang's. It was a funny, self-deprecating story. Likely one he'd told a dozen times already that night. Perhaps it was his go-to tale for every event, it could have been told a hundred or a thousand times. But the delivery was charismatic and intimate, as if the story was for them alone. Nina had to admire his technique. She'd known professional actors who couldn't deliver lines with that kind of authenticity.

Even though Nina had heard him countless times on the radio and in press conferences on the news, there was a presence about him that a cathode-ray tube couldn't convey. It was his gaze. It was affable, focused, and made you feel like you were the only other person in the room. There was a reason he mingled among the donors—three seconds with him made you *sure* you were right to part with your hard-earned cash.

It was hard for Nina to reconcile the genial man before

her and the horror scene she'd seen at The Crucible. This was the individual who had apparently done "something silly" to Alicia Morrison. Even knowing all this, the man in front of her didn't match the profile. Perhaps he was a better actor than Nina had ever been? She wasn't convinced of his innocence, but she was less sure than when she'd signed up for the event. And poorer.

Cindy with the exclamation point was already scanning for the next target, but Nina wasn't going to let this opportunity slide. She wanted to know Tod Bailey more.

"I didn't think an acting mayor could actively campaign for a senate seat."

The question didn't throw him at all, his affability remained firmly in place. "Oh, I'm on sabbatical. My deputy has taken over all official engagements. Once we know the results, I'll either resign or retake my duties."

"Surely you won't be returning, mayor? The polls have you taking the seat in a landslide."

He issued a polite politician's chortle. "One can never be so sure in politics. Anything can happen, hence why we're here." Bailey spread his arms wide, his politician's smile wider still.

"Wasn't it Roosevelt who said, 'In politics, nothing happens by accident. If it happens, you can bet it was planned that way'?"

All heads turned to Nina. An impressed pout creased Bailey's lips.

"That's a hell of a quote." He frowned approvingly. "I hope you don't mind if I steal it?"

"You better ask Roosevelt."

Mayor Bailey let loose a boisterous belly laugh. He placed his big hand on Nina's shoulder, head bobbing in amusement. Heads turned in their direction, jealous of the fun happening in the private little group.

Nina had to admit there was a magnetism to him. A charm that drew people into his orbit. He demanded attention. It was what made him the perfect politician. Or cult leader.

He bid them farewell with a hardy politician's double handed handshake and multiple thank yous before moving on to the next donor. It was a slick, well-oiled exchange.

Despite what they know about who and what he likely was, Nina noticed a small part of her being charmed. A very small part.

"You can't go through life on your own."

Turning to a Lang, who was standing beside her with his fists clenched, Nina assumed he'd been stewing on their previous discussion since being interrupted by the mayor. She mirrored his defensive stance.

"I can and I will."

The two of them stood, arms folded and defiant. This certainly wasn't how or where Nina wanted to have this discussion. The fact that she'd dragged him here for protection and he'd interpreted it as a date of sorts only made it worse.

She forced to herself to soften. "Listen, Lang, you don't have to stay. I'll be okay. There are so many cops here and I'll make sure I get a cab out front where I can be seen, and—"

"I'll stay."

The words were generous, but the tone suggested he'd rather smear honey over his nether regions and be thrown into a rabid bear's cage. She respected him for it, and it only depressed her more.

"I don't want you to." She went to touch his arm, but he

recoiled. "I'm sorry for dragging you here, getting you caught up in all this, everything really. You really are amazing, and you deserve—"

"Don't." His face softened. "Please." He cast his gaze to the high ceiling. "I hope you find happiness, Nina, even though you think you don't deserve it. I'll always be there when you need me," he gave her the saddest smile Nina had ever seen, "but I know you won't." He kissed her on the lips for what she knew was the last time. "Goodbye, Nina."

Watching him walk away, Nina felt stifled by a sadness she hadn't felt in the longest time. It wasn't a lamentation of failed relationship—another one—nor the fact she wouldn't see him again. It was what she'd put the poor bastard through. She truly believed she was toxic. Against her better judgment she'd let Lang in, and it had only scarred him. Never again, she vowed. After all this was done, she'd do some research about becoming a nun. She already wore a lot of black, surely it wouldn't be that different?

Time moved slowly as she watched the mayor schmooze his way around the room, regaling donors with his garage door story, his actions the same every time. He had the schtick down pat, but it worked. By the time he left, everyone in the room had been charmed, and he'd convinced the already eager crowd they'd placed their money on the right political horse.

The well-greased machine gave her no opportunity to talk to him again. Was the mayor a cold-blooded murderer? According to Rachael the waitress, he certainly was.

No doubt the night's festivities would continue for some time. She may be able to find a member of his staff or family to talk to, but she didn't like her chances. Unsure if the exercise had been worthwhile, Nina debated whether she should wait to see if Mayor Bailey made an encore appearance or just cut her losses and leave.

"Excuse me, Miss?"

Nina turned to see Cindy with the exclamation point. "Oh, hi."

"Ma'am, your boyfriend has asked us to come get you. He's fallen ill and requested you come assist him. He's downstairs, not well at all."

I told you not to touch those canapés.

"Thank you. How did you find me among all these people? You must have spoken to hundreds tonight."

Cindy replied, "He said to look for the stunning woman in the green dress."

Nina shook her head. "Smooth."

Regardless of how she'd ended things, Nina still cared for Lang. If he was sick, she'd look after him and make sure he got home safe. It was the least she could do.

Cindy motioned for Nina to follow, so she put down her champagne, picked up her purse and was led to a different elevator than the one they'd ridden up in. Cindy pressed the button for her and gave a sympathetic press of her lips before turning away. She was already craning her neck, searching the crowd for her next donor to schmooze.

When the lift arrived, Cindy disappeared into the sea of the rich and powerful without even saying goodbye. Alone in the elevator, Nina hit the button for the lobby, overcome with concern for Lang. He must have been in a dire way to come back, and even more so to request her assistance.

She'd take him to his sister's place in Encino, but wouldn't stay. That would send far too many mixed messages for the poor guy. Suddenly exhausted, she longed for her own bed, but then remembered Pellicano and Valentine. Titus's pull-out couch would have to do.

The elevator doors slid open and Nina stepped forward, lost in her thoughts, then stopped herself when she realized it wasn't the ground floor. The elevator had stopped on the third. Stepping back, she pressed lobby again. It didn't light up, nor did the doors close. Nina tried hitting the door close button, but it didn't work. She pressed the button for the lobby again, then for the floors above and below. Nothing. She tried the 27th floor from where she'd come and got the same result. There was no call button, the elevator was too old for that. Despite hitting all the buttons on the board, including *Emergency Stop*, the elevator remained completely stationary.

The corridor before her was lit up, as was the elevator, so the electricity was clearly still working, but the elevator refused to move.

What the hell?

There were no doors in the immediate area, just an empty reception desk facing the elevator. Behind that was a long dark corridor with no doors along its length, except for one at the very end.

"Hello?"

The only response was an empty echo. She reluctantly stepped out of the elevator and headed for the reception desk. Picking up the handset, Nina's briefest moment of hope was dashed when she didn't hear a dial tone. Knowing it was a useless movie cliché, she nevertheless jiggled the button in the cradle, but the telephone stayed defiantly dead.

Nina felt more and more like a rat in a maze. Hand delving into her purse, she extracted her Beretta. If she was going to be a lab rat, she was going to be a lab rat with teeth.

Making her way down the wood-paneled corridor, past

black and white photos of Los Angeles of old, Nina's foot-falls reverberated off the walls. She eventually reached a door stenciled with the number 300. When she came within knocking distance, the door swung silently open.

If Nina wasn't already gripping her pistol tightly, she would be now.

"Hello?"

The dark office was lit by a solitary banker's lamp on a desk in the center of the room. Its walls were lined with bookshelves and paintings of starched white stiffs in stern poses. A lone figure sat behind the imposing desk. Their features were draped in shadow, but Nina had no illusions as to the person's identity.

Taking a step into the office, Nina held her gun in front of her. "Listen, I don't know what sort of sick game you're playing at here, but—"

The door slammed behind her. The veiled figure retracted his hand from a button concealed beneath the desk. The only part of his face she could see wore a conceited leer that hadn't been present when she'd seen him an hour before.

"Hello, Miss Maddox." The mayor's tone was even and well-practiced; pleasant. "I think it's time you and I became better acquainted."

"Can I offer you a drink?" The mayor motioned to an antique globe drinks cabinet in front of a floor to ceiling bookshelf.

"Thank you, no," Nina replied faux pleasantly, "I've given up drug-laden alcohol for lent."

Bailey shook his head with faux amusement. "I assure you, Nina, you have the wrong idea about me."

"I assure *you*, I don't. Unless you give all your constituents fake news about their date's health, hijack their elevator, and lock them in your office, I'm pretty sure I have a *very* accurate idea about you."

"All I want to do is talk."

"The rapey self-locking door says otherwise."

"I'm interested in you, Nina."

"You are? From what I hear, I'm a little old for your tastes."

At least that got a reaction. For the briefest of moments there was a drop in his self-assured deportment, a slip in his armor. It lasted a fraction of a second.

The mayor regarded the gun in her hand. "Are you going to shoot me?"

"The thought had crossed my mind."

"Well, it's certainly your prerogative. Here I am, unarmed and defenseless, the most respected politician in the city—not an extensive brag, to be sure, but a correct one. With witnesses upstairs, surveillance footage of you entering the lift, coming into my office and shooting me with your own gun, no less. Who brings a firearm to a fundraiser, I ask you?" He shook his head. "I wonder how shooting me dead would turn out for you…"

"Maybe I could just wound you," Nina suggested. "Like, shoot you in the dick?"

"Quite vulgar, aren't you?"

"If you think that's vulgar you're in for a fucken' ride." Nina huffed. "I'm sure I could explain a great many things that would get me out of it."

"Is that so?" Bailey asked, like a man who knew the precise answer to his question. "Even after you fled Mickey Boehler's house in such mysterious circumstances?" He reveled in Nina's shock. "Fleeing the scene of a crime can be a serious criminal offense, you know? And you've confessed that particular crime to an officer of the law. That's a felony conviction; you're likely to do prison time."

Damn you, Birmingham! Nina didn't know if he'd just done his job by reporting her phone call to his superiors, or if he was working directly with the mayor. She had more important things to worry about right now.

Why had Bailey cornered her? Had he drawn a link between Mickey's death and her work as a private investigator? That's what he wanted to know, Nina realized; what she knew.

"My, you are creating quite the ruckus, aren't you Ms

Maddox? All these murders and there you are, right in the middle. Such an amazing coincidence, don't you think? Are you sure you'd be able to talk your way out of the murder of a senior civil servant in cold blood?"

Nina ground her teeth. "What's all this for, luring me here? What do you think you're going to achieve?"

"I want to get to know you, that's all. Get a measure of you. Ask you a few questions."

"What sort of questions?"

Placing his palms flat on the table, he leaned forward, the sole lamp illuminating his face. "What's the worst pain you've ever felt?"

The abrupt pivot shocked her, as did the question itself. Nina suddenly felt very cold, and very, very alone.

Nina hoped she portrayed more bravado than she truly felt. Not that she'd ever give Bailey the satisfaction of knowing this, but she was terrified. She felt trapped, overwhelmed, and suffocated. The office walls seemed to be closing in around her, like an invisible cage, where the very thought of breaking free only tightened the bars around her. Yes, she held a gun, but Nina couldn't shake the fear of being trapped alone with this man. He truly was the personification of evil. The air grew staler with each passing moment.

"You like to inflict pain, do you?" The gun was heavy but secure in her hand.

"It can be most blissful when delivered by an expert hand, believe me." He settled into his seat, either reveling in the subject or in Nina's reaction to it. "So long as vital oxygenation and nutrition is maintained, one can suffer pain to the point of syncope—that's fainting, for the uninitiated—over and over again. There are ways to prolong the experience for virtually unlimited amounts of time. The pleasure can run on for days, literally."

"Only, when you're the one inflicting the pain it's not pleasure, it's torture."

"Oh, please. I thought you would be more open-minded than the plebians and prudes." He leaned forward, warming to the subject. "Pleasure and pain are inexplicably interlinked, both tied to the interacting dopamine and opioid systems in the brain." He slowly ran his fingers up his arm, closing his eyes as if reliving an experience. "They regulate neurotransmitters which drive reward-driven behaviors. Our brains are literally built for it, you just have to experience the right... stimulus to be unleashed from the pedestrian Protestant mores." He opened his eyes, as if remembering Nina was there. "Pain can open your mind. The experience can set you free."

"I've seen how your pain experiences turn out." Nina gripped her weapon tight. "I won't let you get away with it."

"What exactly am I getting away with, my dear?"

"Alicia Morrison."

That gave him pause. Not even his decades of experience with press conferences and debates could enable him to conceal the blatant shock on his face.

"Oh, that poor girl who turned up dead?" He gave a phony concerned shake of his head. "Such a waste. You look like her, you know?" He leaned back and waved a lazy hand at her. "A few more winkles, years under your belt. Shame the two of us didn't meet ten years ago."

"I would have been sixteen."

He shrugged with a sleazy smirk. The man was the human equivalent of slime.

"The little performance you do for the crowd, the aww

shucks genial nice guy act, it's all to mask what you really are. How many other underaged girls have you got in your closet, mayor? How many other Alicias are there?"

He swallowed hard, doing a reasonable job of regaining his composure. "I do hope you're not insinuating what I think you are?"

"I'm not insinuating anything." Nina lowered her gaze, her voice like a steel hammer. "I'm saying it right out loud: you murdered Alicia Morrison."

"Well, that's…" He rubbed his smooth chin, then straightened up as if he'd given himself a pep talk. "You have no proof of these wild allegations, of course. If you did, you'd be speaking to the authorities, not crashing my event. For you to suggest that I had anything to do with that young woman's disappearance is preposterous in the extreme. I'll have you sued for libel sooner than you can say—"

"Have they told you yet?"

His annoyance at being interrupted was evident. "Told me what? Who are you talking about?"

Nina weighed up how much to give away. Then again, the alternative could push Mayor Bailey into believing she had more than she actually did.

"Pellicano and his security goon from The Crucible. The ones who recently took over Mickey's operation of the club."

She watched the cogs clicking within his skull. His face showed recognition at the name, not confusion. So Pellicano had probably been introduced to Bailey at some stage. He knew who she was referring to.

"And what about them?"

"Have they told you about the video they have of you?

The video of you in the Arbuckle Room with Alicia? When you murdered her?"

There was no masking the panic in his face. The pure, unadulterated fear. "The what?"

"You look pained. Is that pleasurable for you now?" Nina frowned. "Seems you don't have all the facts, hey Tod? Didn't you wonder why new management took over recently? Why all the rooms got a tiny bit smaller?"

"I... I..."

"See, they put in cameras, behind those new mirrors in the rooms. They've been filming members. Blackmailing them. They were going to blackmail you with Alicia's murder, but some knuckleheads stole the videotape. That video is why they killed Mickey, the man you called in to clean up your mess. You're the reason he died. And Mickey's not the only one they've killed. The body count is up to five now. All because of the video of you murdering Alicia Morrison in cold blood. And they want that video back. To blackmail you."

Nina neglected to add, *but it got destroyed because one of the aforementioned knuckleheads hid it in Hank Trank's oven, like a total moron.*

The mayor's mouth seemed dry all of a sudden. He grew pale.

"You're bluffing."

"Why else would they kill Mickey?"

"He owed them money, or something. Or he fucked someone's wife, or made too many shitty movies. I don't know, and I certainly don't care."

"The perspiration on your forehead tells a different story there, Toddy boy."

"So, you came here to blackmail me? Is that it?"

"No, not at all. I came here to get a measure of you. I have that now. So, I'll be on my way."

Nina took a step toward the closed door.

He stood up quickly. "This videotape you claim exists—a forgery, for certain, but—"

"I know exactly where it is. It's in my possession."

Nina wasn't lying about that, at least. The mayor stepped around the desk, but kept his distance, an attempt not to scare her. He addressed her with open palms.

"If you know where this obvious forgery resides, I'm sure I can arrange for it to be removed from circulation in a way that would satisfy all parties involved."

"I'll tell you what, mayor, you open that door right now and let me get the hell out of this rape den unharmed, and I'll think about it." She waggled the gun in her hand as a reminder. "And just so we're crystal clear, my people have strict instructions outlining what to do with the tape if I don't arrive at a designated place by a certain time." She checked her watch. "And oh gee, I better get going or the headline in tomorrow's *LA Times* is going to be a doozy."

She stared him down until he retreated to the other side of the desk and pressed the button underneath it. The door swung open silently.

"Maddox."

Nina turned to the marble face of death.

"If there's one thing I know in politics, it's that the smart ones always play the long game. And I tell you now, I'm playing the long game with you, Missy. You have no idea who you're dealing with. You fuck with me again, you'll find out just how long I can play this game for. You understand me?"

Nina turned and walked out of the room. The entire city, the country even, thought they knew who he was.

They didn't. They had absolutely no idea. But Nina knew. He was the personification of evil.

She made her way down the paneled hallway, glancing over her shoulder to ensure the mayor stayed in his office. Nina made herself a promise. She would make him pay for what he'd done. Even if she had to burn the whole stinking city down to do it.

NINA TOOK FOUR CABS, swapping in public places, cutting through buildings and doubling back to ensure she wasn't followed. All the while, she was consumed with one thought: she'd come face to face with pure malevolence. No amount of showers could wash away the filthy veneer coating her skin. She felt hollowed out, like all the good in her had been cleaved away, never to return.

How had he been able to operate in public life for so long? Given his reactions, she doubted Alicia was his first victim. Perhaps she had been, and there had been a slow progression to that murder over the years, each step more heinous and diabolical than the last. Or maybe he'd been murdering for years, his public easygoing persona a shield against being discovered.

Nina had no more evidence than when she'd arrived at City Hall. Rachael had witnessed the murder scene, said Bailey made her call Mickey to clean it up, but she'd already fled the country. But evidence wasn't everything. Nina knew to her very core that Tod Bailey had murdered Alicia Morrison. Now all she had to do was prove it. As the cab turned onto Titus's street, Nina tapped her teeth, racking her brain as to how to do exactly that. All she ended up with was a headache and sore teeth.

A relieved Trank and Phoebe greeted her with bear hugs and questions. Phoebe's face was lathered in an overnight mask, and Trank wore Titus's home remedy cream to heal his shiners. It seemed to be doing the job—he was less bruised than he had been hours before.

Over cocoa, she debriefed them in the kitchen. Titus joined them, claiming he was there for the cocoa, but he followed every thread as Nina brought them up to speed.

Once she was done, even though it was late, Nina called Lang's sister to ensure he was alright. She confirmed he'd made it there fine and didn't have food poisoning, but he'd refused to speak to Nina. Nina asked his sister to pass on her thanks for the evening and to apologize, for everything. The sister agreed to do so, though her confusion was evident in her tone.

Nina rubbed her temples, suddenly exhausted. Her brain was fried from the information she'd uncovered, the interweaving threads and possible strategies to take. She needed sleep. She needed this to be over.

Bidding her friends goodnight, she went to the bathroom to wash her face and brush her teeth. She found it amusing that Trank and Phoebe were sharing a bedroom. Her bestie was sleeping in her childhood bed while Trank slept on an equally small mattress on the floor. It was a far cry from his gargantuan bed in his mansion, though Nina knew he was in no hurry to sleep in that bed again.

As she finished in the bathroom, Titus propped himself against the doorframe, arms folded and casual.

"Hey, Nina," Titus's voice was its usual molasses laced with shards of glass. "Sounds like you got yourself plenty of enemies. Gangsters, ex-CIA security, the mayor, who knows who else. You don't got a lot of muscle on your side." His large brown eyes peered deep into her soul. "I wanted you to know, you got me."

Nina's heart swelled. "That means everything, thank you Titus. You're worth more than all of those bastards combined."

Titus gave her a tilt of his head and sauntered to his bedroom.

Buoyed by the big man's rare words of support, Nina made up the pull-out couch in the lounge. Her very bones were tired. Burying herself beneath the sheets and musty-smelling blankets, her head hit the pillow and her heavy eyes fell shut.

But sleep didn't come.

She rolled onto one side, then the next. Eventually, she gave up and stared at the ceiling, completely awake. *Shut up, stupid brain, I need to sleep.*

Her stupid brain didn't listen. Its cogs clicked and whirred, unable to be still. For the next three hours, Nina sifted through facts, theories, strategies, memories, and fears. A ceaseless cavalcade of information.

Somewhere around 3 am an idea hit her. A ludicrous, absolutely bananas idea, so much so she literally laughed out loud.

After churning through the various permutations and consequences, she was reasonably sure her ludicrous plan *might* work. It was certainly on the bold side.

Her inaction may have cost Mickey his life, and she sure as hell wasn't going to make that mistake again. She had to take the fight to the people who'd caused this immense loss of life. Hanging around and hoping for the best was no longer an option. She would do whatever it took.

When she could think of no further counterarguments for her plan, she stood and walked down the dark corridor to her best friend's childhood bedroom. Without a word, she flicked the light switch, waking Phoebe and Trank, who both jumped with a start.

"What the hell!" Phoebe rubbed her eyes. "This better be an earthquake or so help me god..."

"What's going on?" Trank was bordering on adorable in Titus's old-school nightgown.

"So, you know The Crucible?" Nina asked.

Phoebe's sleepy face creased into confusion. "The what?"

"The Crucible. You know it?"

Blinking several times, as if her brain was booting up as slowly as her clunking computer, Phoebe said, "The place where those guys who actively want us dead hang out?"

"Yeah, that place," Nina replied energetically.

"What about it?"

"I want to break in there again," Nina slapped her hands together, "tonight."

CHAPTER

TWENTY

"This may be the dumbest thing you've ever made me do," Phoebe said nervously, staring at the exterior of The Crucible from the front seat of her Toyota Shitbox.

"No way." Nina took a bite of her roast tomato, basil, and parmesan mini quiche. "Remember the time we went to your work Christmas party dressed as characters from the *Rocky Horror Picture Show*? I've never seen so many accountants choke on their cheese and crackers in my life. You'd think we turned up naked."

"You practically did."

"Okay, yeah, I can see that, but did I bring it or what?"

"Oh, you brought it." Phoebe flashed Nina a broad grin. "I'm not sure they knew what *it* was though, or indeed, what to do with *it* when it arrived."

"Fucken' squares."

From the back seat, Trank took a pastry from the Tupperware container Nina offered him and shook his head. "As previously stated, you two have a very strange relationship."

Unlike the first time Trank said those words back, his statement now was laced with affection. Having been through so much in a short amount of time, they had formed a close bond. They'd fallen into casual banter like they'd been a team for years.

It had taken little effort to convince the pair to come onboard with Nina's harebrained scheme. They both jumped in feet first. Nina wasn't sure if it was the persuasiveness of her argument or their friendship that propelled them to agree so readily, but gratefully accepted their help either way.

Nina had tried to talk Trank out of coming along. While his physical wounds were healing, the internal ones would require a lot more time. And therapy. But Trank had refused all reasoning and insisted he come along. Nina was thankful, as his presence was comforting, but also essential.

It was close to 5 am. As they had last time, they waited for the last of The Crucible's stragglers to leave before the staff and security closed up for the night. At least this time they had better snacks. They munched and waited. Waited and munched.

Eventually the last of the limousines pulled away, followed by the staff. The last vehicle to exit was a black van. Exiting the front seat, Mr Crew Cut himself, Valentine strode up and locked the roller door before sliding into the driver's seat and leaving.

Nina hadn't spotted Pellicano in any of the vehicles, but that didn't mean he hadn't been chauffeured away in one of the cars with tinted windows. They waited another fifteen minutes before Nina cracked her neck.

"We ready, gang?" she asked.

"Uh, what about Tony the tiger in there?" Phoebe asked.

"What the what?" Trank asked, sitting up.

"Last time we were here we had a run-in with a tiger."

"Define run-in."

"It attacked us, but we managed to trap it in the gambling room. It seemed pretty cozy, liked it hung out there a lot."

Trank rubbed his stubbled chin. "I've heard guests brag about petting a tiger in one of the rooms, but I always assumed it was the drugs talking. Are you saying there's an actual tiger roaming the halls?"

"Potentially. But this time we'll be ready." Nina hefted a plastic-wrapped mound of meat.

"Ah, what's that?" Phoebe asked.

"A four-pound beef roast."

"I mean, where did you get it?"

"Titus's fridge."

"Pretty sure he was saving that for Sunday roast."

"I think we'll make better use of it."

Nina was still worried about the beast, but wanted to move on quickly before the others became too spooked. Images of Mickey's death motivated her to keep going. She wouldn't wait for fate to come for her; she'd attack it with all she had.

"Are you two ready?" she asked.

"Hell yeah!" Phoebe responded enthusiastically.

"I guess."

Nina and Phoebe turned to Trank, who held up his hand defensively.

"I'm here for support, it's just, every time I go anywhere with you Nina, I get shot at, kidnapped, or tortured. Now it sounds like I might wind up being mauled to death."

Phoebe raised her eyebrows. "The man has a point."

"Dude, I tried to talk you out of it!"

Trank was smiling now. "I know, and I love you for it.

But this all started with me, and I'm going to help you end it. You've been through so much, the very least I can do is protect you."

"You know you're not really Vengeance Inc., right?"

"Two Emmy nominations say otherwise."

The three exited the car. Nina carried her usual break-in bag, Phoebe carried a new bag with everything they'd need to execute Nina's daft plan. She nudged Trank playfully, thankful he was here. The action star really wasn't one for actual action. Nina knew how hard it must have been for Trank to come back to this place, where he'd once enjoyed a debauched, carefree time but that now held sinister memories.

Trank had nearly died at Valentine's hands. Beaten and broken, he would have been tortured to death if not for Nina. This place was no longer a sanctuary, but a reminder of how close to death he'd come. Yet here he was, walking beside her into the last place he'd want to be. Nina wondered if it was, at least in part, to win back a piece of himself. No longer a reluctant accomplice, on this mission Trank was actively engaged. It may have been his kidnapping and subsequent torture, or it may have been the growing friendship, Nina wasn't sure, but Trank was fully committed to bringing those responsible for their plight to justice.

Phoebe gave Nina a friendly nudge of her own. "He said he loved you." She flicked her head in Trank's direction. "Hank and Nina, sitting in a tree…"

"What are you, like, twelve?"

"I've had a lot of Kool-Aid and I have to pee."

"Good to know."

Making their way across the street, they scanned for any sign of Valentine. Having mastered them once, Nina worked the locks more expertly this time. They made their way across the parking lot and through the front doors. The big bolt that had previously been closed was completely absent, and the main door was open. Still, they entered cautiously, braced for a tiger attack at any moment.

The place felt darker this time, more sinister. It had only been three days, but it seemed like months.

They carefully searched the place twice, ensuring no one else was present and there were no tigers.

Their earlier banter was absent now; the reality of what had taken place within these walls made frivolity distasteful. They had a precise mission, and nothing would distract them from it. Except for when Phoebe had to pee. After *that*, nothing could distract them.

It took less than an hour to do what they needed to. When their mission was complete, Nina felt both repulsed and relieved. Though she was unsure if her plan would work, they'd done everything they needed for it to at least play out, and then it was out of her hands.

They descended the stairs, each lost in their own thoughts. Phoebe was ahead of them, particularly eager to leave. When she reached the ground floor she froze, staring at the bar. Nina heard a distinct clink of glass, followed by a grunt of frustration.

Nina stuck out her hand to halt Trank's descent. Before he could utter a word of protest she thrust her index finger to her lips, silencing him. Her wide eyes conveyed the message all too clearly: *we're not alone.*

"Oh, hello," the disembodied voice in the bar said in a friendly tone.

Phoebe's head turned slowly toward her friend. She knew who was in the bar and she didn't want to be there. Nina recognized the voice and didn't want to be there either. Nina and Trank were stuck like statues, halfway down the stairs, unwilling to move for fear of alerting this new party to their presence.

Nina racked her brain. They'd checked the rooms twice; the newcomer must have entered when they'd been otherwise occupied. Frozen in place, Nina knew they had to make a move, *any* move. They couldn't leave Phoebe, and besides, there were no exits upstairs, no doors or windows to the outside. In the end, it was a decision they didn't have to make.

"Are you lot coming down or not?"

There was no hiding now, they'd been made. They could only face whatever lay in wait for them. The three of them had a destiny to confront.

Nina descended the stairs, joining Phoebe and clutching her hand tightly. She heard Trank's size-fourteen shoes clumping behind, moving at a glacial pace as if eager to delay the inevitable. They slowly made their way into the luxurious bar. Behind it, a dish towel over his shoulder and a cocktail shaker in hand, was Valentine. He wore his full tuxedo, though his tie was undone and hanging from his collar.

He put the shaker on the bar. "I've made mojitos, I hope that's alright with everyone." As if reading her mind, he jiggled his Desert Eagle pistol and aimed it directly at Nina. "Bags on the floor and hands in the air, thank you."

He rounded the bar, pistol at the ready. As she and Phoebe raised their arms, Nina noticed Trank's were sagging limply by his sides.

"Hank." Nina lifted her hands to emphasize the point.

He just stared at her blankly, as if she'd spoken in Swahili. Trank was in shock. The man who had kidnapped, tortured and had certainly been going to kill him was now before them, holding a gun. Trank no doubt suspected, like Nina, that Valentine was intent on starting the whole process again. The man was frozen in fear. Nina didn't blame him.

Valentine gave them a cursory frisk and returned to the bar to pour four cocktails. "With everything going on, I couldn't sleep, so I came back for a nightcap. And what did I hear? You lot, clomping around upstairs. I swear I thought it was the Harlem Globetrotters practicing up there." When no one said a word, he went on. "I assume you're the ones who locked the tiger in there the other night." He motioned to the gambling room. "Always thought the tiger was ridiculous, to be honest, but the new owner insisted it added an outlandish element. Given that it proved to be completely ineffective as night security, we sold it to some exotic zoo in Oklahoma." He waved his glass, dismissing the subject. "Now, the only question I have is," his face twisted into a sinister sneer, "who's going first?"

With zero leverage and absolutely no chance of rescue, Nina decided to call on her acting skills and do the only thing she could. Bluff.

"It's over, Valentine." Nina projected a boredom she most certainly didn't feel. "The authorities have it all—Pellicano's takeover of the club, the mayor, the murders of the stuntmen, everything. Your little house of cards is falling; by the end of the day there'll be nothing left but a pile of, well, cards. I'm going to give you the chance you wouldn't give us. I'm going to let you walk out of here. It's a one-time offer, so walk now or bring everything down on your own head. You have ten seconds."

Valentine chuckled. "Damn, woman, I have to say, you got some big hairy balls on you." He handed each of them a glass, never lowering the Desert Eagle. "To even try that when you're unarmed and have zero leverage, you must be one tough bitch."

Nina crossed her arms. "I'm so tough my tampons are made from C4."

"Jesus fuck, Nina," Phoebe said, half amused, half shocked.

"Too much?"

"Too much, girl."

"Should I have said barbed wire?"

"Maybe you could have said nothing at all."

"No, that doesn't sound like me."

Amused by the exchange, Valentine took a sip of his mojito, which also appeared to please him. Trank, on the other hand, stood mute and quietly terrified.

"What made you come back here?" Valentine asked casually. His faux-nonchalant manner belied his tension. He was a lethal spring, ready to murder at the slightest provocation.

"Curiosity. I hear the chicken wings are to die for."

Valentine ground his teeth, his growing agitation evident. "Why are you here? Surely this is the last place you should be, either of you." He gestured to Nina and Trank. "I mean, we IDed you, we've been searching the city. Why on earth would you come to the one place you knew we might be?"

Phoebe glanced at Nina. "You can't argue with that logic."

Ignoring Phoebe, Valentine moved on. "So, Miss Maddox, why are you and Mr Trank here?"

Nina couldn't reveal the true nature of their break-in; that would ruin the surprise for everyone involved. Her brain was still searching for an out.

Admiring the gun in his hands, Valentine said, "And

before you answer, know that the time for witty quips is over." He raised the gun. "Don't make me ask you a second time. It's late, I've been drinking," he hefted his glass for emphasis, "and my patience is very thin."

He had been drinking, Nina could tell. And not just in the last ten minutes. His words were slurred, his movements sluggish. He wasn't exactly drunk, but nor was he completely sober. Nina recalled when he and Pellicano had murdered Mickey. Valentine had been drinking that night too; his boss had chastised him for it.

Think, Nina rebuked herself. *Use this.* Why was this buttoned-up, ex-CIA agent getting a buzz on at his place of work, alone, at six in the morning? His line about not being able to sleep was thin at best.

Was he a closet alcoholic? Was this a usual activity for him, drinking the boss's liquor? Was it guilt over what he'd done to Mickey and the others? Nina dismissed that notion. He could have simply said no and walked away if he'd deemed it distasteful or immoral.

What then? Could it be that Nina's bluff was more accurate than she suspected? Was the house of cards falling? *What's changed?*

The sound of shattering glass interrupted her thoughts. Valentine had thrown his mojito across the room, and now he rounded the bar, face red and taut. Nina had taken too long to answer.

Waving the gun in her face, Valentine screamed, "I asked you a goddamn question!"

Nina wasn't entirely sure how the next few seconds unfolded.

One moment, Valentine was advancing on her, the next he'd lifted into the air and was hurtling toward the wood-paneled wall. Trank had dipped a shoulder and charged at the security manager like a demented line-backer. The tackle caught the man on his side and propelled him into the wall with the force of a battering ram. The impact dislodged Valentine's gun, which flew from his hand and clattered to the parquet floor. The stunned man collapsed like a rag doll, leaving a cracked indent in the wooden wall.

Trank wasn't done yet.

He grabbed Valentine's limp right leg. There was no protest; the prone man was dazed. Trank gripped the man's ankle in his meaty left hand, raised his right elbow and then, like a wrestler in the ring, dropped his full body weight onto Valentine's extended leg.

The crack was as loud as a whip crack.

His primal scream engulfed the room.

Trank rolled himself off the writhing man, furious tears streaming down his cheeks. Valentine's exclamations of pain disintegrated into pathetic keening as he cradled his broken leg. Trank scrambled across the floor to the discarded pistol. Rising to his feet, he shuffled toward the prone man, gun arm rising as he did.

Valentine was in shock, but conscious enough to cower as Trank aimed the gun at his head. An unhinged Trank pulled back the hammer.

Nina stepped between them, hands raised, non-threateningly. "Hank..."

His frenzied eyes swung toward her.

"You don't want to do this. You don't want to become like him."

Trank remained mute for a moment before unleashing a toothy grin. "Oh, I'm not going to shoot him." Everyone in the room relaxed, except Valentine. "I'm just going to hold it here for a while."

"How long?" Nina retained her position between the two combatants.

"A century, maybe two."

"Won't your arm get tired?"

"We could take turns."

"Or," Nina stepped forward and delicately extracted Trank's sweaty hand from the pistol, "we could…"

Nina was going to suggest taking him to the nearest police station, but that didn't work with her other plan, which was currently in play. They couldn't leave a man with a clearly broken leg writhing in pain. Nor could they let him go.

Think.

Nina did exactly that. As the plan coalesced in her mind, a wide grin spread across her face. Trank and Phoebe reeled. Valentine just whimpered.

"Hey Hank, you mentioned there was a buffet of drugs here for the members. Where's that at?"

Coming out of his stupor, Trank asked, "Is that wise for someone who's had their leg broken?"

"I don't know," Nina replied. "Do you care?"

"Actually, no, I don't."

"There you go."

Trank walked over to a large antique dresser and opened the drawers. He came back with several small vials.

"Uh," Phoebe raised a finger, apprehension clear on her face, "what's going on?"

Nina explained what she had in mind. Her two friends stared at her blankly.

Phoebe was the first to speak. "Will it work?"

"There's only one way to find out." Nina tucked Valentine's pistol down the back of her jeans. "It's time to bring this whole thing to a close." She motioned to Valentine. "He wasn't part of the original plan, but he's in it now. Listen," she softened her tone, seeing her friends' concern, "none of us chose this, none of us want to be caught in the middle of this nightmare, but we're here now. These powerful men think they're untouchable, but we're going to show them they're mistaken. The mayor, Pellicano, they're not untouchable, they're not invulnerable. They're just men. Petty, frail, fallible, imperfect little men." She lowered her gaze. "And we're going to take them all down."

CHAPTER

TWENTY-ONE

"Hello?"

The voice echoed against the antique beveled mirrors and oak wainscoting. The man entered the elegant bar tentatively, taking in the red leather booths, the antique brass lamps. He noticed Nina and Phoebe, but his attention was immediately drawn to the motionless body on the parquet floor.

"Let me guess, Maddox, another dead body?"

"Not this time, Birmingham. This one's alive."

"My, haven't you changed?" As he drew closer, the homicide detective noted Valentine's glassy-eyed stare and the odd angle of his leg. "He doesn't seem to be in a good way, though."

"I haven't changed that much."

"What's all this about?"

Scratching the back of her neck, Nina motioned to the bar. "I think you're going to need a drink."

"It's seven o'clock in the morning."

"And?"

"I'm fine."

The detective wasn't in a receptive mood. Nina didn't exactly blame him. Over the last week she'd given him the run around with half-truths, misdirection, and outright lies. It was time to come clean. It was time to show all her cards.

"Where do you want me to start?"

"The beginning would be good."

"It's not going to be as easy as all that."

"Try." He folded his arms, and his features settled into his trademark resting scowl.

Nina tugged at the end of her ponytail. "I keep calling you with dead bodies and whatnot…"

"I'm well aware of that."

"You might need adjust the body count a smidge."

He pointed at Valentine. "I thought you said you'd changed."

"I'm not reporting another dead body. How about I raise one from the dead for you instead?"

Birmingham blinked several times. "Have you finally lost your mind, Maddox?"

"That body you have in the morgue."

"You're going to have to be more specific."

"The first one. Trank."

"What about it?"

"It's not."

"Not what? Dead? I think the medical examiner knows what he's doing."

"No. It's very dead. It's just not Hank Trank."

Nina watched Birmingham's face intently. There wasn't the usual anger, just exhaustion. He made a noise she couldn't quite name. It may have been the sound of his brain short-circuiting.

"What the hell are you—"

"The body you have in the LA morgue is Seth Wagner. He was staying at Trank's place as a guest. He was his stunt double, hence the similarity between them. Hank Trank is alive and well."

Like the good actor he was, hearing his cue, Trank entered the bar from the office. He flashed his pearly whites like it was a red carpet, extended a hand and offered a chipper, "Hello!"

Birmingham's jaw dropped like a cartoon cat. His head swiveled to Nina, then to Trank, back to Nina, back to Trank. He glanced at Phoebe, who waved, then he turned back to Nina.

"What the actual fuck is going on!" He placed his hand on the back on a booth. "You're... You're going to give me a heart attack, woman. I can't..." Birmingham's gaze drifted to the bar. "I think I'll have that drink now." He pointed at Nina. "Start talking."

Nina did. Over gin and tonics, she told Birmingham everything, leaving nothing out. By the bottom of the second G&T he'd stopped shaking his head. When she finally finished, there was a full minute of silence.

"Even if I believed every piece of this cock and bull story..."

"There's definitely more cock than bull, I assure you."

"... most of this is a legal nightmare."

Nina turned to the prone body on the floor. "Everything I said is true, isn't it Valentine?"

The ex-CIA agent's head flopped like his neck was made of Jell-O. He turned toward Nina and gave her a sloppy thumbs up. "Correctamundo, Cap'n. I killed 'em all, except for Mickey Bolger. Boggler. Boligler. That guy. Pellicano did the 'ol pew pew on him," he slurred, making finger guns.

Nina turned to Birmingham and thrust her palms toward the pleasantly glazed Valentine.

Birmingham led Nina away, out of earshot, toward the open door of the gambling room. The cop cut himself short and stared at the room, slack-jawed. "Jesus. What is this place?"

"A den of sin and iniquity. What did you want to say?"

The homicide detective flicked a thumb at Valentine. "He's hopped off his brain, any confession would be inadmissible."

Nina steepled her fingers and placed her index fingers on her chin. "True, but Pellicano doesn't know that."

Still distracted by the gambling tables, Birmingham turned to Nina. "What?"

Nina's smile was as broad as her idea. "Call Pellicano in. Tell him Valentine has confessed everything, which is technically the truth, you won't even be lying. Then you separate them and play them off one another. Say Valentine is going to throw him under the bus unless he lays down some truth. Pellicano'll sing like the Partridge Family. They already despise each other. Valentine hates that he's been forced to kill all these guys; he's become an alcoholic. They'll turn on one another, guaranteed. You'll have the full story. Slap down a confession in front of them and they'll rat one another out, you watch."

Birmingham shook his head. It wasn't his usual disgruntled demeanor, it was slightly more amused. "Damn, woman. You're thinking like a cop."

"I have absolutely no idea how to take that. How many female homicide cops do you have?"

"Including the last one we hired?"

"Yes."

"None."

"Thought so." Nina inhaled deeply. "So, what happens now?"

"I call everyone in."

～

AN HOUR LATER, the private and intimate club more closely resembled a bustling police station. Multiple divisions fell over themselves to gather evidence. Vice, narco, homicide, gambling control, bunko. Nina wouldn't have been surprised if they'd thrown in highway patrol for the hell of it. Every available law enforcement resource was sent to pick over the rotting corpse of The Crucible. The law enforcement officials who had taken bribes to look the other way—and there would surely be plenty of those—couldn't prevent the shitstorm that was about to rain down on the once-secret club.

The entire building was writhing with cops. Gambling control were inspecting the gaming room, narcos were taking inventory of the drugs cabinet, beverage control were all over the bar. Several departments were poring over the hidden cameras, exploring the extortion angles that implied. The Department of Justice was investigating the prostitution ring, especially the underage aspect, and Alicia Morrison in particular. As was homicide. Nina had shown them to the Arbuckle Room upstairs and they had begun their preliminary investigations.

Paramedics were attending to Valentine, but had been given strict instructions that he was to remain onsite until otherwise advised. Downstairs, Phoebe was running two forensic accountants through her findings on the computer system, relishing her central role. Her grin was the widest Nina had seen on her friend in a long time.

Trank had been secreted into a side anteroom, away from the sea of people flooding the building. His presence was being kept a well-guarded secret, at least for now. When the time was right, the world would know Hank Trank was still alive and well, but not yet. He was examined by a paramedic who had been sworn to secrecy. As the man treated Trank, he was the dictionary definition of gobsmacked. Nina understood why. It wasn't every day you got to patch up and trade jokes with a dead man.

Nina wasn't entirely sure why the medical examiner had turned up—it wasn't like there were any bodies to examine. She figured it may have been to verify any findings homicide may uncover. The forensics photographer arrived soon after. Lang entered the hive of activity like a guilty golden retriever. Nina caught his eye and gave him a reassuring nod. She hoped it conveyed, *it's okay, for all they know this is the first time you've been here, and I've left your name out of it, just be cool.* Nina had to admit it was a lot to communicate in one gesture, but she did her best. Lang traipsed upstairs to the room he'd already photographed once before.

There was a lot going on. Perhaps too much. Nina sought Birmingham out.

"Won't all this scare Pellicano off?"

Birmingham frowned. "I asked nicely."

Nina raised a skeptical brow.

"I sent him a very nicely worded letter. Most respectful and professional. I even dotted the i's with little love hearts."

Nina folded her arms.

Birmingham shook his head. "Fine. You got me. I *did* actually ask nicely," he gave Nina a less-than-innocent grin, "and I also sent four squad cars."

"Ah." Nina smirked.

Birmingham pointed to Valentine, who was sitting up on a stretcher, paramedics checking his blood pressure. "We have more information on that guy. He really is ex-CIA. He was fired in 1981 for gross negligence, mainly alcohol-related. He's been kicking around a few odd roles since, all short-lived. It's likely Pellicano was the only one who would hire him."

"And he hated that. And he especially hated Pellicano."

"Which we're using to our advantage. The guy's already singing, but we have to wait for him to come down from the little drug cocktail you made him. We'll make sure he lawyers up so it's all above board, but it's plain as day he has no loyalty to his weaselly boss." Birmingham turned toward the entrance. "Speak of the devil..."

One would think being majority owner of an illegal private club crawling with cops would be cause for alarm, but Pellicano entered The Crucible like—well, like he owned the place. He strutted in with a wave and a phalanx of lawyers, each of whom sported expensive haircuts, expensive suits, and expensive briefcases. None of which guaranteed expensive minds.

Pellicano was all bluster, right up until he spotted Valentine, leg in a brace, sitting up on the stretcher. The change in his braggadocio was momentary, but Nina saw it.

"Who's in charge here?"

"I am," a gray-haired, gray-mustachioed officer replied. "Grant. Chief of Police."

Nina hadn't spoken to Grant. The towering chief could have been a body double for Herman Munster.

"Great." Pellicano elbowed a weaselly slick-suited lawyer by his side. "Put him first on the list when we sue the lot of them."

Grant's stoic bearing remained resolutely in place. "You're most welcome to try, sir, as it is your prerogative as an American citizen. I will, however, point out that this establishment has been operating as a purveyor of alcohol, narcotics, prostitution, and gambling, none of which has been approved or even requested of the good and great city of Los Angeles. As owner, you are responsible and will be prosecuted to the full extent of the law. We're still accumulating the list of charges, which, I might add, is extremely long."

"I'm shocked, shocked, I tell you." Pellicano waved his arms about. "I was advised this was a legitimate business with all pertinent licenses and permits. This was all set up by my business partner, Mickey Boehler. You should be hauling him in here."

Nina had to admit Pellicano was pretty good. Not Oscar-worthy, but he was putting on a reasonable act. If she hadn't personally seen him shoot Mickey in the face she might almost be convinced.

Grant cast a sideways glance at Birmingham. Nina wasn't sure what the gesture conveyed, but there was something behind it, she was sure.

"You admit you are partners with Mickey Boehler in ownership of this club?"

"Don't answer that!" one of the weaselly lawyers shouted, no doubt in an attempt to justify his excessive fee.

Pellicano gave him an indifferent wave of his hand. The paperwork would prove it anyway. "Yes, I'm part owner of this establishment with Boehler." Pellicano's attention drifted toward the office, where several officers were rifling through filing cabinets. "A very silent partner."

At least he had the good sense to try and distance

himself from the mess. Nina knew it wasn't going to fly, but the guy was giving it a good old-fashioned try.

"I haven't heard from Mickey in days. Do you know where he is?"

Pellicano's acting had descended into B-grade movie territory.

"You ever been to his house?" Grant asked casually.

There it is. Nina did her best not to smirk. They were setting him up.

"Why no, no I haven't."

Behind Pellicano's back, Birmingham did his best to hide his satisfaction. Nina knew what he was thinking. With all the paperwork, Valentine's confession, and testimony from The Crucible staff, and from Nina and Trank, along with the likelihood they'd turn up Pellicano's prints at Mickey's—they had him. No amount of swagger, no gaggle of lawyers was going to save him now.

Phoebe emerged from the office with a bespeckled uniformed cop and noticed the ruffled feathers. She moved closer to the center of the action, next to Nina. It was the first time she'd seen Pellicano and measured up the little man.

"I would kindly ask you to accompany us to the station to answer some questions, if you'd be so kind." Grant turned to the shiny-suited men surrounding Pellicano. "And your lawyers, of course."

"This is outrageous! I'm not guilty of any of this."

Phoebe hefted a computer printout in the air. "Facts say otherwise, fuckface."

"Who the hell is she?" Pellicano asked Grant.

"Your worst nightmare, bucko."

"Okay." Nina gripped Phoebe's arm and led her away. "Time to stand down, Dirty Harry."

She guided Phoebe to the corner of the bar. "This is thrilling!" Phoebe practically hopped on the spot. "Accounting has never been so exciting."

"Glad you think so."

Birmingham made his way over. "I'm heading back to the station with the chief. He wanted to pass on his personal thanks to you both for your help in this matter. He also wanted me to make it exceptionally clear to you, Nina, that you are to take no further action. He will, and I quote, 'throw every fucking book in the precinct at her skinny ass if she tries any more stupid ass stunts,' end quote."

"Hmmm."

Birmingham scowled. "What? What's that hmmm mean?"

"Oh, nothing."

"What have you got cooking, Maddox? The chief's serious. There'll be hell to pay when the press get wind that this club was operating under his nose. Believe me, he's dead serious. He needs to control this now, he can't have you going around and fucking shit up. I'm serious."

"Oh, I'm sure you are."

Birmingham grunted loudly. "But you're still going to try some dumb shit, aren't you?"

"Maybe."

"Alright, what is it?"

She told him.

Nina didn't know it was humanly possible for a someone who was still living to turn that pale, but there it was. For the longest time, Birmingham's mouth flapped up and down but no sound came forth. When it finally did, it was a high-pitched screech.

"You can't be serious?"

"I am. That's the plan."

"It's the most insane thing I've ever heard in my life."

"Again, that's the plan."

"Birmingham!" Grant called from across the room.

Giving a wave of acknowledgement, Birmingham turned back to Nina. "You can't go up against the mayor, and certainly not with that crazy scheme. You can't."

"Birmingham. Now!"

"Coming, sir!" He turned to Nina. "Promise me you won't go through with it? It'll never work."

"We are, and it will." Nina leaned forward. "Today, Alicia Morrison gets justice."

CHAPTER

TWENTY-TWO

The Los Angeles Ballroom at the Century Plaza Hotel had hosted the Emmys, Grammys, and Presidential dinners. Reagan stayed at the hotel so frequently the media had dubbed it his Western White House.

Nina walked around the ballroom, hardly surprised to find it decked out in the only possible color scheme: red, white, and blue. In keeping with the hyper-patriotism of the Reagan Era, the rally was an explosion of bunting, pro-USA jingoistic slogans, and, of course, American flags.

The ballroom was almost at capacity, with perhaps four or five hundred loyal supporters and press crammed in together. Initially she'd wondered why the event wasn't being held at a larger venue, before realizing it was always better to have a smaller venue full than a larger one half-empty.

The atmosphere was overwhelmingly buoyant, with most attendees sporting supportive buttons. Several speakers had warmed the crowd up, priming them for the main event. The crowd hooted and hollered whenever someone walked onto the empty stage, even if it was only the microphone technician. They were ready for the man they'd come to see.

Nina wondered how friendly the crowd would be in about twenty minutes. Not very, she imagined. She zipped up her leather jacket and strode, head down, toward the front of the room.

Above the stage was a giant net containing thousands of balloons, colored, unsurprisingly, red, white, and blue. Scattered around the corners of the room were uniformed police. Nina hoped they weren't trigger happy.

Exiting through the main door, Nina made her way past the stragglers rushing to enter before the 2 pm show time. A pimply teen stood next to a side door, attempting to dislodge some lost Confederate gold from his nasal cavity. Nina flashed a pass and the kid didn't even remove his finger as his unencumbered hand motioned for her to enter.

The long, whitewashed brick hallway led to the backstage area. She passed two relaxed security guards who gave her pass a vague check and waved her on. They probably assumed she was the daughter of someone important, and it's usually a good idea not to detain anyone important.

In short, security was appalling. Then again, why would anyone want to disrupt a campaign speech by the wildly popular Tod Bailey, mayor of Los Angeles, who was guaranteed to win his senate run?

Nina smiled.

⌁

ONCE AGAIN TO the tune of Fleetwood Mac's "Don't Stop", Tod Bailey strode out to a cheering crowd, waving and smiling like only a politician can. He entered to thunderous applause and shouts of ardent allegiance, his wife Margarette ten paces behind. The spotlight followed him all the way to the podium. He didn't immediately say anything, swept up in the adulation and support.

The production was slick. It had turned out the stage manager was an old gaffer from Nina's Scream Queen days. She'd always been friendly with crews, so convincing him had been far easier than she'd expected. She'd explained exactly what she had in mind, and most importantly, why. Once she'd shown him photographic evidence from the Arbuckle Room and everything else they'd gathered, he was onboard wholeheartedly. He explained that he had two young daughters of his own, and was only too happy to procure Nina a backstage pass and collaborate on the plan.

Network TV cameras were positioned at the center of the room, on a raised platform to provide sweeping views. Press photographers were at the front of the stage, ready to capture mid-rally gestures and the obligatory end-of-speech raised arms in victory with his wife.

Everything was in place.

It was time to bring the bastard down.

Bailey quelled the supporters' cheers with two downward facing palms, his shining white teeth glimmering in the spotlight. When the crowd had quietened, he tilted the microphone toward him and spoke. No sound came from the speakers. He tried again. The crowd began to murmur.

Visibly annoyed, Bailey glared at the stage manager, who stared back at him, arms folded in defiance. The mayor shot a confounded expression to his aid on the other side of the stage.

"Ladies and gentlemen," the booming voice said, "Mayor Tod Bailey!"

The crowd erupted in another round of applause, if

somewhat muted. They thought it was time for speeches, not more applause.

"All-American. Ex-Marine. Patriot. Future senator."

The crowd cheered, even more subdued now. Then Nina stepped on stage, microphone held to her mouth. Bailey's jaw dropped.

"There are some things you good people don't know about your mayor. Would you like to hear them?"

Some people cheered, most didn't. There was audible confusion now; the audience sensed this wasn't how things were meant to run. Press cameras clicked, unsure what was going on but capturing it all the same. Bailey was glued to the spot, unable to move from his position of power. Or perhaps it was panic that had frozen him.

Nina heard someone in the crowd ask, "Is that Nina Maddox?"

She ignored them and strode toward the man of the hour.

"Did you know, for example, that our mayor is an avid stamp collector?" She frowned theatrically to the crowd like an MC would. "It's amazing what some folks are capable of, and you just don't know what they do behind closed doors. Isn't that right, mayor?"

Bailey was angry now, even those in the cheap seats could sense it. A few people booed while others still cheered, such was the confusion in the room. The audience members weren't the only ones who were confused. Bailey's security were poised to move, but were visibly unsure if this was part of the event.

"Our mayor here has so many talents, so many interests, I want you to know what they are so you can get a real sense of this esteemed civic leader and devoted family man. For all his selfless duty to our fair city, this trusted public servant also has some special hobbies I'd like to share with you."

Bailey pushed himself away from the podium and marched toward her, fists clenched. Nina highly doubted he'd take a swing at her in such a public place, but she hoped he would.

Undeterred, Nina continued with her cheesy MC routine. "I'm here to tell you folks, Tod Bailey's two most passionate pursuits are, of course, rape and murder."

The room dropped into a deathly silence; the only sound was the constant whir of press cameras. Bailey reached Nina but stopped short. He turned and shook his head, even tried a flash of his pearly whites, but there were no cheers. There was no applause.

Like a viper, he grabbed at the microphone and wrestled with Nina for control. With her hand still on the mic, he leaned down and strained for his voice to be picked up. "It's a lie. This woman is a liar."

"Yeah? Well, how do you explain this?"

The crowd turned to stage right as a man wheeled in a cart with a TV screen at the top and a VCR beneath it. If the crowd was already confused, that was nothing compared to when they realized that the man wheeling the screen was none other than Hank Trank. The apparently very deceased Hank Trank.

Gasps filled the ballroom; one woman screamed. People turned to one another, trying to figure out what the hell was going on. The trouble was, no one else knew. They were glued to the stage, waiting for whatever was about to happen to unfold.

Bailey managed to wrestle the mic free of Nina's grasp. "Ladies and gentlemen, we're all victims of some sort of prank. Is Allen Funt going to jump out now?" His attempt at humor drew a tomb-like silence from the audience. He turned to Nina and Trank. "I don't know what these two think they're up to—"

Phoebe's disembodied voice from offstage cut him off. "Shut up and watch the tape."

Trank gave the startled crowd a friendly wave and pressed play on the VCR. A brief flicker of static was replaced with a clear picture. The image on screen was of the interior of the Arbuckle Room. On the bed was a white-robed figure, face just out of frame. Stepping into the scene with their back to camera was a blond woman in a long red coat. She sashayed seductively toward the bed.

As the scene unfolded on screen, Phoebe's voiceover narration kicked in. "On the night of the second of September this year, your mayor frequented a club called The Crucible. Don't bother looking it up. One, because it was an illegal underground club for the elite, and two, because it was raided by the Los Angeles police department this morning."

Nina didn't know what shocked Bailey more, the fact that the club had been raided or the scene on the TV screen. His panicked gaze darted from Nina to the screen and back again. His wife didn't get a look-in.

"Police!" Bailey screamed. "Help me."

Nina turned to the place in the crowd where she knew Birmingham stood. Every other cop in the room turned to him at the same time. Very slowly and deliberately, Birmingham shook his head. Every cop in the ballroom resolutely stood their ground.

Phoebe continued. "On the night in question, as can be seen here, Alicia Morrison, famous movie actress and all of fifteen years old, was raped and murdered by Tod Bailey."

"That's a lie!" Bailey screamed into the microphone.

On the TV, the red-coated blond woman continued her slow saunter toward the white-robed man on the bed. The crowd was silent as they watched, mesmerized, unable to look away.

Bailey gestured to his assistant to join him on stage, but he didn't move. Bailey's desperate, frantic denial was doing little to garner support from even his most ardent devotees. He was in a downward spiral, and the last thing you do with a drowning man is attach yourself to him.

"I'm going to sue you all! You can't treat me this way!"

"It's still better than the way you treated Alicia." Nina stepped forward, her eyes blazing embers. "Tell me, why did you do it? Was it the thrill? Did it get you off? She was fifteen, and you corrupted her, murdered her. Her blood was sprayed across the room."

There were moans of despair from the crowd. Bailey tried to swallow, abject terror smacked across his ashen face. His once-dignified politician's stance was shrinking by the second. Nina couldn't stop. She drew closer to him, making sure the microphone picked up her words.

"That girl had her whole life ahead of her. You took it from her. Why? The thrill? The power? What?"

Bailey shook his head now, unable to speak, his petrified face searching for someone to come save him. No one did. Certainly not his wife, who quietly made her way off stage with nary a backward glance.

Nina thrust her finger toward the screen. "Did you mean to kill her? Was that the plan all along? Why did you kill Alicia Morrison, Tod? Why?"

In a childlike, timid voice, Bailey said, "It was an accident."

The microphone started to slip from his hand; Nina

caught it. All strength seemed to have been drained from his body.

"What was an accident, Tod?" Nina asked, her voice laced with sympathy she didn't feel.

"I didn't mean to kill her."

Several people screamed. As one, the entire room recoiled in shock.

"You killed Alicia, but it was an accident?" Nina asked, making sure she wasn't obscuring the TV cameras. "Is that what you're saying?"

Bailey's head dipped in agreement and the room erupted into pandemonium. Journalists leaped forward shouting questions. The crowd turned ugly and began screaming abuse, some at Bailey, but just as many at Nina. Cops swarmed the stage, two grabbing Bailey by the arms.

That jolted Bailey out of his dream state. He bolted upright.

"What? What did you do?"

He tried to shake the cops loose, straining toward Nina. He managed to free himself from one, and his hand lunged for her throat. Luckily the other cop's grip held fast.

"I'll fucken kill you!"

Nina placed her hands on her hips. "I thought I was too old for your tastes?"

"I think we have enough, yeah?"

Everyone turned to the TV screen where the voice had come from. The blonde red-coated figure turned to the camera. It wasn't the face of Alicia Morrison, but Nina Maddox. She removed the wig and said to camera, "I think we can cut it there, Hank."

The screen returned to static.

Bailey's head snapped back at Nina, his face twisting with pure venom. "You said there was a tape!"

"Yeah, I did." She leaned in close to make sure he could hear her over the baying crowd. "If there's one thing I know about this city, it's that the smart ones always play the long game." She waited until he recognized his own words repeated back to him. "Shame you didn't have any idea who *you* were dealing with. Enjoy the spotlight while you can, mayor, you're going to spend the rest of your horrible little life in jail."

Whether it was on a timer or someone in the crew had a sick sense of humor, that was the moment the net above the stage released the balloons.

Tod Bailey was dragged away, kicking at the cascading balloons. Cameras flashed, no doubt grabbing images for the front page of every newspaper in the country.

The crowd was a cacophony of confusion. Eventually, they began to disperse awkwardly, like a couple after an unsuccessful attempt at forest sex. No one made eye contact.

Journalists flooded the stage, swarming Nina and pelting her with questions. Others sprinted toward the non-dead Hank Trank. He ignored them and, like the football star he once was, used his impressive bulk to carve his way through the crowd to Nina's side. His big arms surrounded her as he embraced her in a bear hug.

"Are you okay?" he asked softly.

Nina hugged him even tighter. In her planning, this was as far as she ever got. She had nothing further. The torment of the last week was at an end. Valentine, Pellicano, and Bailey would all face justice for the crimes they had committed. The families of all the victims would soon know the truth.

It was finally over.

Trank released her from his hug. Nina stood among the

chaos—and balloons—being pelted by a barrage of questions. She felt utterly exhausted. All she wanted to do was feed her cat and sleep for a million years.

"Ladies and gentlemen..."

The clatter of the room subdued a little, but didn't die away completely.

"... if I may have your attention for just a few more moments." Trank held the microphone. "You must have many questions about the events that transpired here this evening. No doubt more information will be forthcoming in the press in the coming days and weeks. However, before all that becomes known, I want to thank the woman who's responsible for bringing the truth to light. That woman is Nina Maddox." He made a grand sweep with his arm to Nina beside him. "Nina Maddox is an unparalleled private investigator who uncovered not only the truth about Alicia Morrison, but about the murders of Mickey Boehler and others, too."

Nina didn't know if the press could have glowed more if they tried.

Trank went on. "If not for Nina's tenacity and expertise, I, no doubt, would have been a victim alongside the others. Therefore, I can think of no better recommendation for your private investigator needs than the Scream Queen Detective Agency."

Trank dropped the microphone, gave Nina a wink and walked off stage with a pack of journalists at his heels.

Nina shook her head. *You son of a bitch.*

In a single speech, Trank had given her struggling agency the kind of publicity not even a thousand publicists could provide. She had it made.

Pushing her way through the journalists and cops, Nina

joined Trank offstage. The cops formed a barrier, giving them a brief moment of privacy.

"You didn't have to do that."

Trank tilted his head toward her. "Yes, I did. You're going to draw a lot of attention now. You're welcome."

Her hand gripped his forearm. "Thank you."

"Least I could do."

Phoebe joined them and the three hugged once more. She jutted her chin toward the yapping throng. "You ready for this?"

"No." Nina inhaled deeply. "But I'm going to do it for Alicia and Mickey." She turned to Trank.

"And for Seth?"

"And for Seth. And Diehl and Kaufman too. I'll even do it for Leonard."

"Alright then."

They stepped around the cops and turned to face the press.

"Who's first?"

TWENTY-THREE

The barrage of questions went on for an hour and a half. It only stopped because the newspapers had to file before deadline and the TV crews wanted to make the late news bulletins. When Nina, Phoebe, and Tank left the stage, the ballroom felt exceptionally large and exceptionally empty.

Exhausted and exhilarated at the same time, Nina walked away with a fist full of business cards and requests for interviews from the big boys, *20/20, 60 Minutes, Good Morning America*. She'd decide over the next few days if she wanted to put herself in front of the cameras again. Her first foray into celebrity had not been a pleasant one.

Poor Titus was going to be inundated with phone calls. Maybe she should invest in an answering machine after all.

Once the crowds had cleared, one man stood in the corner near the stage with his arms crossed, taking it all in. Nina left Trank chatting to Phoebe and approached him.

"Quite the show you put on."

There was less malice in Birmingham's tone than usual. That didn't mean it wasn't present.

"What can I say? Once a theatre brat..."

"You know you just embarrassed my entire department."

There wasn't a question mark at the end of the sentence.

"Not your entire department, surely? What about Kevin who gets the coffee?"

Birmingham gave a shake of his head. "He quit, got a repeat extras job on *Night Court*."

"Well, I guess it is the entire department then."

Folding his arms, Birmingham said, "You're enjoying this, aren't you?"

"A little bit."

"It won't last, you know."

"Is that what you say to your wife?"

"Yes." Waiting a beat, Birmingham pointed to the last of the press as they left through the main doors. "They think you're the bee's knees now—"

"Did you just say bee's knees in an adult conversation?"

"— but it won't last. They'll turn. They always do."

"Thank you, Captain Sunshine. I'll deal with whatever comes."

"Now you sound like my wife."

"Please don't tell me you have a sense of humor, Birmingham. I don't think I'm ready to live in that universe."

"Be at the station at ten tomorrow, we'll continue our questioning. There are still some gaps." He pushed himself off the wall and turned to face Nina. "You repeat this to another living soul, I'll deny it." He leaned in closer. "You did good, Maddox. You did real good." Before Nina could reply, he added, "Don't make a habit of it, okay?"

Unable to find the right words, Nina gave him a nod of thanks. Without another word, he walked toward the exit, not looking back, not deviating from his path. Nina didn't know if it was the fatigue or the release of everything coming to an end, but she found herself overcome with emotion at the gruff man's words. Trying not to dwell on the feeling, she made her way back to Trank and Phoebe. They looked as exhausted as she felt.

"Can I offer the woman of the hour a lift home?"

Nina's shoulders slumped. "Tomorrow I'm going to have to pay Greasy Steve a visit and see how many lungs I'll have to sell to get my car patched up."

"Your lungs or someone else's?"

"To be determined. Getting the bill isn't going to be fun, but I need my beast back. I can't be this cool-ass private investigator getting lifts in a dinky little Toyota Shitbox. No offense, Phoebs."

"Why on Earth would I take offense to that?" Her friend gave her a playful shoulder bump. "Maybe with all this newfound attention, I could graduate from associate member of the detective agency?"

"You're serious?" Nina had always hoped to bring her friend onboard, but never saw it as a reality, until now.

"Yeah, I think so. I had a ball gathering the evidence and everything. Even the scary bits were still exciting. Try as it might, accounting just doesn't have the same thrills. Can we at least talk about it in the next few days?"

"You bet!"

Nina yawned. Her eyelids felt weighed down by lead weights. "But first, we're going to go home and sleep in our own beds."

"My own bed and not Dad's single bed?" Phoebe said, threading her arm through Nina's. "I may tear up."

The only one who didn't appear to relish the thought of sleeping in his own bed was Trank. In fact, when Nina mentioned bed, his pace slowed, his mannerisms somehow sluggish. Nina understood why. When she'd first found Trank, confused and alone outside his own house, one of the first things she'd asked him was who she could contact. He couldn't think of a single person. She linked her arm in his.

"Hey, Hank." Nina waited until he turned to her. "Dinner tomorrow night at mine. Say, seven? Bring a bottle of something. Wear pants. Sound good?"

The smile on the man's face was the warmest Nina had ever seen. "I would like that very much."

EPILOGUE

The man turned off the late-night news after the sensational story about the mayor. He'd wanted to hear the results of the Mississippi Valley and Kentucky State game, but didn't get that far.

As soon as he saw her, he forgot all about football.

He forgot about the grilled cheese sandwich on the hotplate.

He even forgot about the redhead tied up in the bedroom.

All he could concentrate on was the face on the screen. A face he hadn't seen in years. She'd been blond back when he knew her. A few more pounds, but he approved of the new curves. He liked a bit of meat on the bones.

He'd seen the old *Scream Queen* posters around, of course. Seen bits of the movies when they showed horror flicks late at night. But he hadn't seen her in the flesh since he'd slashed the throat of her whore of a roommate.

What was her name again? Jane? Janet? He really wished he could keep a list, but only amateurs left evidence.

The man felt a twinge, a familiar primal pang he didn't get from the disappointing redhead in the bedroom. That whore was all manufactured enthusiasm and gossamer-thin declarations of love. It made him sick. She was as fake as her disgusting cheap chipped nails.

He craved the real deal. And from what he remembered about Nina Maddox, she was exactly that.

Licking his chapped lips, the man decided he would pay Nina Maddox a visit soon.

Real soon.

THE END

FADE OUT

To be the first to find out when new novels arrive and to win prizes and get free stuff (who doesn't like free stuff?), sign up for my VIP Book Club at:

https://davesinclair.com.au/newsletter/

ACKNOWLEDGMENTS

There's a running joke amongst my close knit writing mates — affectionately called the G-Mob - that whenever one of us is on a writer's panel someone from the tribe will invariably grab the microphone in the audience and ask, "Where do you get your ideas from?" It's one of those questions authors ALWAYS get asked.

Where did I get the idea for Nina from?

The answer is simple – desperation.

I was contacted by a production company who were eager to get Eva Destruction on screen (big or small) and optioned the rights to all the Eva Destruction novels – woot! As part of those discussions, their literary team asked what other ideas I had. So I pitched them four ideas - three I had fleshed out pretty well, the other I kind of slapped together a tagline and a paragraph or two but that was all I had. One of those ideas was about an ex-scream queen who became a detective in 1980s Los Angeles which was the one that resonated with the team — and of course, the one I had absolutely nothing more than two paragraphs and some vague ideas. From there, Nina Maddox was born. See, sometimes writer's CAN tell you where their ideas come from!

And now - the acknowledgements!

Always first is my incredibly supportive and gorgeous wife, Kristi. I wouldn't be writing today without her support, drive and love. Monkey, heart, unicorn.

To my amazing and brilliant girls, Quinn and Esther, big love!!! I'm loving seeing them grow into amazing women. My youngest Esther was finally old enough to read one of my books (the first Atticus Wolfe novel) and turned to me and said, "You're a really good writer dad". It probably would have meant more without the heavy note of surprise in her voice though...

As always, to my tribe, the incredible G-Mob who are brilliant writers and even better friends. To Craig, Justin, Luke, Nathan, Kat, Joel, Amanda and Amanda, thank you for your support, encouragement and laughs. And booze.

A big up to my editor Vanessa Lanaway for removing all my mistackes.

Thanks to the team over at 99 Designs and my amazingly talented artist Didi who did a fantastic job on the covers for the whole series.

Stay tuned to see what comes from the writer's cave! https://davesinclair.com.au/newsletter/ for all the latest news!

Don't be afraid to reach out on Facebook, Instagram, carrier pigeon, mental telepathy. It's always great to hear from readers. You can stalk me at all these semi-reputable places:

www.davesinclair.com.au

https://facebook.com/DaveSinclairAuthor/

https://www.instagram.com/davesinclairauthor/

https://www.goodreads.com/author/show/22167525.Dave_Sinclair

https://www.bookbub.com/authors/dave-sinclair

If you can, please drop a review, it is greatly appreciated. It helps new people discover my work.

Thank you and here's to many more adventures!

Dave